ERIN ZH

Plus SIZE *in*

PARIS

Dearest Niamh,
Thank you for supporting
this story. It means so very
much!
Love
Erin Zh xxo

A The Plus-Size Series™ Book
© 2023 Erin Zhurkin

The world is full of impossible beauty standards, and Abby Allerton is here to challenge those standards one city at a time. Although this book is a work of fiction, the continuing narrative that there's one perfect body type is sadly not, so the good fight continues worldwide.

To request permissions, contact the author at erinzhurkin.com.

Published by Dépaysement Publishing

Paperback ISBN: 979-8-9881885-0-6
Ebook ISBN: 979-8-9881885-1-3

Cover design by Liam Fitzgerald: frequency.studio
All chapter ornament illustrations by We are Lapin: wearelapin.fr
Interior design by Liz Schreiter
Edited and produced by Reading List Editorial
ReadingListEditorial.com

For Katie Sturino, Remi Bader, Stefani Nicole, and so many other influencers that are fighting the good fight by putting themselves out there online every single day so the rest of us feel seen, valued, and most importantly not alone. Paris wasn't so hard in my body when I was able to see how you all were in yours.

*How many cares one
loses when one decides
not to be something
but to be someone.*

—*Coco Chanel*

ONE

Mais Oui

Abby's never been to Paris, so frequenting her local imitation French café, Wholly Crêpe, is the closest thing she's got. Now, sitting in her favorite spot, where they should probably have a nameplate in her honor because she's there so much, she's doing her favorite thing—the thing that brings her back here time and time again—which is to watch the chef and owner, Philippe, and hopefully flirt with the handsome waiter, François, while she works.

Like clockwork Abby watches Philippe desperately try to keep his national identity alive. He does this by torturing the diners at Wholly Crêpe with his singing. He sings—or rather shouts—a weird mash-up of Edith Piaf lyrics and "La Marseillaise." If the mood is right, she'll join in for a verse or two. Listening to Philippe, Abby can't help but wonder if his singing isn't a coping mechanism, a kind of scream of the soul that he ended up here after his premiere culinary training at Le Cordon Bleu in Paris. Cue another somber chorus of "La Vie en Rose."

Just at that moment, Abby sees François stop scrolling on his phone and look over to her table. In his black waiter's suit and long apron, he looks like a tall, sleek, out-of-place penguin. Of all their usual customers, she's got a hopeful hunch that she's his favorite. With that thought in mind, she adjusts her hair, highlighted blonde with just the right touch of brunette lowlights, so that it falls gently on her shoulders. Abby is curvy and falls into the super silly, outdated fashion-world category "plus-size." Always sitting up straight thanks to her yoga practice, she gives off the vibe that her body is her home, and in her home she's undoubtedly comfortable. Her dreamy brown eyes with their long, naturally curling eyelashes are often noticed by others, and people are drawn to her because of them. She's been described as a cross between Blake Lively and Aidy Bryant.

Today she is wearing a colorful top that dips in front with just enough calculated cleavage to be what her mama calls "elegantly sexy—not town hussy sexy." Out of the corner of her eye, Abby sees François quickly run his fingers through his wavy, dark hair and adjust his stereotypical moustache before heading over to greet her. She gears up to place her usual order and to feel the flirty François butterflies that appear in her stomach whenever he is near.

"*Bonjour,* Abby. *Ça va?*"

"*Très bien, merci!*" Abby says. François gives a sigh in response.

"Goodness. That sigh seems loaded. Are we a cranky French waiter today?" Abby says.

"Well, one could say I'm over it, *ma chérie.*"

"Oh no. Do you want to talk about it? I like your scarf," Abby says.

"I didn't wear my scarf for a few days, and I think I've caught a *boog,*" François says as he adjusts his linen scarf tighter around his neck. Abby smiles at the way he says *boog* for *bug.*

Being able to take in François's accent is a delicious side dish for all the customers of Wholly Crêpe, and Abby is no exception.

"You are having the usual, ma chérie?"

"*Oui, mon monsieur . . .*"

"Philippe, two sugar crêpes with lemon and side of crème Chantilly, *and* don't forget that Diet Coke because balancing our nutrition is important." François winks.

"Ouch. I think you might have a bit of *le cranks* today." Abby has just thought of that term and is waiting to see how it lands.

"*Le cranks?* Really? Mademoiselle, I took you to be a little more cultured than that."

"I like to keep things interesting," Abby says.

"*Mais oui . . .*" Following a good tug of his black penguin-esque vest, François adjusts his scarf again and moves on to the next table.

Now settled in and ready to roll, it's time for Abby to do her Insta post with links to her website and peruse the new offers of sponsorship and partnership waiting for her in her inboxes.

Her blue-checked verified accounts—Femme Fatale, at last count a half million followers, and Plus-Size Real, with upward of 450,000—are her life's yin and yang. Femme Fatale is all things Parisian style, all things skinny, subtly using vintage pieces she acquires. She also uses third-party photographers from France. Femme Fatale has been her monetary star thanks to her gorgeous layouts and ability to add just the right touches to the pics. Using vintage pieces has allowed her to make quite a profit adding affiliated links to her posts. Plus-Size Real, on the other hand, is the antithesis to Femme Fatale for obvious reasons; the word *skinny* is never mentioned, nor is the desire to achieve thinness allowed. It's all about being real.

Still, she recognizes she's in her sweet spot with her influencer business and doesn't want to do anything to mess it up. She wants to get Plus-Size Real to 1M, but it's been a little stagnant for some reason. She clicks over to her Google folder for Femme Fatale content to see what new photos have been added by her partner photographers in France and elsewhere. Just at that second, one from Pascal (her fave hired Parisian photographer) pops in. It's good but not exactly right.

@FemmeFatale: Bonjour! Can you make it a little more vivid? It feels a little drab to me. And maybe on the next round put the flowers to the left of the model?

@ParisPascal: Bonjour, FF! I can try, but it is not vivid in this part of Paris. It is between two old buildings, and the light is limited. The small streets here as you know are hard to capture with good color, but the vibe is clear and simple industrial chic! Do you like the model's look?

@FemmeFatale: Yes, she's perfect. Very cool. Isn't it brighter in Paris?

@ParisPascal: In summer yes, but you asked for a winter shot, and I delivered. Haven't you been to Paris?

Abby sits back. Time to lie. Again. She straightens up, sitting tall and strong, and types a response.

> @FemmeFatale: Of course! I just remember there being more light. My bad. Merci. I'll make it work.

> @ParisPascal: Pas de problème!

Abby takes the photo and starts to work her editing magic, adding the tags and links to ensure what's shown is accessible to her followers—where to buy the trench, where to buy the cliché beret, where to buy the cute gold pointed-toe flats. Then, like clockwork, she quickly pops back on to Google to initiate yet another flight search to Paris. She's looked at flights for years without following through, but lately it seems to be a daily occurrence, like brushing her teeth. François is back with her Diet Coke.

"All sarcasm and pending sicknesses aside, what's new with you, mademoiselle?"

"Um, I think you are already looking at it, François . . ."

"I'm sorry, but I couldn't help but see it with your huge screen."

Abby laughs as she's using the smallest, most compact version of the MacBook on the market.

"Are you planning a trip to Paris?" François says as he leans in even more.

"Oh, I'm just doing some fun searches as I work. I've always wanted to go. I think I told you before that I missed my high school trip to Paris because my mama was sick. One can dream." Abby sighs.

"Paris is always a good idea, Abby. Especially for you."

Abby crinkles up her nose and asks, "Mmm, why do you say that? I feel a smidge of snark coming, François, and I'm pretty sure you've hit your cranky French waiter limit at my table today."

François puts his hand to his heart, and with a slight bow he smiles gently, letting her know he's in a better place. Abby swoons as his thick, dark hair falls forward over his piercing blue eyes that are now looking straight through her.

"You should go because you've never been, and you will go all doe-eyed like that emoticon with hearts for eyes. You are the *perrrfect* visitor." François slowly straightens, keeping her gaze.

"I've never been overseas," Abby says as she breaks his gaze and shrugs.

"Really? You seem so worldly to me."

"Wordy? That's funny you said that. Did I ever tell you I was spelling bee champ all through middle school? I was so hated for that and other reasons, but I didn't care. Never underestimate a good speller."

"So many miscellaneous facts come from your mouth during our little visits. I said *world-lee* with the *lee*, the letter *l* and *ee*, *worldly* as in the world we live in, the planet, the earth."

"Oh, right! Sorry. I guess it was an accident with your accent."

"Oh, mais oui . . ."

"You think I'm worldly?" she asks.

"Oui, but of course," he says back to her matter-of-factly.

At that moment, François's phone buzzes in his pocket. Abby's intrigued.

"What's that buzzin' in your pocket? You saw my screen. Show me what's in your pocket making all that noise."

"Oh, mademoiselle, we don't know each other well enough for you to know what is going on in my pocket," he says as he moves away.

"Well, that's not true, I've been coming here for a few years now, and you've been here every time, so I'd say we know each other relatively well, *non*?" Abby says.

François moves his body in what appears to be an attempt at a hip TikTok dance and then puts his hand in his pockets. Abby laughs. She grabs at his apron and gets the phone. Once the phone is in her hands, she sees there is a notification from Femme Fatale on the screen. She quickly fumbles it back to him. She had no idea that he followed one of her accounts.

"Sorry. I shouldn't have grabbed it from you. I'm not usually that aggressive, and you're not feeling well."

"It's okay. I like when women grab at me."

Abby can't help but laugh. He's just too cute.

"You should go to *Par-ee*, Abby. It will be good to you—or for you. Damn your English prepositions. You can finally put all those mediocre French classes you took in school to good use."

"You know why I like coming here?" Abby asks.

"Because of the chef's songbird singing voice and *moi*? The sexy waiter?" François says.

"Oui, all those things, but mostly because it reminds me of a place I've never been. Coming here, I travel there." Abby points to the big Eiffel Tower on the wall. "It's a little trip without the hassle, trouble, and goodbyes—and I do love a good crêpe!"

"But life is trouble, Abby. Without hassles, life is not truly lived. And if you don't say goodbye, you can never have a new hello. I think that was said by some guy named Pico or Paulo, so it is not all my philosophical genius, and therefore I can't take *all* the credit, but hassles are needed so that you can enjoy the other side of life."

"Did you get all that from a su-*PEAR* positive Insta account?" Abby smiles as she says it, attempting her own French accent.

"Oui! From the @MeaningfulQuotes profile. It has, like, three million followers. Totally legit, so positive, and making the world a better place, what's not to *j'adore*."

"Thought so." Abby takes a sip of her Diet Coke and then sighs with delight.

Their frequent banter with accents has become a kind of visceral experience for her. She could speak to him all day, just asking him to repeat certain words in French and then in English with his accent in full swing. She's often wondered what would be sexier—him speaking in English with a French accent in bed with her, or him in bed speaking the real deal, full-on French. She starts to blush a bit and focuses back on François.

François's apron pocket buzzes again.

"Are you going to grab it? Please grab it! It will certainly be the most exciting thing to happen to me today!"

A different customer, an old lady, sits upright, and says, "I'll grab it from you. Come on over here."

Abby gestures for François to go over there. François turns to the lady and smiles confidently. "Non, ma chérie. There is not enough of me to go around. *Désolé*." He turns back around to Abby.

"As tempting as it is, I'll keep my hands to myself this time. You can do that little move you were doing earlier, though." François smiles and shuffles off. Both Abby and the admiring old lady laugh as if to say, "Once again, day made at the Wholly Crêpe café."

Abby closes the tab on Paris flights and shelves that away once again so she can focus on getting her Instagram post done. She wants to get this latest post online so she can move on to something else. She's learned that with influencing, discipline is key. Keeping things fresh and fun for her followers must be her daily goal. She can't help but recognize the irony that she's starting to feel in her own life that it's time to post and move on.

With her AirPods in and the volume up on Meghan Trainor, who has been her mantra in human form for years now, she starts typing as fast as she can, capturing the thoughts as fast as they come. This post is a hassle and a trouble that she's *over* encountering on a daily basis.

Buttoning up a shirt is one of those thoughtless, mundane tasks for a woman. But put a plus-size woman, whether she's voluptuous or not, in that scenario, and it can make or break her day. No matter the color or style, there's always a guessing game as those buttons move up that fastening line of fantasy thinking. "No gape, no gape, please god, no gape!"

Often, when a significant boob gape appears, spiraling ensues: "The shirt's too small, which means my boobs are too big. If I just had smaller breasts! I'm fat, so no good design-abiding shirt will ever fit me if I'm this weight and shape." And finally, down the rabbit hole to research the latest detoxes and diets, starting tomorrow! "I'm not okay," "I need to change," and "I'm not enough" have taken residence in our hearts once again. All this madness from a silly, thoughtless design flaw. Before we find ourselves in an all-out boob-gape mental state requiring us to call in sick to manage our breakdown, there is an option. Because ladies, we always have options! The option is simply not to spiral. We deserve shirts that fit and don't gape! Society and its hugely overwhelming stigma of what constitutes a normal body, an acceptable body, is the problem. Not designing for *real* women is the problem. Now here's a list of brands that boob-gape and a list of brands that don't. You got this!

"I've so got this!" Abby says, louder than she realizes, as she does a little jig, adjusting her body in her chair. She looks up after posting and sees that others are watching her. She smiles and double waves to them. All five of them wave back, and that's inclusive of Philippe and François. After posting to Insta, Abby quickly maneuvers through her post to then link it to her story, all the while shimmying in her seat to the music blaring in her ears, and starts to type the text:

PLUS-SIZE REAL: BUTTON-BUSTED LIST REVEALED!

As she continues to masterfully click around the keyboard with her hot-pink manicured nails, she realizes this offers her the perfect Instagram Story shot with the caption "Writing in pink this morning." She quickly takes a photo at the perfect angle, so her fingers look sleek and long, and adds it to Femme Fatale's Story. She's a master at this, and she knows it. She looks up and notices François watching her.

Just as she's about to shut down, she decides to check her accounts once again, on her phone, to make sure all looks pretty and on brand. She scrolls through Plus-Size Real first.

"Seriously?" Abby says to herself as she scrolls down and sees she's once again being trolled. She reads the comment:

@plussizereal: If you're all about empowering women, how about you empower them to lose weight! It's not empowering to be fat—it's just being fat. Lame.

Abby narrows her eyes and starts to formulate a response. So many trolls and so little time. She's used to it now and has become an apt responder.

@winner123: How about you be a REAL winner and stop the objectification of women and worry about your own body? Oh, and you might want to come out from the basement at your mom's house and do the dishes. Peace and love, my brother, because I'm pretty sure you are a man.

She clicks Reply, but the feeling of good comeback swagger is short-lived for her on this one. What she wrote to the troll hit too close to home.

TWO

Twinkie Talk

"Abby? What's coming up?" Charlene, Abby's therapist, tilts her head slightly down to meet Abby's gaze on the cushy white linen couch across from her.

"I feel guilty," Abby says as her eyes fill with tears.

"Can you tell me more?" Charlene says.

"I feel tight. Everywhere. I feel guilty that I hate her sometimes, when she's the one that gave me life." Abby wipes a waterfall of tears gently streaming down her cheeks. "I feel guilty that sometimes during her illness I wish she would've died. How awful is that?"

Charlene hands her a tissue. Abby wipes her tears with it and now has black streaks resembling tire tracks across her eyes. Charlene hands her the whole box.

"It's natural to feel all those feelings, Abby. What's not natural is to dwell there. And that's why you're here."

"I guess I feel with things being better, with her better, that something's got to give. But then I get pulled back in and I feel selfish. I live this strange dual existence with them."

"How so?" Charlene asks.

"From my room, I've built and manage two successful Instagram profiles with literally hundreds of thousands of followers. I mean, I love what I do, I loved getting my degree, I just don't love the isolation of it all. It's strange, isn't it? That I'm living this way? I feel like this stupid troll I was responding to recently. I felt like I was responding to myself."

"In what way?" Charlene says, holding eye contact.

"Because I'm the same. I have one life online and another in real life. It sounds cliché, but it's how I feel."

"What do you need to do to feel more authentic, for yourself?" Charlene asks.

"I'm not sure. Do you think I'm having a quarter-life crisis? I saw this whole Reel on it and listened to a podcast about it. Is that a thing?"

"Could be. What do you do when you feel those feelings of being inauthentic?" Charlene asks.

"It's weird. I kind of double down and work harder on my accounts. I go to this café, Wholly Crêpe, a lot just to get out of the house, and then . . . there's the Twinkies." Abby's eyes move down to the floor. A slice of shame about those Twinkies permeates the room. She sees Charlene's eyes still holding hers in the most loving way. Abby knows she won't let that go.

"Do you want to tell me about the Twinkies, Abby?" Charlene says.

"They were always put in my lunches and given to me after school. My mom used to give them to me when I was young. When I felt sad, or when things were hard. They were kind of a go-to treat for us."

"How do you feel about them now?" Charlene asks.

"That maybe I don't want them anymore," Abby answers.

Bull's-eye. Charlene leans back.

Abby's cat, Chloe, pushes the door to enter Abby's room and jumps up beside her on her desk. Abby picks her up to give her a gentle nose rub. In a red bra and dark-blue silk pajama pants, it's another day, another dollar in the online world. With her being what's called a mid-tier influencer, who gets anywhere between five hundred to five thousand dollars per post, she's done well for herself, and one of the benefits, she must admit, of living at home is that it has helped her be a savvy saver. She loves working first thing in the morning and is almost always half-dressed while doing it. She's just finished some morning journaling or morning pages, as Charlene recommended, and is feeling particularly focused and positive.

"I need a new gig, Chloe. I do not want to turn twenty-five like this. Isn't it time for me to *live*? I want my joie de vivre." Chloe resumes her usual position on the desk, ready to interrupt, in the same way Abby resumes her usual position at Wholly Crêpe, waiting for François to interrupt. She smiles to herself at this realization.

Abby looks around her room. It's professionally set up with an eclectic flair. There are vision and mood boards full of mini-printer pics organized by hue alongside ideas for her next posts on magnetic boards. There are strings of lights across the boards and long mirrors along her walls that give optimal views from every angle, which help her recreate Femme Fatale looks for Plus-Size Real. It's a curated space that percolates with creativity around her centrally placed diploma in Fashion and Art Design from Watkins. Memories of good years, good times alongside the sad and hard going on at home. Always pursuing her creative life kept her going.

Chloe stretches and rolls all over, attempting to overpower the keyboard. Abby types around her as if she's not there. She pauses, looks at Chloe, and says softly, "At least I'm not in the basement. I mean, this is a cool space even if it is in our parents' house, right?" Abby creates a camera lens box with her hands and looks through it at different angles of the room. "Ah, doesn't matter how you angle it or shoot it, Chloe. Living with my parents is indeed sad." She flaps her arms down on the sides of her chair and does a stretch that lets her arms dangle and her neck fall back, but then after a few seconds, she starts her 5, 4, 3, 2, 1 countdown she learned from listening to the Mel Robbins podcast. That helps catapult her forward in every challenge, and today is no exception. She rockets herself straight up and gets back to work. She gives Chloe a final gentle stroke before the cat jumps down in her dismissive way.

"Hey, Siri!" Abby says.

"Uh-huh?" Siri answers.

"Play *Abby's Je t'aime* playlist," Abby commands. Siri confirms that she's now playing the playlist, and Abby scrolls down and opens multiple files in her IG Femme Fatale posts archives on her MacBook Pro. After perusing the pics, she clicks over to Notes to prepare her post for the profile and quickly writes the heading:

FRENCH GIRL CHIC FROM PHARMACY TO TRÉS JOLIE

She moves a few curated pretty pics of pharmaceutical skin-care products around on her screen, then goes into her archives to see if @parispascal sent her any shots that go with the products she's highlighting this morning. She's due to post them today, according to her sponsorship calendar. She comes across an old pic, one that she herself took when starting this account. It's a memory of how Femme Fatale came to be, and it's perfect. Just then, a DM comes through.

@HeatherBeather: Hey, I didn't get my payment this month. Just letting you know.

@FemmeFatale: Hi, how are you? I was literally looking at some of our old pics. It's been a while. I'll check on it.

@HeatherBeather: I'm fine. Thanks for checking on it and letting me know.

@FemmeFatale: Sure thing. You didn't tell me how you are doing. My mama's better, and things are better, and I'm thinking of making some changes with Femme Fatale. Can we meet up soon when you are in town? I'd love to fill you in.

@HeatherBeather: I'm happy to hear about your mama. Let me know what you find out about the payment. Sorry to be short, but I've got to go. Thanks.

Abby throws her phone on the bed. This needs to stop. The fact that Femme Fatale is her more lucrative account makes it hard to give up the facade. This arrangement with Heather is like a stale piece of gum that's been chewed too hard and too much. Her so-called "perfect scheme" of keeping Heather the face of the account but Abby behind the scenes doing all the work seemed genius at first—they simply went their separate ways due to creative differences, keeping the account and its brand on the money for both of their benefits. She clicks back over to the Femme Fatale post, with the vintage pieces beautifully placed, and adds the accompanying link to Insta to finish it off. As she does, the memory starts to play in her mind once again, as if an assistant director on a movie set were fiercely wielding the clapboard and calling out, "Biggest fuckup so far—take 119."

"Okay, so let's go with the pale-yellow shirt, the turquoise pendant and bracelet, and add the men's chapeau for a campy feel," Abby says to Heather, her best friend since ninth grade, as she throws the items her way across the bed.

"Got it. I love that combo. You are so good at this, Abby," Heather says with a thumbs-up.

"*Merci, mon amie.*"

Heather puts them on in front of the mirror, and Abby jumps back to look at her more closely.

"Why don't you do this?" Heather asks.

"Do what?"

"Dress yourself up and post photos? You're the one with the style sense. I'm beginning to feel like you only want me for my body." Heather laughs.

"Well, you do have a killer bod. We both know that, and I would be stupid not to want it."

"Really?"

"Well, yeah. I mean, your life is so much easier because of the body you have."

"How so?" Heather says.

"Well, because you're skinny and petite. That's like winning life's lottery ticket."

"What are you talking about, 'life's lottery ticket'?" Heather puts the phrase in air quotes.

"I mean, how often do you get made fun of, or used in games of truth or dare because you're the fat girl? I've never even been asked to a dance," Abby retorts.

"Abby, I can't believe that you think my life is easy because I'm skinny and petite, which I can do nothing about—it's just my genes. Don't you think that's, like, kind of limiting me as a person?"

"I just think it's true, genes or not. It's just the way it is. We aren't even on the same planet when it comes to that stuff," Abby says as she prepares the images.

"Says who? You?"

"Well, yeah. I'm living it, so I'd say what I think is worth something," Abby snaps back.

"Abby, my life isn't easier just because I'm skinny."

"Um, yes, it is. You don't have to deal with what I deal with. I thought we understood that. This is the exact reason we have the arrangement we do. Otherwise, why would I go to this length to hide who manages an account that's super skinny-focused and a completely unrealistic ideal of how we should look?"

Heather stands frozen for a second and then looks around the room.

Abby turns around and finishes up the pictures and then downloads them to her iMac. She then starts to impose them on a fake background with some masterful Photoshop moves. Then she posts them to the account.

"*Voilà!*" Abby leans back in her chair to show Heather, who is already back in her old clothes. Abby turns around to look at her.

"What are you doing? You can stay in them a bit longer, or you can even have them, as always, because you know they're sponsored," Abby says, unsure of what's happening.

"I'm good. I've got more than enough of these. Did you get everything you need?"

"Yes. Is there something wrong?" Abby asks.

Heather breathes heavy and then spews. "There's a lot wrong with this. Don't you see it? I can't believe I didn't see it earlier. You're using me, and not only that, you're also hiding behind me to not be you. Is this why you are my friend? For this stupid account?"

"No, Heather, please. I didn't mean it that way. I'm such a jerk."

"You're not a jerk, Abby, but I don't think I want to do this anymore."

"Do what? Benefit from everything I do?"

"Whoa. That was cold, Abby." Heather steps back. "Do you realize that you aren't even showing my face in these pictures? Look at them. It's only my body, or you're showing me from angles that you can't see me, who I am. I just realized how weird this is."

"Heather, can you just chill for a second?" Abby says, putting her hand up to deflect what's coming at her.

"And then you always want me to be this buffer of yours to deal with the questions that come through on email. This was your deal, not mine."

"Heather, please."

"No, I can't chill, Abby. You know how hard my life is at home and how boys at school are with me—it's far from winning a lottery. I mean, Josh called me a plank the other day, and it wasn't because I was doing a good plank, either."

"Well, he called me a whale, so . . . ," Abby says. There's a painful pause as Abby searches for something else to say in return, but she's got nothing. Just then, her phone buzzes with all the notifications coming in. She shows it to Heather. With tears welling up in her eyes, she says, "It's a hit," and puts the phone back down. Heather picks up her courier bag.

"I'm happy for you, Abby, but I think it's time for you to find a different model or face or whatever it is you are trying do here. Or maybe just put yourself out there. That might be more honest."

"But Heather, you're my best friend. We did this together. Why is this even a thing? You're skinny, I'm not. End of story. Why are you mad about it? It's not like I just suddenly became a bigger body today, this very minute. Right?"

"It's almost the end of the year, and I'm heading off to summer jobs up north after graduation, so I guess my body—the one that won the lottery of a lifetime—won't be available."

"Heather, wait, please. Seriously, I'm sorry." Abby wipes a single tear.

"Me too. I'll see you around." Heather leaves abruptly.

Shaking off the memory once again, in one fell swoop, her hair is up in a messy bun, and she clicks over to Plus-Size Real, which has served as a kind of salve to the memory and hurtful truth that she still hasn't come clean to her followers that it's she, not Heather, who is running Femme Fatale. She sees the "Button Busted" post continuing to rack up the likes and comments twenty-four hours later. That boosts her spirits, because in that online world she is herself. She looks at her DMs, as she prides herself on being open and connected with her followers on Plus-Size Real. She is drawn to one of them and opens it.

> @Aubsinaustin: Hi, I've been following you for a few weeks now, and I want to say thank you. I hate my body. Do you ever feel that way? My mom told me to go on Weight Watchers or

WW—whatever it's called—but it's full of boomers with big flower shirts and white pants. I know it's dumb of me to write to you. Just delete this and forget it. You probably don't even read DMs.

Abby reads it again. She wants to respond thoughtfully, because after looking at the account, she's pretty sure this is from a tween, based on the number of unicorns and rainbows and the random skull in their bio.

@plussizereal: You are so brave to write to me, and yes, I do read these! I created this account for you, for me, and for all of us that for some reason have been told by society that because our bodies are out of the so-called "normal" size range, we aren't acceptable. I'm going to get preachy now, so hold on to your attention span because it's important!

I believe the perfect body is the body where you feel at home, free to be yourself and free to be who you are, no matter what. I'm a size 16, 18, and even a 20 depending on whatever is happening in my life and the clothing label I'm wearing at the time. I do yoga on the regular. I walk every day, too, and I'm flexible, like almost can do the splits flexible, you feel me? My larger body doesn't limit me, nor does it hold me

> back. To me, being loving to myself is the ultimate glo-up.
>
> Be brave, be true to you, and be kind to your body. It will never work going harsh on your body—I believe it only responds to love. And go easy on your mom. With all their best intentions, sometimes, moms get it terribly wrong. Those unicorns and rainbows on your bio show me you're a dreamer. DREAM BIG, bigger than what society thinks you should be and tells you to be. Peace and love, my sister. Xx

Abby finishes it, smiles, and hits Send.

"Abby, dear? Are you coming down to breakfast?" calls her mama, Betty Lou, from the kitchen. This jolts Abby back. She changes out of her pajama pants and into some cute boyfriend jeans and puts on her favorite shirt—ironically not a button-down but a flowy, colorful top with her signature color, hot pink, highlighted in the center.

"Just a second, Mama." She grabs her designer tote bag and stuffs it with her MacBook, journal, and planner.

"I need to head out for a bit, so don't worry about me," she hollers from her room.

"Again? Okay then, but you are missing some fine cookin', isn't that right, honey?" Betty Lou fishes for support.

"Ya sure are, sweet pea," mocks Abby's father, Steve.

THREE

Soufflé au Chocolat

Abby walks into Wholly Crêpe feeling a little edgy. She sees that her usual spot is taken by two older women wearing extravagant hats, as though they are dressed for an afternoon tea. She diverts to a different table and flops down, almost throwing her bag on the opposite chair. François heads over.

"Bonjour, mademoiselle, looks like it's your turn to have a case of the—how did you call them—le cranks?"

"Oui, that's me. Mademoiselle Crank," Abby says with a sigh.

"How can I assist you? Your usual?"

"Non, mon monsieur, I'm tired of the status quo."

"Well, this is very exciting. What would you like?"

"Surprise me."

"Surprise you? You mean . . ."

"Yes, surprise me. Knock my socks off, François. Take me on a culinary adventure courtesy of Philippe."

"I would love to, but to do such a thing during the day is no good. This requires planning, and I think in the evening it's much better, non? Will you come back for this exclusive experience in the evening, say, this Saturday at eight p.m.?" François immediately yells back to Philippe in French to confirm the day and time. He smiles and nods in agreement.

"Um, yeah, okay. I'd love to," Abby says.

"*Magnifique,*" François says in his debonair way with more pep to his step as he heads back to the kitchen.

"Did I just agree to a date?" she says to herself out loud. François turns around and winks at her. The two cute space invaders catch her eye and wink at her, too. She sits up straight and smiles. "I did, didn't I? Huh, didn't see that one coming."

"Well, he sure did," one of the ladies loudly whispers across the room. Abby laughs.

"I love your hats. They are so chic. Did you make them yourselves?" Abby asks.

"Oh no, who's got time to make hats? Would you like to borrow one of them for your date?"

"You are very sweet, but no thank you. I'll come up with something on my own." Abby has a sudden urge to run, and she packs up her things. She heads toward the door and turns around to say goodbye to François, who, thankfully, is in the back. A slight awkwardness has hit her, and she needs some space. She waves and mouths "Au revoir" to Philippe. He waves back to her, as he's in the middle of a verse of "Boum."

Back at home, Abby starts to look through her closet, multitasking as she pulls out all kinds of fashion scenarios for her continuing, sly adaptation of Femme Fatale looks to Plus-Size Real. She peeks at herself in the mirror, fluffs her thick hair a bit, and does a little dance move ending in her giving herself a high five in the mirror. She's got a little spring in her step and puts on some music to complete the mood rising inside of her. It seems the stars are aligned, and she and François are potentially headed in the right direction. It's been a few years since she started going to Wholly Crêpe to work and get out of a house that was heavy with sickness. François has been a sort of saving grace to her sadness, and she's excited to see where this might lead.

.· .·+ ·+ + ·· ·.

Abby pulls up to Wholly Crêpe and sits in her car for a second as she turns it off. She gently puts her head on the steering wheel. She's feeling a little jittery and nervous. She remembers the fling during college a few years ago with one of the hipster graphic design majors—the kind of guy who wore black, thick-rimmed Warby Parkers, who then friend-zoned her after she helped him formulate his project and then fulfilled his horny needs after a night of bar hopping downtown on Broadway when no one else was around or available. She pushes that thought out of her mind and puts one hand on her heart and takes three deep breaths. She sits up straight and looks in the visor mirror, applying the latest deep-rouge lipstick from the trendy Violette_FR because it seems apropos. She gives herself a self-love high five in the mirror and snaps the visor back up into place.

As she leaves the car, she smooths out her cute black dress that's waisted just below her bust, her cleavage highlighted by two lines of delicate, hot-pink ruffles that she added herself for that extra little something. She walks up to the door, and the place is completely dark.

"Weird. He did say Saturday, right?" She pulls at the door. It opens. She enters with caution and goes through the little entry hallway, just like she's done a hundred times before now, then steps into the main room.

"François?" she says, now standing in the middle of the room.

"Oui, mademoiselle." François's voice is behind her. She turns around, and the lights go on, only it's not the overhead lights, it's hundreds of twinkle lights all around the room, highlighting fake trees, red gingham tablecloth–covered patio tables with huge teddy bears sitting in the chairs, and delicately placed vases of roses. A French chanson playlist is playing in the background. There are even twinkle lights lining the horrible painting of the Eiffel Tower on the wall, giving it the upgrade it desperately needs. Abby turns around and takes it all in with her hands over her mouth, slightly smudging the very bold red on her lips. She stops her spin at François, who is leaning up against the doorway, still by the light switch and dressed in his normal clothes, not a waiter's uniform. Abby sees him. Totally a date. She scans what François is wearing—dark blue jeans, a brown leather belt, a crisp white button-down, and a blue blazer with brown brogues. Her decision: *He looks* très élégant *and very handsome.* Abby continues to take him in as he walks up to her.

"Care to join me at the table with the Eiffel view?"

"Oui, monsieur."

"Please, mademoiselle, tonight I am François, and I'm off duty." He smiles and brings Abby over to her chair. He pulls it out for her. She sits down. Then he sits down across from her. Abby looks over at the Eiffel decal and sees a part of the second floor falling and steps back up to smooth that part of the decal back in its place.

"Voilà!" she says enthusiastically. François laughs.

"Merci, mademoiselle. All of France thanks you for restoring our most treasured monument."

"Pas de problème, monsieur. Vive la France," Abby says, smiling as she cutely sits back down. Philippe enters in a waiter's uniform with a chef's hat on. Abby laughs.

"Are you wearing many hats tonight, Philippe?" she asks.

"Mais oui. François was very particular about the menu tonight, so I will be your chef and your waiter. I expect a very good tip." Philippe winks.

"But will you sing?" Abby asks.

"Non, mademoiselle, very strict instructions that I do not sing. Désolé." Philippe saunters off, and Abby shakes her head in acknowledgment as she puts her napkin in her lap. François takes the wine bottle from the little table next to them that has a basket of baguette. Abby points to the baguette basket. François passes it to her, and she takes a piece and puts it on her appetizer plate.

"This is beautiful. Wholly Crêpe never looked so good," Abby says sweetly.

"That is not true. It always cleans up well when you walk in the door." François smiles back. "Wine?"

"Of course," Abby says, smitten.

"I have prepared for you a menu from my past life in Paris. You asked to be surprised. Maybe you will be, or maybe you won't be, but in any case, we will pretend that we are in Paris at some typical Parisian café together, preferably just off the Seine where we can people-watch but of course with a view of the Eiffel while we enjoy each other's company. What do you think?"

Abby is completely mesmerized by him. She's into this evening and into off-duty François, big-time.

"Sounds divine," Abby says.

Philippe brings the first course, which are salmon canapés topped with delicately placed sprigs of dill. Abby takes one and pops it into her mouth.

"Mmm, those are so good."

"Oui, he makes the canapés himself. With the exception of the cheeses, because it costs too much, all the things he creates here are with ingredients shipped in from Paris. He's quite dedicated, our Philippe," François says as he pops another one in his mouth. Abby watches him. "Magnifique," he says, doing the chef's kiss that is widely known as the French approval, the five-star review all in one cupped-hand kiss from the lips. Abby laughs, smiles, and takes another sip of her wine.

"How did you end up here?" she asks as she puts down her glass.

"Where? You mean here with you? I asked you, mademoiselle." He smiles.

"I mean here, like here. In this little gem of a café?" Abby asks, taking a sip of water this time.

"Oh, mademoiselle, that's such a long story with many layers, involving a friend of a friend that's no longer a friend," he says, taking a piece of baguette that Philippe snuck on the table without them realizing it.

"That resonates, I must say," Abby says as she takes a piece of baguette, too. They both instantaneously make the "mmm" sound, signaling that Philippe got it right. They continue to enjoy each course, taking in the culinary artistry that Philippe has prepared. When the cheese course comes around, François jokes that the cheese basically sucks in comparison to what is available in France, but they did the best they could.

"Well, mon monsieur, I wouldn't know the difference," Abby says with a slight smile, looking away from him as she watches Philippe prepare to bring them the next and what seems to be final round of all-out Frenchness.

Philippe, breaking his promise not to sing, is belting out "Paris, je t'aime d'amour" as he walks over with the final course, which is dessert. It's a gorgeous *soufflé au chocolat* that is delicately hanging over the edges of the ramekin just so. Abby turns it around to take in the precision with which it's been prepared. Philippe stands and waits. Abby takes a bite. She closes her eyes and lets the taste sink into her tongue. It is transportive. It's light, like air, but with a rich chocolate density that melts in her mouth so quickly it's gone before she has a chance to fully enjoy it, which makes her want to spoon up even more. Abby opens her eyes and sees François watching her, and then she looks at Philippe.

"Philippe, this is . . . there are no words. *C'est magnifique.*"

"Merci, mademoiselle. The fruits of my labor at Le Cordon Bleu."

"I know, and I feel privileged to be able to partake of it. Merci, mon chef."

"*Je vous en prie,*" Philippe says as he heads back to the kitchen, but not before he takes his phone and puts on the song "La complainte de la butte" by Zaz. François stands up and offers his hand to Abby. Abby shifts her body toward him, takes his hand, and stands up. They move across to the empty space of the room and start to slowly dance.

"This has been an amazing night, François. *Merci beaucoup.*"

"Ce n'est pas un problème, mademoiselle." François spins her around and dips her but then pulls her back up. They are both looking at each other straight on. François moves her in the same rhythm as him. The song ends. They slowly keep moving without music.

"I have a question for you, mon monsieur," Abby says.

"Hit me," François says, as they continue to sway.

"Why are we doing this? I mean, I've been coming here for a while now, and we've been, you know, flirty pretty much every time," Abby says, looking at him straight in those blue eyes.

"Le coeur a ses raisons. You seemed open to it at that moment with the grannies in hats, and the way you said, 'Surprise me!' It was like you and the universe sent me a message, a message in a bottle but with no ocean or water . . ."

"I get it, go on," Abby says.

"I seized the day! Other moments didn't feel open to be seized because you seem with heavy heart or always so busy on your MacBook," he says as he puts his cheek close to hers. She feels his skin on her cheek, and it's warm with some stubble. She closes her eyes.

"It's eleven p.m. Time for madame to sparkle!" Philippe shouts as he goes to the Eiffel on the wall and hits the switch, which makes all the lights on it frantically blink. It's a little much, but so is Philippe, so it's all good. Abby laughs, leaves François's dancing embrace, and sees him glare at Philippe, letting him know his timing is the worst ever. Abby goes over to her purse to get her phone to take a video of it all, as it is such a sweet yet comical scene. It's pure magic and one of the best evenings she's had in a very long time. She grabs her phone and sees an email notification on the screen with the subject line "Official Invite to Influencers Event—Paris Fashion Week."

"What the . . . ?" Abby says out loud and sits down on her chair. François heads over.

"What is it?" he asks, concerned.

"I got an email. A strange email with an invite."

"To what?"

"I'm not sure."

"Well, open it," François says, sounding a little annoyed because this message, along with Philippe's crazed lighting, seem to be hijacking his otherwise perfect evening. Abby slowly opens the email and reads it out loud:

Dear Ms. Sampson,

We would like to invite you to take part in our first-ever behind-the-scenes experience for exclusively selected influencers with compelling and chic profiles. You are on our first round of invites because of your Femme Fatale brand. It is a very elegant style, incorporating vintage designer looks with modern scenes.

This is an opportunity for you to become fully immersed in one of France's premiere fashion houses, leading up to and inclusive of their exclusive, elite haute couture fashion show. Some quick points of what is offered:

You will work with a group or cohort of fellow influencers for the duration of the time, exchanging ideas and possibly doing mutual account takeovers.

There will be a stipend offered to cover basic expenses as well as access to other benefits outlined in the offer attached.

As we partner with Air France, you will be flown to Paris in business class, a true luxury not everyone is so privileged to enjoy.

Please review the attached document outlining what we expect you to do while here in return for you using your account the entire time you are under this agreement and as we dictate to you. The point of this event is to educate the world on Paris Fashion Week in a different medium through the eyes of influencers who may not usually attend or be a part of it.

Please reply promptly if you are interested. We can assure you there is no place on earth better than Paris in the springtime, and there is certainly no better fashion week on the planet. We await your reply but won't wait too long because there are so many like you on the internet to choose from, and we chose you to ask first because of your eye for trends.

Cordialement,
Sophie Dubois
Claudette Couture

Abby finishes reading and stands.

"I'm speechless."

"Me too. Who is Ms. Sampson? Aren't you Allerton? And it's you that runs Femme Fatale—I had no idea. So many new realizations with just one email," François says.

"*Oui, c'est vrai, monsieur.* It's very confusing and dumb on my part, but this is so très cool, right? What do you think? It feels like I won a contest I didn't enter. *C'est incroyable!* This is surreal." Abby sits back down on her chair, holding the phone tightly. She's zooming in and out on the email message.

"It's amazing. Do you think it's real?" François asks.

"Oui, mon monsieur, it is from Claudette. You have to know the label, right?" Abby stands again. She's zooming in and out, rereading the sentences over and over. Fashion show. Two weeks' accommodation. Stipend. Her anxious excitement permeates the room.

"Ma chérie, you are hopping up and down like a jumping bean. You are so excited. Focus. So, you will go?"

"I will. I think it's real, which is why I can't believe it."

"It's great for you, Abby."

Abby stops, looks at him, and then looks around at this crazy, tacky room lit up with sweetness.

"Because I'm so wordy?" She smiles sweetly at him.

"Oui, because you are wordy . . ." He smiles back.

FOUR

Don't Like Change

Abby wakes up and grabs her phone first thing. She pushes up her sleep mask and opens the email once again to read it. She needs to answer. The initial excitement is waning, because during her sleepless night she kept having to admit that it is in fact an invite for someone like Heather. *Not her.* She drops the phone back on the bed. She slowly gets up and does some simple yoga stretches and puts on her robe, leaving the sleep mask in place with her hair still messy. Still half-asleep, she follows the aromas of a good old-fashioned country breakfast into the kitchen.

"Good morning," Abby says, yawning.

"How are you, my dear? Rough night?" Steve winks.

"Yes and no." Abby attempts to give him a fist bump and misses. Steve gives Chloe a little piece of sausage. Abby plops down on the chair and sighs. "Let me guess. Biscuits, bacon, and gravy with sausage and eggs?"

"You don't sound excited about the prospect of your mama's amazing cooking," Steve says, looking up from his Kindle.

"It's what we have every Sunday."

Abby rests her face in her hands and then takes a drink of orange juice.

"Sweet pea, would you like some?"

Abby knows that her mama hates it when anyone rejects her cooking. She's standing there with her spatula at the ready.

"When are you going to stop calling her sweet pea?" asks Steve.

"Never. Isn't that right, *sweet pea*?" retorts Betty Lou.

"I'm in my midtwenties, Mama. Maybe it's time?" Abby gives up and grabs a biscuit.

"Over my dead body. No pun intended. If you live in my house, you are my sweet pea!"

"Okay, then, glad we talked." Abby puts a little butter on her biscuit. They are hard to resist.

Betty winks at her and moves over to manage the new espresso machine that Abby got for them with some sponsorships she nailed for Femme Fatale. It's new to the house. One of Abby's attempts to modernize the kitchen.

"Where did you get this thing? Can't we just use the old one? My Folgers worked just fine."

"Mama, please. Embrace change. It's the best cup of coffee you'll ever have."

"Your mama doesn't like change. Haven't you figured that one out yet? Let me give it a shot. Get it? A shot?" Steve winks again.

Abby rolls her eyes affectionately and sits back to watch how this will all play out. Steve moves over to Betty Lou and pinches her butt. Abby smiles, as there's a sweetness to their relationship even if her mama is Southern and her daddy is Northern right down to his liberal views with a touch of tree hugging.

"Stop that! Not in front of Abby!" Betty Lou playfully slaps him.

"Mama, I've seen more than that, and frankly I've done more than that," Abby responds, deadpan.

Betty Lou turns around with her mouth hanging open and says, "I don't want to know."

Abby shakes her head, laughing in disbelief.

"Listen, sweet pea, I like change, just not with things that don't need changing. And my Folgers coffee is one of those," Betty says.

"We got that, Mama. Which is why you've never left home for how many years now?" Abby regrets saying it as soon as she says it.

"Well, I couldn't leave for a lot of years."

"I know, Mama. I'm sorry."

Betty walks over to Abby and takes Abby's face in her hands. "Why do I need to leave home anyway, Abby? I've got everything I need right here. This is home."

"Well, I'm thinking about doing something crazy." Abby stands up.

"Marrying that boy down the street?" Betty Lou interrupts.

"Seriously, Mama. It is not 1956. People get married to people from different countries, different religions now, and not just people down the street."

"Well, down the street could just as well be a different country now. It's changed a bit over the years," Betty Lou retorts.

Abby looks over at Steve, and he shakes his head sympathetically. The two of them have always agreed that they need to take Betty Lou on a trip somewhere—at the very least across the state line—to get a bigger and broader perspective, but they both know that "ain't goin' to happen," as Betty Lou quibbles every time they mention it—usually after she says something

like she just did, something backward, outdated, and border-
line discriminatory.

"I got an invite," Abby says.

"To what?" Betty Lou says as she stops fiddling with the
food on the counter.

"To a fashion thing." Abby positions herself to stand
up straight.

"In town?" Betty Lou asks.

Steve jumps in, "Are you going to New York, Abby? I've
been telling you, with all your talent, you should go there.
We'll help you get settled. You're the real deal, Abby girl!"

"Thank you, Daddy, but I make enough money. You don't
need to help. I've told you that. I'm thinking a little farther."
Abby points for emphasis.

"Well, don't hold us in suspense, sweet pea . . ." Betty
Lou's now leaning in and looking over her quirky glasses, still
with spatula in hand but now enjoying a piece of her personal
masterpiece, the biscuit. The espresso machine shudders into
action, making Betty Lou jump back.

"Oh, my Lord. It's like a truck!" she says loudly in disbelief. "It sounds like it's alive!"

Abby straightens, stands up, opens her arms wide, and says
playfully, "I'm going to Paris!"

"Paris? Which one? Paris, Tennessee, or *the* Paris?"
Betty asks.

"Oui, *the* Paris, the one in France," Abby says, still with
arms open wide, waiting dutifully for the reaction she's hoping
she'll get.

"We what?" Betty deadpans. No such luck.

"No, Mama, seriously, that's French for *yes*," Abby answers.

At this point, Abby can see that Steve is at full attention,
taking in the dynamic that is playing out between her and

her mama. It's still respectful, but it could go one of three ways: very wrong, very right, or all-out sideways. The last one is what will most likely happen, as it has many times before with much simpler and mundane topics. Abby headed to Paris? That's a doozy. Going sideways for sure. Abby watches him slowly put his Kindle on the table and take a deliberate sip of espresso, which leaves him with a perfect, milk-frothed mustache.

"When did you learn French?" Betty Lou says.

"Mama, I took it all through middle school and high school. All the French vocab words all over my room."

"Oh, right. I remember. I thought it was a phase, like everything else was, and well, I was sick."

"Not a phase, Mama. Just had no place to use it," Abby says as she tightens her robe.

"So, is this like a study abroad, or is it for your fashion biz?" Betty Lou says, looking over her glasses once again.

"My successful Instagram accounts? Yes, Mama. As much as I love you both and enjoy watching you being forced to embrace the modern world, you and others have helped me realize that I need a change. A drastic, new, over-the-ocean change!"

"It's those children's books Aunt Doris read to you when you were little. The one with the little orphans in the straw hats?" Abby can see that Betty Lou is struggling inside. They both knew this would happen one way or another, but Abby's pretty sure Betty Lou thought it would be somewhere else in the South, not across the Atlantic Ocean and in a country where they don't even speak English. Abby knows what's going to happen next. Betty will try to discourage her, even though she knows in her heart that the right thing to do is to let her go. This must be when being a mother is tough.

"There've been so many terrorist attacks there recently, and the French don't like us. Remember that whole French fries scandal?" Betty says.

"The one where some of the people in the US wanted to change the name to 'Freedom fries'? I can kind of see why they hate us. Mama, it's time. I need a new gig. This place is starting to feel claustrophobic. I need some space with some new scenery and adventure. Can I tell you the details?"

"All right, then. C'mon with it." Betty Lou turns from the counter fully to face Abby straight on.

"So, I've been invited to an influencer event to show the world the behind-the-scenes preparations for the Claudette haute couture fashion show during Paris Fashion Week! Isn't that the coolest?" Abby turns to both her parents to get their reactions, knowing that they have no idea what any of that means.

"Wow. That's amazing, Abby girl," Steve says.

"Claudette? Wow. Even I know that designer. Your Grandma Lillian had a beautiful brocade jacket from them. It's that old and classy," Betty Lou says.

"I knew you would know them. Isn't it great?" Abby claps her hands in excitement.

"It is, sweet pea. That's wonderful," Betty Lou says as she turns to take some bacon from the skillet and puts it on a plate with a single paper towel on it. Abby grabs a piece and takes a bite, using the other part of the piece as a kind of thinking wand, ready to deliver her most prized idea.

"So, I've been thinking all night that I'll use some of my savings and go over earlier for a month or so. What do you both think?" Abby asks.

"Where will you stay? Hotels are expensive anyway, and I'm sure France is no exception," Betty Lou says.

"I'll look for a longer-stay option on Airbnb or something. I feel like something will work out. I got a good feeling about it. Well, most of it. I've got to work out some stuff with Heather first." Abby takes another bite of her bacon.

"I didn't know you were still in touch with Heather, sweet pea," Betty Lou says.

"Well, we're not besties anymore, more like business associates, and I need to deal with that."

"You seem to have all but decided," Steve says.

"I think I have. It's a little gift to myself. I think I've earned it." A palpable pause comes across the room. Betty Lou stops.

"Earned it? What do you mean by that?" Betty Lou says, taken aback.

"I just mean that I've worked hard, and I'm ready to do something fun with all the money I've earned, that's all."

Steve gets up and goes over to Betty Lou and gently says to her, "I think it's *go* time for our Abby girl, and we need to support her."

"I didn't realize you thought having a mama with cancer was a duty or a job," Betty Lou retorts.

"Mama, I didn't say that. I didn't mean that at all. Of course it wasn't a duty."

"I didn't ask for cancer, sweet pea—or, I'm sorry, excuse me, *Abby*. I'm sorry you had to live with a mama that was sick by no fault of her own." Betty Lou turns off the stove, slides the pan in the sink with sausages still in it, along with the spatula, and starts to head out of the kitchen.

"Mama, I know that. I didn't mean to come across that way about it. I just need to do something with my life now that you are better, and I can feel comfortable leaving. That's all."

Turning to Steve, Betty Lou says, "Can you take those biscuits out of the oven when they're ready? I need a minute." Betty Lou exits the kitchen with her all-too-familiar passive-aggressive fog following her.

Abby stays put, feeling like she's fifteen again, triggering her mama by simply stating how she feels. She half smiles with hurt at her daddy and says, "Well, that didn't go well," and leaves the kitchen as if she's been punished.

Once back in her room, she sends a DM to Heather.

> @FemmeFatale: Hey! Can we FT in the next couple of days? I really need to talk to you about this account. Something's come up that's time sensitive.

She hits Send and puts the phone on her desk. Chloe is in her usual position, and Abby gives her a couple of hard strokes, maybe a little too hard, as Chloe promptly jumps down. There's a text alert.

> @HeatherBeather: Hi Abby, I'm busy with my dissertation right now. What is it about? I finally got my monthly payment from you. Looks like we had some solid sponsorship deals this month.

Abby reads it and shakes her head. "We? By that, you mean *me*." Abby shakes her head. She texts back.

> @FemmeFatale: I understand, but this is important and it's time sensitive.

She clicks Send and waits. The agonizing three dots that indicate someone is typing appear.

@HeatherBeather: Ok, let's talk tomorrow afternoon? That work?

@FemmeFatale: Yep. I'll text you after lunch. Thanks.

⊹ ⋅·+ ⋅ ✦ ✦ ⋅ ⋅ ⊹

Back at Charlene's office, Abby is sitting in her usual spot. "I've worked hard for this. Really hard." Abby stops, takes a deep breath.

"What's stopping you?" Charlene asks.

"I don't know." She shrugs.

"Will you try something with me?" Charlene holds eye contact with her.

"Sure, is this about the Twinkies?" Abby asks.

"Let's see where it leads. Take that pillow next to you." Abby grabs it and strokes it softly, as it's a nice light-pink chenille.

"Give it a good squeeze to your chest," Charlene says. Abby holds the pillow tighter, with a little more enthusiasm than Charlene expected.

"Now I want you to close your eyes and take a couple deep breaths. Put that pillow close to your heart and talk to that part of yourself that's holding you back." Charlene leans in.

"This is so weird, Charlene."

Abby peeks through one eye and can see Charlene is focused as she says, "I know. Keep an open mind. Take a couple of deep breaths. Good. Now, think of yourself in Paris. What does that feel like?"

Abby strokes the pillow, and her face softens.

"I feel excited and pretty, like full of light," Abby says, smiling with her eyes closed. "I see myself walking down the cute streets, completely immersed in the different styles and scenes. It feels like I'm in a movie," Abby says, still with her eyes closed.

"Good. Now keep that feeling safe in your heart. You got it?" Charlene asks.

"Yes, it's locked in," Abby says.

"Great. Now, holding that feeling, let yourself think about staying. What does that feel like? How do you see yourself?" Charlene asks gently.

Abby's face tightens.

"I feel like I can't breathe," Abby says with her hands clasping the pillow.

"Are those feelings bringing up anything else?" Charlene asks in a gentle voice. Abby's eyes start to fill with tears, and one falls down the side of her face slowly, softly but ever present.

"What's coming up, Abby?" Charlene asks her.

Abby grips the pillow tightly, her long, curly eyelashes holding steady.

"I'm remembering something that happened when I was about ten or eleven maybe," Abby says, wiping away the tear.

"Do you want to share more?" Charlene asks. Abby's face with her eyes still closed is slowly blushing and becoming a deep shade of red.

"I remember being in school. In a bathroom stall, and the windows in the bathroom were open, but the stall was enclosed, so no windows. I was peeing. I finished and I farted. That's when I heard them."

"Heard who, Abby?"

"The three girls. They were whispering, thinking I couldn't hear them or that I wouldn't see them underneath the doors of the stall."

"Keep going, Abby. What happened next?"

"I flushed the toilet, and by the time I turned back around to open the stall door, they were holding it closed. I kept pushing it, thinking it was stuck, because who could be so mean and stupid as to hold a door like that."

"I'm with you. You are safe here. What happened next?"

"The first girl says to me that I have to go on a diet to get out, and the second one chimes in and says you'll have to lose a few to get out of here, and then the third one says . . ." Abby at this point is sobbing, holding the pillow, roughly petting it, desperately seeking a way out of this, its softness on her palms and fingertips.

"It gets worse."

"How so, Abby?" Charlene asks, then takes a drink of water quietly.

"I lunged at the door so hard I hurt my arm. I kept yelling, 'LET ME OUT! LET ME OUT!' and I kept lunging and lunging and falling over the toilet. I was crazed. I was so angry."

"Take that pillow, Abby, and put it down. Punch it. Punch it with everything you need to say to those girls."

Abby starts to punch at the pillow.

"Let me out, you little bitches. Let me out!" Abby hits the pillow a couple of times. She then stops and looks over at Charlene.

"One of the girls said that if I gave them my underwear, they would let me out. She said they were going to use it for my before and after pictures. Said the ones I had on that day would be my before ones. I just lunged at the door once more. They kept holding it. It was three against one. And then . . ."

Abby looks up at Charlene and sees her eyes full of love, right there with her.

"And then what, Abby?" Charlene says, completely engrossed.

"And then . . . the bell rang. Recess was over. I never loved hearing that bell so much as I did that day. It distracted them right when I lunged at the door again and . . ." Abby takes a breath. Grabs a tissue and blows her nose.

"So, you got out?" Charlene says and takes a breath.

"The door gave, and it fell on top of them, and I was on top of the door. I smashed them, hard." Abby's face is a beautiful mess with those tire tracks of mascara, her cheeks red hot, flushed with blood, but there's an underlying smile of achievement after sharing that part of the story.

"I pushed the door so hard that the hinges fell off, and that was that." Abby blows her nose again but is still looking down. Abby gently strokes the pillow now on her lap. After a few seconds of silence, Charlene gently starts to speak.

"What's going on now, Abby?" Charlene asks.

"I always feel confined. I still feel it at home, in my business with my friend, and I mean I created that confinement. I didn't have to do that," Abby says as she shrugs.

"I see it differently," Charlene says.

"How so?" Abby asks.

"Back then, you took control for yourself, and you busted down that door. And you literally and figuratively smashed the shaming and humiliation that was happening."

Abby lifts her eyes to Charlene's again. She sees Charlene's eyes full of compassion and love.

"I did. Didn't I?"

"You sure did. What if you reframed this? Saw this as an opportunity to break down another door."

"I didn't realize that was still in me."

"Our bodies hold it all. If you reframe it now and use it to get unstuck, and unravel from the life you live here, what does that look like?" Charlene leans back.

"How? What does that mean, like in real-life living?" Abby puts the pillow down and guzzles some water from the glass on the table next to her.

"Go toward the feelings that bring you the light and excitement, not the shame and humiliation that want to keep you in the bathroom stall."

"And talk to me as a pillow?" Abby blows her nose.

"If that works for you. Maybe occasionally check in and see what that amazing middle-school-aged girl in there needs to feel heard and valued." Charlene has her hand over her heart now. "What does she say about this opportunity and about the relationship with your friend now?"

"Feels weird, but I'll give it a try. It did feel awesome when I smashed that door down. I still have the scars." Abby shuffles on the couch to show Charlene the mark on her arm and pulls down her pants slightly to show one under her hip line.

"Those are battle scars. I feel so excited for you. You already broke through so much with your influencer platform. You smashed down a huge door for others and gave them a voice, too. Doors are there to be opened or closed. I wonder, though, if this is the middle schooler inside of you and the high schooler inside of you, too, that was never was able to launch? What doors would she open and what doors would she close?" Charlene smiles.

FIVE

Bon Voyage

There's something calming about sitting in one's own car and having time to be quiet and still. Abby, holding all that she just went through in Charlene's office, needs that space once again. She's parked just down the street from her house. This invite is the perfect springboard for her, even if it's only technically for a month or so. She feels raw and broken open and doesn't have it in her to go back inside the world that she wants to leave just yet.

She can see Betty Lou working on her flower beds with a renewed fervor. Watching her methodically dig and pull up weeds, Abby sees Betty Lou's favorite headscarf is starting to fall off. She instinctively wants to move the car forward so she can help her put it back on and make it perfect again, as she's done so many times before.

This time she turns the car off and watches. The scarf slides off slowly and falls to the side of Betty Lou, exposing the small patches of grayish-blonde hair growing back in for all to see. Abby continues to watch Betty Lou as she frantically puts it back on, looking around to see if anyone saw her. But then out of nowhere a pause happens. Abby watches her mama stay on her knees and look up at the trees, the clear blue sky, and the sun. She watches as Betty Lou closes her eyes and smiles, looking upward as if she's taking in every ounce of warmth from its rays. And then it happens. Betty Lou looks down, removes her garden gloves, and then, looking back up, she ties the scarf around her neck with perfect precision. As Betty Lou runs her hand through the soft patches of hair, Abby's eyes well up. Abby zeroes in on the scarf that's now daintily tied around Betty Lou's neck and no longer on her head.

Abby starts the car and slowly pulls up to the house and into the driveway in her designated spot just to the left of the double garage. She gets out of the car with her Goyard bag of business on her shoulder and heads into the mudroom off the kitchen.

"Hey, Mama, how's the yard?" Abby says, entering the kitchen as Betty Lou is washing her hands. Abby notices that the scarf is still around her mama's neck. Abby drops Chloe on the floor and her bag on the counter, then she pours some lemonade for both herself and her mama from the large glass pitcher on the countertop.

"Beautiful. I had some diggin' energy in me and was determined to get in there and get it pretty." Betty dries her hands, takes the glass from Abby's hands, and drinks almost all of it.

"Well, it looks amazing out there, Mama. I love your scarf. It looks great there."

They take another synchronized drink and say nothing for a couple of seconds, offering the perfect picture of a rare moment when a mother and daughter feel comfortable in their own skin together. Betty Lou puts her glass down, and turning back around, she unties the scarf from her neck and starts to put it back on her head. Abby turns around and without even thinking takes her mama's hand before she makes it to her head. She catches her eye and smiles warmly. Betty Lou holds her gaze, and Abby notices tears forming in her mama's eyes. As Abby puts her mama's hand with the scarf still in it slowly back down to her side, she takes the scarf from her mama's hand and in one sleek motion chicly ties it around her own neck.

"What do you think? Looks good?" Abby does a little pose.

"Beautiful."

"Well, I am your daughter. It would be impossible to not look beautiful, right?"

"Well now, we do have to give your daddy some of the credit."

"Do we?" Abby says as they both laugh.

Abby hesitates, then she blurts out, "I'm going to go to Paris, Mama."

"I know," Betty replies.

"I feel like things are happening serendipitously. It's kind of cool."

"Well, that's a big word." Betty Lou laughs.

"I won a spelling bee with that word."

"Oh, that's right, I remember. Was it fifth grade?"

"No, Mama, it was seventh grade."

"Oh, this brain of mine, but I'm gettin' better," Betty Lou says as she gently pats Abby's cheek. "I'm going to go cool off from all that weeding and take a shower. Later, gator."

"Later." Abby takes another drink of her lemonade. She looks at her phone and opens her emails and goes into the Femme Fatale account. She rereads the Paris Fashion Week message once again. Then she clicks over to her DM's with Heather, trying to confirm their FT call, but still no response. She clicks over to the Femme Fatale Insta account and reads through the different posts that have Heather in them that's she done over the years, noticing the many images of Heather phasing out and more generic images from @parispascal using sleek, beautiful linen mannequins in ways that highlight the use of the vintage pieces that are chic and elegant. She feels proud that what she incorporated and developed without Heather is what got Femme Fatale the invite. She reads one post that she remembers writing long ago, and it's good. Just then, a text comes through from François.

> François: Bonjour, ma chérie! What is the status? Are you headed to Paris?

Abby hovers over the message with a smile. She responds.

> Abby: Bonjour, mon monsieur! Technically, I'm still thinking about it, but honestly, I'm already there.

> François: Of course you are. So, you will need some courses on how to be a Parisian and how to swat off the French men that find you as irrésistible as I do.

> Abby: Stop. You are making me blush.

> François: Good. Send me some details. I'll plan. And you decide, because opportunities in life come at you fast, and you need to take them before they pass you by.

> Abby: @MeaningfulQuotes again?

François: Oui. ☺

Abby: Later, gator. ☺

François: Tchao-tchao

She sits down at the kitchen table and remembers the last time she and Heather met and the desperation she felt to keep Femme Fatale's brand of chic, skinny, and perfect and Heather's resistance to it until she offered her a deal. Looking back down at her phone, she scrolls through and reads all the cold and cryptic messages between them, and then she clicks over to her Venmo to see the amounts of money she's sent Heather. She hovers over her current balance and sees the ample sum in big, bold numerals. After a final click over to Plus-Size Real, seeing her own images and her creative shots curated perfectly with purpose and pure heart, she declares, "Screw it. I just need to get there." She clicks over to her drafted response message in the Femme Fatale inbox.

Dear Ms. Dubois,

Thank you very much for your offer. I am very sorry for my delay. I am pleased to accept your invitation, and I will send you the signed agreement in the next couple of days. If it's possible, I'll make the flight arrangements for myself, and you can reimburse me, as I'd like to come much earlier to practice my French and spend time in Paris before the event begins. I'm looking forward to this great opportunity.

Yours truly,
Heather Sampson—Femme Fatale

At that moment, Chloe jumps on her lap. It's done now. Abby stands up, and, holding Chloe like a baby, she rubs her soft belly and says, "I wish you could come, too, Chloe and be like Chloe in *The Aristocats*."

. . + . + + . . .

Abby, sitting outside on her porch, is waiting for François to show up. They've agreed to meet at her place today for another "Parisian pointers" session. She's perusing Airbnb, looking at places she might be able to rent for her time before the event begins. She's also been reading some very concerning posts about Paris Airbnbs being completely derelict and having squatters in them when people enter their fully paid-for places for the first time. François pulls up and hops out of his pet project, a semi-restored vintage Ford Mustang. He plops himself down next to Abby on the porch swing and glances at her MacBook.

"Mmm, that one's nice," he says to her, smiling. Abby laughs.

"You are so nosy. Always looking at my screen. Do you poke around in your other customers' business like this?" she asks.

"Have you seen my other customers? Not much to poke." He smiles. Abby looks at him sweetly. He smells like possibility to her. And she's decided to leave. Ugh.

"So, ma chérie, let's talk turnkey."

"Turnkey. Do you mean turkey?" Abby says, trying not to laugh.

"Turkey? No, I mean turnkey. Like we are going to turn this topic to what it needs to be."

"The expression is 'let's talk turkey,' but I'm happy to do whatever you want." Abby winks at him, smiling.

"What? All this time I thought it made sense, but now you are telling me it makes completely no sense. Why is it turkey? I mean, I always thought it was a little weird, but now you are telling me it's turkey. Which is even weirder. There is no logic to that. What does a turkey have to do with talking straight? Are they especially honest birds or something?" François says, exasperated. Abby is laughing so hard she's almost crying but then realizes that François is in fact not joking around and is looking at her for solid answers. Abby's got none.

"The last time I spoke to a turkey, I couldn't figure out if it was a straight shooter or not. Must have been all the gobble, gobble sounds making it hard to discern. Désolée." Abby smiles.

"*So* funny, mademoiselle. I'm how you say, splitting my stitches over here," François says sarcastically. He directs her back to her Airbnb page, and she starts to scroll again as she giggles over his last sentence.

"So, you want to rent an Airbnb, yes?"

"Oui, there are some cute ones on here." Abby keeps scrolling through.

"Ah, wait a minute! Hold the phone! I just remembered something. I think I can help you. I have a friend, or a *cousine*, that has a place in Paris, and I think she's going to Amsterdam for a few months, last I heard."

"Wait, is she a cousine or a friend?" Abby's confused, triggered by a twinge of jealousy.

"Mmm, *c'est compliqué*, Abby."

"It's really not, François. It would be weird if you dated your cousine."

"So, let's stay on topic. It is top floor but in a not-so-bad area with some life and love and music and fun. You will love it."

"You seem to know this apartment well. Did you visit often?" Abby asks.

"Oui." François sees Chloe and takes her into his lap and starts to gently pet her. She rubs herself all over him, purring with great intensity. Abby watches and likes what she sees. Chloe has always had the gift of good discernment when it comes to people.

"It's not my favorite view, because as you know from Wholly Crêpe, the Eiffel is everything to me . . . ," he says, rolling his eyes. "But I think you'll like it. I'll connect you two, and you go see it when you are there, oui?"

"Really? That would be great! So should I book a hotel for the first few days or . . ."

"Oui, why not, and then you can transfer to her place if you like it. Good plan?"

"Magnifique!" Abby says, excited. She then types in *booking.com*. "So, is she maybe more of an ex-girlfriend?" Abby asks. She can't help but pry a little more.

"Does it matter? Let's keep it simple," François says. Abby nods and knowingly smiles. "What is your plan in Paris?" François asks.

"Well, I'm going over there basically as someone else, so there's that to deal with first thing . . ."

"C'est vrai. I wish I could be a little fly in the room when that happens," François says as he continues to pet Chloe.

"I want to do some posts around Paris with a theme, but it hasn't come to me yet. I'd love to see how the whole plus-size vibe is over there." She looks up at François. He nods a little bit to the side, hesitantly.

"Do you not think it's a good idea?" Abby asks.

"*Si, c'est très bien.* You will see when you get there. Sometimes it's better to let one have their first raw experience with something for the full natural effect." He smiles. Abby raises one eyebrow. That's certainly fishy. Chloe jumps down.

"Should I be prepared for something?" she asks.

"Non, you do you, ma chérie, and everything will work out. Paris is . . ." He and Abby finish the sentence together, "always a good idea!" He smiles.

·: ·:+ · + + · ·:.

In the back seat of her parents' car, Abby feels like she's thirteen again on her way to summer camp. She didn't have the heart to tell them she wanted to go to the airport in an Uber on her own. She's asked her daddy to stop by Wholly Crêpe on the way, as she wants to say a final farewell to François and Philippe.

Pulling up to Wholly Crêpe, Abby can see through the window that François is there. She gets out of the car quickly and rushes in.

"Bonjour, Abby! You ready?" François says from the pastry counter.

"Bonjour, monsieur," Abby says, smiling. She walks over to the counter. "It's time. I wanted to say a final goodbye once again."

"A *final* goodbye? I think you mean *au revoir pour un mois*?" François says sincerely. "A final means we won't see each other again," he says as he comes around the counter to stand in front of her.

"C'est vrai."

"Remember, ma chérie, be careful of French men, except for moi, of course. I'm one of the only good ones. And crêpes are wonderful, but please try everything! Paris is a place where senses are overloaded. Fall in love with all of it."

"But not the men?" Abby smiles, cocking her head to the side.

"They don't call it the City of Light because it's lonely and dreary—well, it is dreary in the winter. I don't miss that. What I mean is, it is full of fate, and you cannot change fate." François smiles.

"Note taken, mon monsieur." Abby smiles with her François butterflies fluttering through her stomach, only this time they are flying in an air of bittersweetness.

"Remember, my crêpes are just as good as the Parisian ones," Philippe yells from the kitchen. François makes a "no" face to Abby with his back to Philippe, and she laughs.

"I'm really going to miss you two. So much." Abby moves forward to give François a hug.

He stops her and says, "Remember how you do the *bisous*?" He takes her hand and then leans in, kissing her right cheek softly. He methodically moves over to kiss her left cheek softly and then gently pulls back. "The more confident you are doing it, the more respect you will earn." He steps back and releases her hand. Abby touches her left cheek with her hand.

"Merci, mon monsieur. I must go, or I'll miss my flight. *Je t'aime pour toujours.* You are my guru on all things France, Paris, and *romance*." Abby kisses his cheek and then kisses him full on with an intensity she didn't know she had. She steps back, smiling ear to ear, and then blows him and Philippe kisses as she leaves the café. Once back in the car, she notices that Betty Lou and Steve are smiling like they've just been let in on some juicy gossip during their Bunco nights but can't share it because that just wouldn't be prudent. Blushing a little, she smiles at them. Not a word about it is spoken between the three of them.

"Let's go. I'm going to be late."

"You got it," Steve says. They pull out of Wholly Crêpe's parking lot and head off. A text dings for Abby. She grabs her phone, mentally crossing her fingers it's not Heather. There's no turning back now. Sighing out all kinds of relief, she sees it's François.

> François: Oh la la! You swept me off my feet, ma chérie! I'm floating. I'm now François that floats. Wow.

> Abby: That makes deux of us! ☺ Take care of yourself. I'll call you from the Eiffel!

> François: Non, call me from anywhere BUT the Eiffel. Cliché. ☺

> Abby: Understood. ☺

Once at the airport and all checked in, Abby stands in front of her parents and says, "I'm going to miss you both, but I'm so ready for this. Thank you for supporting me, and I hope you'll enjoy this time without me *always* being around." She smiles.

"You will always be around, sweet pea. Right here." Betty Lou touches her heart with the palm of her hand, just like Charlene has told Abby to do in her sessions. Abby's eyes well up. She can't help but feel this is a watershed moment. Something is shifting, she can feel it, and it's scary and exciting all at once. Abby places her palm on her heart as well. They both tightly hug and then release. Abby moves over to Steve.

"You take care of yourself, Daddy." She gives him a warm, tight hug and whispers in his ear, "Get what you need, okay?"

"I will," Steve says quietly.

Abby leaves his embrace and says, "Pinkie promise?" as she puts her pinkie out.

Steve links his pinkie with hers. "I promise, Abby girl." Then they do their secret handshake they've done since she was a tween. Abby heads into the customs area, turns around, and sees them embracing each other and waving with an intensity that is a little embarrassing. Seeing them both from afar, especially Betty Lou with her favorite scarf around her neck and her head au natural, makes her quickly take out her iPhone and snap a photo of them. *Parfait.* She does a final wave and goes behind the screen. She hands her passport to the customs officer and smiles widely as she says, "I'm headed to Paris."

"Well, then bon voyage, mademoiselle," he says in response with a Southern drawl as he hands back her passport and boarding pass. Abby laughs and walks confidently through.

Entering Air France's business-class compartment is like stepping into a Louis Vuitton shopwindow. The iconic pet carrier bags are filled with little dogs that could be mistaken for stuffed ones were it not for their sometimes piercing little barks and snapping at anything that passes. The passengers are all dressed, as if they have run from a fashion magazine photo shoot directly to the plane, evoking images of hurried assistants holding coffees and phones, with snarky undertones. Abby enters with her travel bag from Target, or Targét as she likes to call it, along with every other Southern woman trying to be chic and cute. Thankfully she also brought along her larger monogrammed Goyard tote bag that she got as part of a limited partnership with Femme Fatale. It helps her to feel more acceptable in this very tough fashion crowd. She's wearing a black T-shirt that says *Chéri(e)* in bold white letters. Her blazer looks campy and fun over her statement tee. She's chosen ripped boyfriend jeans and her trusty white Converse platform sneaks for the travel day, anticipating any hiccups along the way. Comfort is king. She's excited and she's ready. It's hard not to notice that every other passenger is wearing big dark sunglasses like the ones you'd wear to a funeral. After doing a scan of the space as she's boarding, she says to herself, "Did someone die today?"

Not to be outdone, she gets her Gucci sunglasses— thick-rimmed red ones with some sparkle—from her bag. By this time, she's noticed that all the surrounding passengers have given her a once-over, ascertaining her value and position within their petri dish of first-class culture. Simultaneously, it occurs to Abby just how much she stands out in this crowd as she is quirky, stylish, and unusual, and she can't help but catch the minor detail that she's at least twice the size of the women around her. She starts to shift around a bit in her airplane seat. She picks up the super chic Air France magazine and starts to thumb through it. More pictures of designer handbags and the little dogs in them. Ugh. She sticks the magazine back in the pocket. Why not just get a cat? The thought of Chloe stops her in her tracks. She misses her already. Suddenly, the little oasis of her parents' house, with her own sweet room that was all hers, seems so far away. It's a surreal mix of sadness and excitement, fear and anticipation. She takes in a deep breath.

She remembers François and their last meetups/dates and that kiss just a few hours ago. It makes her sweetly smile but also sad. Oh well, it's only a month.

The flight attendant, who is giving off next-level vibes in this part of the plane, appears to be dressed better than most of the passengers, with her little red scarf and perfectly coiffed French chignon, and her outfit accented with a few statement pieces of jewelry. She's offering some takeoff treats. Seeing the flight attendant's scarf endears her to Abby. She takes her hand to her heart and closes her eyes, repeating to herself the phrases she learned from Charlene: "I am loved, I am worthy, and I'm okay." Then she shifts to thinking about how decadent and even absurd this is, but so exciting, so she's in for all of it. Besides, she wants to get her money's worth since she footed the bill up front for this seat. She waves the flight attendant over.

"Bonjour, madame!"

"Bonjour! Would I still be referred to as *mademoiselle*?"

"I'm not sure. It's hard to tell."

"I don't think I'm a *madame*. Not yet, anyway." Abby smiles.

"It's good you are so confident. You'll need it in Paris." The flight attendant saunters off to the next passenger with her treat tray. But before she's able to move completely to the row behind, Abby waves her hand again.

"*Uh, pardonnez-moi, madame,* may I have a drink and those treats, too, *s'il vous plaît*?"

The flight attendant stops in her tracks, appears peeved, and swirls around to return. Abby has already started unwrapping the little chocolates that were placed on the armrest at her seat.

The flight attendant is taken aback and speaks without thinking.

"So, you will have the drink, treats, and chocolate? All at once?"

Not understanding the tone of the comment, Abby responds with spunk and humor. "Well, you only live once, right?"

In a more scolding tone, the flight attendant answers, "Oui! Which is why you might want to choose one or the other?" She moves on briskly to the next passenger, leaving

Abby openmouthed with half a chocolate in her mouth and completely speechless.

Abby doesn't know what hit her. She looks around to see if others heard that comment in the same way she did—rude and insulting. She looks over at the lady across the aisle from her, who's smiling at her. Abby smiles back. The lady leans over and quietly says, "Welcome to France. Don't take it to heart too much. It's a cultural thing. You'll get used to it. It's part of our charm."

"Thank you. I'll keep that in mind." Abby smiles back.

She grabs her journal titled *BIG IDEAS* and starts to write down what just happened. It's going on Plus-Size Real.

A little dog in its little bag has been watching Abby the whole time. Abby sticks her tongue out at it. It growls. She shakes her head and laughs to herself. She then grabs the little travel pack and tries the complimentary L'Occitane hand lotion sampler. Just at that moment, the man sitting in the row behind her, who she noticed has been watching her since the second she boarded, taps her on the shoulder.

"Yes, did you drop something?" Abby leans forward to help.

"Bonjour, mademoiselle. Are you enjoying the first-class perks?" He's put his head around the seat, and Abby's turned toward him.

"I am. They are so nice."

"Of course they are. They are French. We only do the very best. Let me guess. First time in first class and first time to Paris?"

"Oui! First time for both," Abby answers, smiling.

"Where are you staying? At the Ritz at Place Vendôme or maybe the George V?"

The man gives her a look that makes her a little weak in the knees and uncomfortable all at the same time. Damn these double-dip feelings. They seem to be everywhere today, and she'd really like them to stop.

"Oh, non. I'm a part of an event for influencers who will be doing a behind-the-scenes at Paris Fashion Week from the Claudette design house."

"Ah, for big woman? Do they do that at Paris Fashion Week? I don't think I've ever seen it," he says, making a gesture of "big" with his hands.

"No, I think it's for successful influencers—like me. I'm trying to say I'll be given housing courtesy of Claudette. It's part of the deal."

"Ah, I see." He's grinning now, like a Cheshire cat. "May I join you?"

Abby's taken aback.

"In Paris? At the hotel?"

He smiles even bigger. "If you wish, but I was referring to the seat next to you. It looks like it will be empty."

Abby calls upon her inner middle-school girl as Charlene suggested and decides to put on some inner armor.

"Are you going to steal something? My French waiter friend warned me about men like you and how you sometimes prey on naïve American women in Paris."

"Do I look like I would steal something from you? Other than your heart, of course."

Abby turns away from him and waves to the flight attendant. As she's doing that, the charming potential shyster makes himself at home in the seat next to her.

She turns back around, and he's there. Before she can even react, she is taken in by all that he's presenting. Her eyes fall upon the top button of his indigo-colored shirt, with just the perfect poof of chest hair showing from beneath it. His stubble is hipster but with a twist: there's a smidge of gray, which means he's a little older than she thought or lives a very stressful life. Either way, she's finding it surprisingly sexy. He's wearing a couple of leather bracelets with vintage silver clasps on his very perfectly proportioned, manly wrist. Abby is completely swept away.

"Keep it together, Abby. Keep it together," she says quietly to herself as she looks around for the flight attendant, who apparently thinks she is Marion Cotillard.

The flight attendant stops. "Oui! *Madame?*" she says, emphasizing the hell out of *madame* this time.

"We'll have to agree to disagree. May I have some champagne, s'il vous plaît?"

"Of course. Would you like some more chocolate, too?"

"Non. Just the champagne." The flight attendant pours the champagne with the flair of a Michelin three-star waitress and saunters off in what seems to be her signature style.

"I like you. Living life to the fullest! My name is Jean-Baptiste." He has his hand out to shake hers. Abby gulps down another swig of champagne.

"Did you say John the Baptist?" Abby says, confused.

"Mmm, I think you'll find I'm not so holy. It's Jean, like Sean, only with a *J*, not an *S*; and it's not John."

Abby's eyes are glazed over. She's kind of following him, but his accent and smell and the champagne are causing her head to swirl a bit. He's reminding her of François but with a different, more bad-guy vibe. She's never met a man who smelled like a combination of lavender and chamomile. She realizes that it's probably the hand lotion she's smelling, but he's still so clean and stylish, and the way he crosses his legs is womanly but in the most masculine way. *Oh la la*. She remains stoic, regardless.

"I'm not sure if I like you yet. You still seem a little shifty to me."

Abby can see that Jean-Baptiste now thinks the infatuation is mutual. He seems enamored with her. "Shifty? Like in a car? I've been known to shift women to some *very* high gears. Vroom! Vroom!"

"Wow! That is not what I meant. I was saying that I still think you might steal something."

"You'd better watch those chocolates of yours." Jean-Baptiste smiles. Abby puts her hands on her cheeks. She's getting warm.

"No way, José, or I mean Jean, or John the Baptist. These are mine." She grabs them playfully and puts them close to her heart. The champagne is hitting her fast.

The announcement stating that the plane is about to take off is now playing overhead.

"Don't worry. I would never take a woman's chocolates. That would be blasphemous!"

He winks cutely.

"Cute. It looks like we're taking off soon, so . . ." Abby shrugs, hoping that will direct him back to his seat. Jean-Baptiste takes the hint and gets up. As he crosses over her, he brushes her knee with that manly wrist and hand and leans in.

"I've got my eye on you."

"I'm sure you do."

"Do you want to frisk me to make sure I didn't take anything?" He's still hanging over her, face-to-face.

"Non, no, I'm good, thanks." Abby holds her power and looks right back at him.

"Good luck with the fashion week. I think you're going to need it." He slides back into his seat, appearing completely amused by what has just happened.

"Why does everyone keep telling me that?" She starts to put her seat belt on. It's not clasping. She keeps trying—clasp, reclasp, clasp, reclasp—and she pinches her finger. Seriously. C'mon. Just at that moment, the flight attendant passes by.

"Do you need some help, madame? Have you flown in a plane before, madame?" Now Abby's pissed. She's had enough of this French-bun bee-ach.

"Of course I've flown before! This belt clasp seems to be stuck."

"Madame, I can assure you it's working. I think you need an extender." Before Abby can respond, the flight attendant is already yelling in French, "Alors! Benoît! Une américaine obèse!" and she's gesticulating dramatically to indicate a passenger the size of a house.

"Listen, I'm at the end of my rope with you and your attitude. I told you it's the clasp, not the size." Dramatically, Abby shows her the clasp and again pinches her finger. "Dammit to hell, seriously."

"Whatever you say, madame." The flight attendant swirls around with vindictive confidence, and the plane starts to taxi. The lady that spoke to Abby earlier says to her, "Remember it's part of our charm. Welcome to France." Abby looks at her in amazement. She finally gets the clasp to work, but her finger is a pinched blue. She takes out her *BIG IDEAS* notebook and writes, *WTF is now Welcome to France!* She jots down some more thoughts, ending with questions: *Why am I going to need luck? What does that even mean?*

SIX

Bienvenue à Paris

Abby scurries out of the Charles de Gaulle customs area toward a little man in a bad black suit and white shirt holding a whiteboard with the name Heather Sampson on it.

"*Bonjour, je suis* Heather Sampson," she says as if reporting for duty.

"Bonjour, madame." He looks her up and down, makes a "mmm" sound, and says, "Follow me." Abby attempts to give him one of her bags, but he's maneuvered a swift turnaround, just in time to avoid helping her. She follows him hurriedly as they weave through the arrival crowds and into the parking garage. He opens the trunk and throws her two suitcases in, but once again the driver has impeccable timing and turns away just as she's about to give him her other handbag. "Okaayy," she says.

As they head out of the airport parking lot and onto the expressway, Abby is snuggled into the back seat of the Mercedes-Benz with soft leather and a nice armrest. She eagerly looks out the window to fields and warehouses, and then as they approach the city, she sees graffiti and trash alongside the expressway. It's dirty and gritty to her. This is something she didn't expect. She sees the driver glancing at her from the rear-view mirror.

"First time to Paris?" he asks.

"Oui."

"You speak French?"

"Un petit peu." She makes the little gesture François taught her during their Parisian French crash courses before she left.

"That's good. You're here for the Claudette event, oui?"

"Yes, I am. Have you picked up others?"

"Non, not yet. You are the first. You are lucky they made *une exception* and let me pick you up."

"Yes, I thought it would be fun to practice my French and have some time in the city before the event starts."

"C'est bien."

"I think so. Is it this dirty in Paris?" Abby asks as she looks out the window at the sides of the freeway.

"Is it clean in America?" the driver quips.

"Where I come from, it's all very clean, pristine, and perfect."

"It's the same here. There are parts of Paris that are clean, and there are parts that aren't. I'm sure you'll only be in the parts that are."

"You never know, maybe I'll explore those grittier places. Can I ask you something?"

"Oui." He adjusts himself to sit up straight.

"Would you consider me a madame or a mademoiselle?"

"Oh, it is a very delicate question for every woman. Especially French women. What do you think you are?"

"I thought I would be a mademoiselle because I'm young, not married, and I have no children."

"Well, my lady, those three things will guarantee you a fabulous time in Paris, but they do not guarantee that you are a mademoiselle. Désolé," he firmly states.

Abby starts to feel sleepy, but she's hanging on as she can tell they are getting close to the city, as the buildings are becoming more and more ornate with architecture that's pleasing to the eye.

"Are you taking me to the hotel I booked? I sent my details to Sophie's assistant."

"Oui, I was told to take you to the hotel that you have provided."

"Great. Thank you."

"Take some candies," the driver says to her. Abby looks around and then lifts the middle armrest to find a colorful array of French mints and hard candies. She unwraps one, puts it in her mouth, and looks back out the window. Coming around the bend of the expressway, she sees the Eiffel Tower in the far distance. "Wow. There it is!" she says out loud.

"It is the best view of the city for people like you, in Paris for the first time. I like to see people when they first see it. It's like a religious experience." Seeing him look at her through his rearview mirror, Abby takes out her phone, positions it to take a picture of the view from the backseat. With the city view and Eiffel out the front window and the driver's eyes peeking through the rearview mirror, she taps the big red dot. Perfect.

"My first view of Paris," she says as she puts it in her folder for a later post. She looks out the window, remembering that weird long-haul plane ride and feeling like she must have long-haul flight funk all over her, and thinks how she desperately wants a shower and some sleep. Still, she is completely full of excitement that she's made it here! Finally.

. .+. ✦ ✦ . .

A week later . . .

Abby's alarm clock goes off, but it isn't an alarm clock at all but rather the rhythmic pounding on the wall from the headboard in the next room. She's pretty sure she knows "Yes, yes, yes" in about six different languages. All this courtesy of the couples that have stayed in the next room.

"Not again. I mean, I'm all for a good time, but jeez are they keeping hydrated?" she says as she slowly pulls herself up out of bed and once again feels the heart pang of missing her cat, Chloe, rubbing up against her leg to wake her up. She stands up, does some stretches, then steps over to the little coffee tray cabinet and mini fridge. After looking at them apathetically, she shuts the cabinet door. Now dressed in a cute terry jogger outfit from Yitty, she heads over to the "Eiffel view"—that is, a small window in the bathroom that is blocked by a pair of huge trees. The hotel room is the size of a matchbox, and it's nowhere near "five-star clean," as her mama says.

However, the array of wines in cute little bottles, petite sample cheeses, and decadent dark chocolates in the fridge every afternoon after they mediocrely refresh her room are still quite impressive and giving her life when she comes back to the room after a day out in this city.

After bumbling down the pretty stairs to the lobby, Abby heads over to the hotel desk. She sees the clerk straighten her suit jacket and adjust her name tag with *Fantine* written across it in fancy lettering.

"Bonjour, Fantine!" Abby says.

"Bonjour, Ms. Allerton, is everything okay with your stay?" she responds as she looks down at her screen.

"Oui, but I have an unusual question," Abby says.

"Yes, how can I help?" She looks up and adjusts her jacket again.

"Is there a way for you to not book people next to me that make a lot of noise?" Abby asks, smiling, as she knows she's walking a thin line here now. She's already complained about her room not being clean enough, that the housekeepers seem to be helping themselves to her designer makeup samples that she's sprawled all over the tiny bathroom counter, and that she needs some air conditioning or a fan.

"Mmm, I'm afraid we must book all rooms that come available. In what way are they loud?" the desk clerk asks, tilting her head and adjusting her Tom Ford eyeglasses.

"Well, they're, you know, loud. Like, physically loud," Abby says, giving her a knowing look.

"I don't understand. Are they punching each other?" the clerk asks.

"Non, non, no punching. I mean, I don't think so. It's more passionate, I guess," Abby says, smiling and blushing a little.

"Passionate?"

"Oui, passionate."

"You want me to rebook people away from your room for being too passionate? In Paris?" Fantine says incredibly.

"Well, they are waking me up every night/early morning, and I'm exhausted," Abby says.

"Madame, I would suggest that sleep is not what you need but rather something else entirely," the desk clerk says with the look of a deadpan comic as she continues to type on her keyboard. "Is there anything else I can help you with?"

"Non, non, I guess that's it. Merci beaucoup." Abby slowly steps away from the desk.

"*Bonne journée,*" Fantine says cheerfully.

Abby heads out to the street, intuitively connecting the dots that the hotel receptionist may be deliberately putting honeymooners or one-night stands or whatever they are in the room next to hers to teach the valuable lesson that in France being a complaining customer may not be the best way to get results.

Just then a text from Sophie comes in, addressed to Heather Sampson. One after another more texts from Sophie flood in with dates of when and how to report to the event and what she's to be doing. She walks down the street toward the Starbucks that's been her refuge the last few days. It's felt like home, strangely, in the same way Wholly Crêpe felt like home for her back home. She's noticed they spell her name wrong. Every. Single. Time. While waiting for the barista to incorrectly yell out her name yet again, she sees a magazine called *Paris Expatriates* and grabs one to leaf through.

"Barbie! Chai latte *sans eau!*" There it is again. She throws the magazine in her bag.

Taking a sip of her extra-hot chai latte and then a bite of the warm, fresh croissant from the local boulangerie she hit before going to Starbucks, she finds herself meandering past the Eiffel Tower once again. It's official: she's totally in love with it. Seeing it in person after seeing it in pictures and movies and on the wall of her beloved Wholly Crêpe café, well, it's truly something to behold.

Having taken some more steps, she is now standing right in front of the Eiffel Tower on the Champ de Mars. The backdrop of sunshine glistens through the metalwork. She's brought out of her euphoric moment by the most peculiar sound coming from the dirt under the low-lying bushes. She moves closer, her face all contorted, and thinks she is seeing some worms of some type, like at home after a spring rain. Then she realizes with horror that these aren't worms at all—these are tails, and they are attached to *rats*! There must be twenty of them feasting on leftovers from picnickers. Wrappings of brie cheese, crackers, and Camembert are everywhere. Even the *rats* in Paris dine well. They all scurry out at once, and Abby screams, hopping from foot to foot like she's doing some kind of modern dance interpretation. She and the rats part company, the rats seemingly annoyed since she crashed their elegant breakfast of leftovers. Abby can see there is a group of older men watching, amused, from a bench with their cigars and scarves. This is the best thing they've seen in years. One yells to Abby in French: "Mademoiselle, they only like fine cheeses and olives. They are discerning and only dine in three-star hedges." Abby nods and smiles but keeps moving to get the hell out of there. She rushes off in the direction of her hotel. Once back in her room, she pulls out her phone, looks up François's cousine's contact info, and determinedly sends her a message stating that she needs to move on from the hotel in the next day or so. She hits Send, and immediately there are three dots . . . hovering. Hovering. Then gone.

SEVEN

C'est Compliqué

S taying true to her goal of visiting every arrondissement in Paris while she is here, Abby is in the 17th today, looking at the street sights as she nears Parc Monceau. It's packed full of children playing and joggers running around its tree-lined circular path. Stepping through the high, wrought-iron entrance gates is like entering palace grounds. This is just a city park, and yet it's so regal and majestic, with its manicured lawns, beautiful flowers and trees, and a pond at one end. There are kids throwing sand in the sandpit and moody teenagers pouting and smoking. She decides to head over to the cute kiosk and get something. She tries her hand at ordering an ice cream in French and gets an apathetic look. Why are they not understanding her? She always got through to François. They don't seem to understand a word she's saying, so she resorts to the gestures and pointing at pictures yet again. The thought reminds her of how much she misses François and their little chats. Once on the park bench, she decides to FaceTime him.

"*Allô?* Abby? Is that you?" François says with his face a little too close to the camera.

"Bonjour, mon monsieur! Je suis à Paris!" She's nervous to speak to him, as it's the first time since she left.

"Oui! I know. I encouraged you to go. How do you like Paris?" He keeps moving the phone back and forth to find the perfect frame for his face and adjusts himself to give her the best view.

"I don't know. I love it, and then I don't. It's weird. I'm in a hotel that could be participating in a prostitution ring based on the amount of sex that's happening next door in the very short time I've been here."

"Oh la la," François says and smiles. "Nothing wrong with that, right? Try not to be so American." He winks.

Abby notices a couple on the ground making out. Some boys playing soccer kick the ball, and it lands on them. Without even flinching, the guy just grabs it and throws it back to the kids. They yell, "Merci," and all this is done without stopping his passionate kissing.

"To what do I owe this great pleasure of you calling me and adding such positive energy to my day?" François says.

"Well, I've texted your cousine, and I haven't heard back, so I was hoping you could nudge her a bit. I'd love to move from my hotel as quickly as possible." Abby can hear Philippe, belting out his latest Edith Piaf song in the kitchen, through the phone. It makes her homesick, which is so strange given that she's in Paris and François is not, and he's wailing his woes about not being there, while she's so new and dealing with expectations of not necessarily loving it yet.

"Remember what we said?" François sweetly says to her.

"That people will steal from me because I'm a total target?" Abby responds.

"Eh! Non! We said Paris is *always* a good idea! And it is. Give it some time. Think of it as an adventure—the adventure of a lifetime. With every adventure, there are always mix-ups and frustrations. It's what makes it worth it. And think of the stories you can tell when you are back. You'll be the most interesting person in the town. Even more interesting than me."

"Non, mon monsieur. I can't compete with you. *C'est compliqué*, François. I think if I can just get settled and get to work on my posts, it'll be great. Can you help me with the getting settled part?"

"You will find your place. I know it. Look at me. I found mine here at Wholly Crêpe, and if a handsome Frenchman like me can find their place *here*, then a lovely lady like yourself can certainly find your place in Paris."

"Thank you. You always make me feel better, *mon monsieur*. I have one more question for you before I go because I really have to pee," Abby says. She stands up from the bench and looks for where she might be able to go.

"Oui, shoot," François answers.

"Why don't they understand me? I'm speaking French to them." Abby starts moving. "I'm going to have to go now because I really need to pee, and I need to find a place to pee, which I've discovered is not so easy to do in Paris."

"C'est vrai. It is a sport, finding a toilet that doesn't make you cringe," François says. Abby heads toward the public toilets with François still on the phone. She's moving quickly, so her breasts are bobbing up and down. François is riveted. "Are you speaking how we speak at the café? Because if so, that would be Frenglish, and that it not French, especially in Paris."

"I'm trying to speak proper French, François, and they just go blank on me. Anyway, more later. I'm at the public toilets now."

Abby, now at the public toilets, presses the button, and the chamber door opens. It's like entering a time capsule for urine and feces. The door shuts. She's locked in.

"Merci, François. I miss you."

"I miss you, too," he whispers into the phone, so close she can only see his mustache, and then he pans out again.

He winks at her and starts to tell her to hurry up as the doors on those toilets are timed and will open automatically. She hangs up before he has a chance. Abby's positive disposition has come back. She's now a little more hopeful.

By this time, a few minutes have passed, and she's pulling down her pants to squat over the very basic toilet, taking care not to touch it and hovering her backside about two inches above it. There is nothing like the sweet relief of urinating in this town. She's had to hold it way too much since she arrived here. As she's enjoying the relief and thinking about how much better her conversation with François made her feel, the capsule walls start to make a shuffling sound. The next thing she knows, the toilet flushes, causing some water to splash on her behind. As she jumps up and turns around to see what's going on, the robotic sanitizer hand comes out to clean the toilet. It's all very futuristic. She's standing there with her pants down and bare behind to the entrance when the main door slides open. A group of Chinese tourists is waiting in line to use the facilities. They are now her dedicated audience. She turns around, mortified. Grabbing her pants, she pulls them up and does a quick scan to make sure she has everything before she leaves. Just then she trips and falls on the ground, which is part capsule, part street. The door buzzes. It's about to close in preparation for the next session of public toilet trouble, but she's in the way. She jumps up, ninja-like, to avoid being hit by the door. It misses her by a centimeter. Luckily, she makes it out with all her belongings and her phone. Unluckily, her pants still aren't buttoned, and she's now got a little bit of urine from a previous user (who was too lazy to take the five steps to the toilet to pee) on her pant ankles and shoes. She leaps out, making a sad attempt to redeem herself. The Chinese tourist group parts like the Red Sea to let her through, giving her a round of frantic applause. She takes a hasty bow and scurries off.

Now near the Arc de Triomphe, heading back to her hotel, an overall feeling of meh envelops her. She sits on a bench for a minute with the Arc and two-thirds of the Eiffel Tower as her front view. She takes a photo of it because it's so layered, with the Arc and the top half of Eiffel to the side behind it and the beams of sunshine coming through. *Parfait.*

An elderly lady who's smartly dressed and sitting on the same bench with her little Yorkshire terrier seems to have caught a whiff of an undesirable smell. She picks up her dog and does a butt-sniff check. Not there. She looks over at Abby and scrunches up her nose. At that moment the dog jumps down and prepares to urinate on Abby's leg. Abby bends down to gently shove it away. The lady starts to yell at Abby aggressively and protectively grabs her dog. She scurries off, and Abby sits there on the bench trying to recalibrate by taking in that layered view of the Eiffel Tower. She decides to FaceTime her mama.

Betty Lou picks up, flour all over her face. She's baking, which means she's focused. "Hi, sweet pea! Or should I say, bonjour, sweet pea! What's *sweet pea* in French?" Betty Lou jokes.

"I think it would be *petite pois.* Are you stress baking?" Abby's asks. She really needs her mama right now.

The phone is showing only Betty Lou's eyes and forehead. Abby looks at her mother's flour-covered forehead fondly, remembering all the times they baked together.

"Yes, I am. Do you want me to send you some? I mean, I'm sure it's not up to the French seven-star standards, but you can't beat homemade biscuits."

"I called to show you the Eiffel Tower, Mama. Want to see?" Abby rotates the phone, but Betty Lou isn't looking. She's rolling dough with a force to be reckoned with. Abby turns the phone back around.

"Did you see it, Mama?"

"See what, *petit poah*?" Betty looks up quickly but then returns to her task, clenching the rolling pin to conquer a massive heap of biscuit dough. Betty Lou's pronunciation makes Abby smile.

"Never mind. There will be another time. Should I call you later, Mama?"

"You okay, honey? You seem a little down," Betty Lou asks.

"Yeah, I'm okay. Just trying to find my way over here, I guess."

"You know that French waiter friend that you kissed before you left brought us a nice baguette the other day. It was so good."

"Oh, that's so sweet. I was just talking to him earlier. He didn't mention it."

"Well, maybe he didn't want to appear too eager or somethin'," Betty Lou answers as she continues to knead more dough.

"I'll let you go, Mama. I know your biscuits are serious business. It was nice to see you and hear you."

"Why, thank you, Abby girl! We miss you. Listen, you hang in. Remember what I always said to you?"

"Remind me," Abby answers.

"Keep your soul full of sunshine, and all will be all right," Betty Lou says with a smile and blows Abby a kiss.

"Got it. Thank you, Mama." Abby smiles and then hangs up. She drags herself off the bench and walks away from the layered Eiffel Tower view she's fallen in love with just as it's beginning to sparkle. A young French woman with a little pug stops right in front of Abby, looks at her, and gestures for Abby to turn around. When Abby does, her mouth instantly falls open.

"Wow," Abby says.

The young woman winks at her and says in English, "You must never miss the Madame sparkle." She tugs at her pug, who is trying to smell Abby's leg, and briskly starts to walk away.

Abby yells, "Merci beaucoup!"

EIGHT

Merde!

Early the next morning, as the thrusting and sighing continues next door, Abby rolls over in her bed, pushes up her satin sleep mask, which has *Real Deal* inscribed on it, and grabs her journal. She writes:

I miss Wholly Crêpe. I miss François. I miss home. I've only been in Paris for a little over a week, and I feel a little out of place in a place that is truly a fairy tale. Does this mean I don't belong in a fairy tale? Everything feels so mixed up, but I love that everywhere I go I feel like I'm in a movie. It's unreal, but it's real. And the momentum of the city is so invigorating. I have noticed, though, that me and my large body are in the minority. That's kind of strange to me. I want to see if there's something that can be done with Plus-Size Real here. If I'm feeling like I'm not represented here, there must be other women feeling it, too!

She drops the pen on her journal and picks up her phone. She scrolls through some of the pictures she's taken since arriving and chooses one that is elegant and Parisian. She formulates what she wants to say about her arrival to Paris on Femme Fatale, making sure to keep it in line with what she thinks the event organizers would want to see. Two more pictures from her picture roll for a Plus-Size Real post are chosen, and she adds some truth, talking about what it's been like for her so far. All this processing and posting leads to a longing for another session with Charlene and ends just as the couple next door finishes their longing or lusting (she doesn't know which, but she's glad they're done).

"Oh my god. I've got to get out of here." She spins around and sits up on the side of her bed. Her hair, with the eye mask pushing it up, is a bedraggled beehive. She opens her contacts and scrolls to François's "cousine," where she's added the woman's phone number and the address of her apartment. Floundering at the hotel is going to end. Just then, a text comes through.

> Bonjour, Abby. It's Justine. I'm ready to show you the apartment today, and if you are good, you can take the keys. Look forward to meeting you. Ciao for niao!

Reading it gives Abby the adrenaline she needs to make the move. She quickly responds.

> Bonjour Justine, I'm looking forward to it! Merci beaucoup!

"Serendipitous," Abby says to herself.

+ + +

Later that afternoon, dressed in flats and a flowing skirt, with her little box bag hanging diagonally across her body, Abby is walking down the street eating a fresh *pain au chocolat* and enjoying every bit of it. She's decided that, so far, pain au chocolat is one of the best things about Paris because going to get one is an event. The line at the boulangerie winds all the way around the block, with three shop helpers behind the counter shouting at the people in line to keep it moving. The delicious aroma of the long, warm baguettes as they change hands, the display counters full of colorful, perfect petite cakes and beautifully crafted croissants—it's all art. It never gets old, nor does it disappoint.

A favorite part of this process is hearing the final *"Est-ce que c'est tout?"* She loves the accent on *tout*. It evokes limitless possibilities. She loves it because the question is, "Is that all, or does she want more?" She usually does want more, so she has made it a fun sport to think of one more thing, just to be able to respond. The last time she was at a boulangerie, she ended up with a full bag of baguettes, pains au chocolat, croissants, and other decadent *viennoiserie* just because she didn't want to stop the flow of "Est-ce que c'est tout?" She ended up dropping them at a little homeless village on the road back to her hotel.

She pulls out her phone and starts a Reel of the street she's on, holding her pain au chocolat: "Hey there! Can you guess where I am? What I'm holding *and* the street I'm on? I mean, look at this . . . How many perfect spots can one city have for Insta shots? It's just too many. In fact, I feel it's completely overwhelming. But alas, I am at your service, my PSR community. Can I tell you how much I love this pâtisserie?" Abby shows the pain au chocolat and then pans out for the Reel to show the full 360 of the streets. In the background there are people in all different styles and moving at all different paces, some oblivious and some hesitating to see what she's doing. One shoves her aside. *"Oh. Excusez-moi!"* she responds, still recording.

As she's turning the phone, she notices a beautiful old door with the most ornate brass door knocker in the shape of a mermaid. "What do we have here, my friends? Look at this. It's a mermaid door knocker. Isn't she gorgeous?" Abby focuses in on it for her followers to see the detail of it. As she steps forward to take a closer look and get a photo of it, she instantly feels it. The warm, disgusting ooze comes up over her ballet flat to the front of her bare foot. Dog poo. "What the?" Abby turns the phone camera back to her. "My friends, I seem to have stepped in a pile of dog poo as I was trying to show you this gorgeous, ornate door knocker. Paris is amazing, more to come! Au revoir!" She stops the video and throws the phone in her bag. Now, standing still, she fully takes in that her foot is covered in excrement. She opens her arms wide, looking around, hoping for sympathy and outrage from some-one—anyone—but nothing. The elderly spectators are long gone. She then shoves the half-eaten pain au chocolat into her bag and rummages through it to find something she can use to clean this up. A little old lady dressed in vintage designer brands, carrying a basket full of vegetables and a baguette, walks up to the mermaid-knocker door. She smells the stench and sees the poopapalooza on Abby's foot.

"Madame, avez-vous besoin d'aide?" she asks in an uncom-mitted way.

"Parlez-vous anglais?" Abby asks.

"Oui! Yes . . . ," the elegant old lady answers.

"Oh, I'm so relieved. I don't have anything in my bag. Not even a tissue." Abby shrugs with frustration while dangling her foot in the air.

"Come inside. We'll hose you in the courtyard," she says as she ushers Abby in.

Once inside the courtyard, which is a perfect square, Abby looks up and sees all around her what must be fifty open windows. She can hear various sounds emanating from them, resounding around the courtyard.

"Pay attention, dear. I'm about to spray your foot." She turns on the faucet that the building's concierge uses to clean the floors. Abby moves her foot around to clean it all off and examines her shoe.

"Don't worry. Wait right here," the old lady says.

Abby is still dangling her foot, bracing herself against the wall above the faucet, when she hears two women yelling. The helpful old lady returns with the concierge following her, waving a rag in her hands. It's clear to Abby that the woman responsible for the building's maintenance is being accused of something very bad and she's reactive, trying to deflect the blame. Abby's hoping it's because she didn't clean up the massive pile of *merde* she just stepped in, but she can't be sure because they are speaking so fast. The concierge gives Abby the rag.

"Merci beaucoup! Beaucoup de merde!" Abby says, trying to join in on holding the concierge responsible in her own way. She sees the concierge couldn't care less.

"Would you like to come up for some tea, dear?" the old lady asks Abby.

Surprised but relieved, Abby nods in agreement even though she's not a tea drinker. They head up to the second foyer, which is just as grand as the first, then go upstairs. The old lady opens the door, and a huge, puffy gray cat comes running to greet them. The old lady starts speaking to the fluffy fur ball in a nurturing tone that almost makes Abby cry. She picks her up and shows her to Abby.

"This is my roommate, Colette. She's named after the writer. Do you know of her?"

"No, I don't, but I have a cat, too. She's at home, and her name is Chloe. They are very similar. She's my everything, and I miss her so much." Abby takes Colette in her arms. The cat is fidgety and jumps down.

"*Je m'appelle* Abby." Abby extends her hand.

"*Enchantée. Je m'appelle* Angélique." Angélique goes in to kiss her cheek for the customary *bisous-bisous* French greeting. Abby remembers François at their goodbye and knows just what to do. She finds it a little uncomfortable, so she's a bit stiff, but she complies, remembering what a tender teacher François was with her.

"Now, we are formally introduced without *la merde* getting in the way. I'm guessing you are américaine?" Angélique asks as she heads to the kitchen.

"Yes, I am," Abby answers. She knows she should ask something back but instead is distracted by the light and spacious room directly in front of her. Its high ceiling and walls are lined with beautifully crafted, ornate molding. The impressively large fireplace with its beveled mirror on the chimney breast adds an air of elegance and sophistication that she's not seen before. It's an apartment with some interesting history, she can feel it. She gravitates toward the walls, where a series of old vintage design sketches, all framed in black with white backgrounds, are hanging. She stands in front of them, marveling at their detail and intricacy.

"What are these?" she asks Angélique, who is walking back through the corridor with a tea set and some dainty madeleines that have the aroma of being freshly baked.

"Those are from a lifetime ago." Angélique waves her hand dismissively.

"How long ago? Are they yours?" Even without the answer, Abby is already very impressed.

"Yes, they are mine, but I'm retired now and have been for many years. I keep them up there because they remind me of what I once was—refined, elegant, fashionable, and a creative spirit," Angélique says in a wistful tone.

Abby looks at her confused. Based on what Angélique is wearing now, just for a trip to the market to get vegetables and a baguette, she looks like she just stepped off a geriatric cat-walk. It's a sweet reminder for Abby of her mother. Her mama wouldn't be caught dead going to the Piggly Wiggly without her makeup and hair done. Seems Angélique lives by the same ethos, which endears her to Abby (as if her spraying off dog poo wasn't enough to tick that box).

"How are you finding Paris?" Angélique pours tea for Abby, even though Abby hasn't said she wanted any.

"I love it. I love being here. I've only been here a short time, so it's early days, but I'm planning on staying a little longer."

"Why is that?" Angélique motions for Abby to drink the tea she doesn't want.

"I want to practice my French and build my business a bit more." Abby takes a fake sip.

"You didn't take a sip. Do you not like it?" Angélique inquires.

"I'm not really a tea person. More a chai latte," Abby answers.

"I see. Well, I don't have coffee, nor do I have that latte. Désolée," Angélique says.

"It's okay. I'm so grateful to you for helping me with"—she does a swirling hand gesture pointing to her foot—"and then inviting me into your home. It's beautiful and unlike anything I've ever seen. Have you lived here your whole life?"

"Yes, I have. My husband and I raised our family here, but he died about twenty years ago, and my child is long gone. On her own for many years now."

"So, she's an only child. Like me." Abby perks up.

"Oui! I hope you aren't as spoiled and inattentive to your mother as my child is to me?" Angélique puts down her tea, zeroing in on Abby, which makes Abby a tad bit uncomfortable.

"Our relationship is—oh, c'est compliqué, that's for sure—but I'm hopeful. The therapist I've been seeing says it's common with mothers and daughters, and yes, I do therapy because of it. I'm here because of the therapy part." She takes a large bite of the madeleine. Angélique leans back. Abby has literally bitten off more than she can chew, both in conversation and pâtisserie. She's dying for a drink, but there's only the tea.

"Would you like some water to help you with that? Badoit or tap . . . which do you prefer? Badoit is sparkling and tap—well, you know what that is . . ." Angélique stands up.

"Sparkling, please," Abby says, chewing with her mouth still full. Part of her wants to bolt and never see this lady again, but another part of her is telling her to see this through, at least today. At this point, because of the anxious processing going on in her head, a piece of the madeleine gets stuck in her throat. Angélique returns with an elegant bottle of Badoit. She pours it and stands there to watch. Abby's seen these bottles at the cafés but has yet to try it. She takes a huge drink, and it goes down wonderfully. She's hooked. From now on, it's only this water for her. She takes a deep sigh, and all is well.

"All went down okay?" Angélique sits down again. "You know, it is not my place, and I'm not a psychiatrist, but I think you might want to try and enjoy your food more. Eat it slowly, don't throw it down your throat like a hyena."

"Thank you for your concern. *C'est bon.*" Abby straightens up a bit.

"*Alors!* You know, I know a wonderful doctor who helps women to learn this principle. I'll give you her name and number. Go see her. Tell her I sent you. My daughter has gone to her, too." Angélique shuffles through her side table drawer and gives Abby the card.

Docteur Monique Le Vot, Diétécienne

"Thank you, but I'm not sick." Abby adjusts herself again, making sure she has a confident posture.

"I didn't say you were sick. She has an excellent track record. You may even run into a celebrity there. She has many famous clients," Angélique says, still holding out the card to her. Abby reluctantly takes it and puts it in her bag. It's time to go.

"Merci beaucoup, Angélique! It's time for me to go. I'm hopefully moving from my hotel today to an apartment. I hope it will be 'the one' so I can finally leave the hotel life." Abby stands up and heads to the door. Angélique quickly follows her.

"Why do you say 'the one' like that?" Angélique asks with her ear closer to Abby.

"Oh, it's something my mama always said on our trips when going to look at hotel rooms. She said, 'You never settle for the first because you must find "the one" that's right for you.' My mama can be a handful sometimes."

"I see. I don't think she's a handful. I think she has high standards. Nothing wrong with that. You might want to listen and follow her advice," Angélique says in a slightly patronizing way.

"That's another way to look at it. Maybe you're right." Abby smiles.

"May I ask, what is the address?" Angélique asks. Abby pulls out her journal and opens the page with the details on it.

"It's in the 18th, I guess, because the postal code is 75018, and I was told by my friend back home that those last digits are the arrondissement, correct?"

"Indeed. The last digits of the postal code tell the world who you are. The 18th arrondissement is a place of Parisian *bobos*. It's Montmartre or La Butte. Right up the hill. We will be neighbors. Come by anytime." Angélique gives Abby a lovely card with her details on it. Abby is completely charmed. Angélique, being very old-school and very proper, only has cardstock that reeks of class.

"Merci, Angélique. I'd like that." She edges toward the door.

"Go see Dr. Le Vot. She's a miracle worker, I tell you," Angélique calls after her as Abby's walking down the stairs. Abby waves. The French seem to like having the last word.

Abby's phone buzzes, and now out on the sidewalk she stops and takes it out and sees a notification from Instagram. It's a DM from Heather.

> @HeatherBeather: Hey, are you in Paris? I saw your Story and it looks like you're there?

Abby hovers over the screen and takes a deep breath. She moves over and stands against the stone wall of the building she's just left and looks at all the people, decisively, beautifully dressed, walking with determination to get where they are going. This is where she is now, and she doesn't regret it. The physical distance between her and Heather is empowering. She dives into DM land with a response.

@FemmeFatale: Hi! Yes, I'm in Paris.

@HeatherBeather: Wow! How did that happen?

@FemmeFatale: Femme Fatale was invited to come for #BTSPFW influencer event.

@HeatherBeather: Really? Was it a contest or something?

@FemmeFatale: Nope, no contest. Femme Fatale was invited.

Abby waits a second and then hits Send. This could be bad. The message shows read.

@HeatherBeather: Oh. So why didn't you tell me?

Abby starts typing with vigor. She's so done with this.

@FemmeFatale: Because I basically run Femme Fatale.

@HeatherBeather: Why didn't you tell me about the invite?

@FemmeFatale: Because I do all the work with FF.

@HeatherBeather: And I've been the face and front person.

@FemmeFatale: I've paid you for all of that. Just like any other third-party supplier. That's something we agreed upon and you chose. Maybe it's time we stop this arrangement. I don't want this anymore.

@HeatherBeather: I'm sure you don't now that you've made it to Paris.

@FemmeFatale: How about we come up with a reasonable amount that works, and I just send it to you as a final payment and be done with it?

@HeatherBeather: You should've told me, Abby, and not let me find out from a post. And I can't believe you are STILL lying about who you are and in such a big way.

@FemmeFatale: Who said I was lying? I tried. You never got back to me for a FT call. And let's be honest, it's not like we're really friends or anything. This is a cold business relationship. Think about the amount, Heather. Let's keep it on the up and up.

@HeatherBeather: Wow. I wonder what would happen if the event organizers found out that you are lying to them. Maybe that's how we should end it? I mean, if you really want to "keep it on the up and up."

Abby looks up from her phone, shaking her head. She exits Instagram and puts the phone in her bag. She looks at all the people again, and, like a car merging onto a highway, she skillfully merges herself into the Parisian crowd.

NINE

A Punch of *Par-ee*

Now waiting outside the building for Justine, Abby is loading up a prepared Reel with some of the very cool French music she's discovered since arriving. Knowing she's in the 18th and not the 17th, she's noting any differences in the way the neighborhood feels and is set up. She wants to have this apartment done and dusted today! She's got Reels to post, Stories to do, preparations to make, and this amazing city to explore. She yawns because she still hasn't been sleeping well, due in part to the usual neighborly escapades but mostly because of the fear that Heather is going to get in contact with Sophie and mess things up for her. Fumbling through her courier bag, the card that Angélique gave her falls out on the street, but Abby doesn't notice. At that moment, the infamous cousine by the name of Justine walks up.

"Abby?"

"Oui! Bonjour!" Abby responds. "Parlez-vous anglais?"

"Oui! Un petit peu," replies Justine, to Abby's secret relief. Justine is tall, slender, and chic. Like many of her fellow Parisiennes, she looks like she has just stepped out of a poster advertising the elegance of French women—terms and conditions at the bottom letting all other women know that they will never make the grade. Ever. So, don't even try. She's dressed simply, understated yet elegant, with a twist. A round basket bag with a clasp is draped across her body. Her look is so effortlessly put together that Abby is struggling not to take a step back to give her a head-to-toe once-over so that she can take it all in and take notes. She can't get over the simplicity and how it all works together so marvelously. Abby's always felt that she has a good or even great sense of style and fashion, but after this short time in Paris, she's seeing she needs to level it the hell up. She looks at Justine and says to herself, "Totally an ex."

"So, you are a friend of François? How is he? We miss him." Justine smiles as she fumbles for her keys.

"Yes, I went to his café back home way too much."

"Oh yes, the café. I've heard so much about it. I hope it's still going well and prospering. I never saw him as actually owning something, but sometimes people surprise you," Justine says.

"Pardon, you said 'we' miss him so much. Is that you and a dog, or you and your friends?" Abby's fishing as nonchalantly as possible.

"No dog. I don't like to clean up the . . ." Justine grimaces.

"And you said François owns the Wholly Crêpe?" Abby asks, surprised.

Justine turns to answer but sees something on the ground and picks it up. "Is this yours? Did you drop it?" Abby looks at the card and curls her upper lip in frustration.

"*Oui, c'est la mienne*—it's sadly mine."

"Your French is not so bad, Abby, maybe better than my English." Justine smiles. "So, shall we go see the flat?"

"Oui, I'm so grateful to you. Is it yours?" Abby puts the card in her bag. She can't seem to lose this card, either intentionally or mistakenly.

"It was my great-grandmother's. She was an art dealer here in Montmartre, and it's been passed down through the family. It's not big, but it has charm. Shall we? It's on the sixth floor."

There is a tiny staircase that they could take, with stairs that wind up in perfect symmetry all the way up to the top floor. Abby stops and takes a photo of it from below, as it'll make great content for one of her Stories. The stairs are lovely and quaint in their own unique way. Justine stands outside the elevator door, and an older gentleman walks up. The older man is your typical older Parisian man, with round tortoiseshell glasses, a white button-down shirt, and jeans. Brogues with patterned socks complete the look. He's carrying the newspaper *Le Monde* all rolled up, and a little dog sashays beside him on a leash.

"So, I hope you will like it, Abby. I imagine since you are américaine you will see its size as smaller than you are used to, non? François is always talking about the big stores and the big parking spaces and the big buildings," Justine says.

"Huh. I've never thought of it that way. Everything is kind of big there, isn't it? I mean, compared to here. Maybe it's because the US is a huge country, land wise? I guess it's a cultural thing—much like the French, with your cheeses and wines."

Justine smiles and attempts to change the subject, but not before the man waiting for the elevator interjects in French, "Il ne faut pas comparer des pommes et des oranges!"

Abby's not sure she hears him right, so she just smiles and nods. The elevator arrives, and they all get in. It's the size of a tiny kitchen broom cabinet encased in a cage-like structure.

They barely fit, and the little dog starts to growl. The elevator door won't shut, so the man is forcefully trying to reopen and shut, reopen and shut the cage doors, making a racket that echoes through the glamorous hallway and staircase. The dog is beside itself, and so is its owner. Finally, the door stays shut, and the man presses the button for his floor without asking where they are going. Justine pushes the number six. The elevator buzzes. A harrowing buzz. A deafening sound that this elevator is going nowhere.

"Pardon, cela ne vas pas. Pardon, the lift won't move. I think your big size is too heavy for the lift." He looks directly at Abby. It's official. He is dissing her, and in her own language. Nice.

"Perhaps it's the elevator itself, non? These things never work properly in Paris." Abby can see that Justine is trying to recover some semblance of tact.

The man keeps pushing, and the buzzer keeps buzzing. Nothing's changing, but he keeps pushing the button. Abby's entered a kind of fight-or-flight state. She's reliving that middle-school bathroom stall experience all over again, but this time it's with a suave, geriatric asshole and a slim, sleek, most likely ex-girlfriend of François. She's not sure what's worse. Then or now. At least now she can possibly chalk it up to cultural bias and not mean girls, but is that really any consolation? Maybe it's just a convenient way to excuse it.

"Non, non, it buzzes when it's over the weight limit. Someone must vacate. It should be her because *she* put us over the weight." The man adjusts his scarf—the scarf he doesn't need with the warmer weather outside, but it adds some flair, so it seems to make sense, nonetheless.

"I think your dog isn't helping. Maybe you and your treasure could allow us to go, and we'll send it back down?" Justine says.

"*Ce n'est pas possible.* I'm on the housing committee. You can take the stairs, but it may be hard for your friend, non?" Also standing his ground. Abby's had enough.

"As a matter of fact, I welcome a walk up that beautiful staircase. Excuse me, or is it *pardon-moi*?" Abby thinks she's showing off a little French, but what she doesn't know is that she's flown right into his web, and he's ready for her.

"It is neither. One is in English, and the other is incorrect French. Perhaps you missed it in your travel book. We speak correct French in France."

Abby pushes herself out, almost crushing poor Justine against the tiny elevator wall—it's that small of a space. After they are both out, the man slams the door, and as the elevator finally goes up, he shouts to them through the little cage, his little dog growling in the background, "Welcome to Paris! The boulangerie is just around the corner. Award-winning galettes and baguettes are sold there. I'm sure you'll frequent it often."

Abby gives a fake smile and gives him the middle finger behind her back.

When they reach the fifth floor, Abby is out of breath, having walked up all those flights of stairs, the residual baggage of anger and frustration from the elevator encounter making her footsteps even heavier. Justine pulls a small bottle of Evian mineral water spray from her bag to cool her off, as if she is waving a magic wand, and everything falls back into perfect place. Abby makes a mental note to get one of those sprays at the next pharmacy she sees.

There is music behind two of the neighboring doors, one piano and one guitar. Another door has a child-sized micro-scooter, and the next door has a floor mat that reads *FUCK OFF.* Abby makes a mental note to stay away from that neighbor.

Finally, they reach the sixth floor, just as the next-door neighbor is coming out of her front door. She is multiracial, with gorgeous freckles across her cheeks and nose. Her eyes are the color of a cold winter ocean, gray and blue. Again, a feminine creature with an overload of unique beauty. Paris seems to be filled with them.

"Bonjour, Justine. Ça va?"

"Bonjour, Claire. Très bien, merci." Claire runs down the stairs. Abby watches her go, intrigued by her casual but chic look of rolled-up boyfriend jeans, Doc Martens, and a striped St. James shirt under a red blazer. Justine continues to unlock what seems like ten locks on the door, then pushes the door open with her shoulder, shoving all the mail to the side. There are loads of letters, all handwritten and addressed to *Mme Monique Tallier.* Abby steps over them and bends down to help pick them up.

"Non, non, Abby. I will get them."

Justine scurries to grab the letters, then puts them on the old marble-topped stand near the door. Abby crosses the corridor, at the end of which are two rooms, one on each side. A large, circular beveled window graces the end of the hallway and, stretching beyond it as far as the eye can see, is the most amazing rooftop view of Paris. The chimneys are perched across the skyline like building blocks on the dark-gray zinc roofs. Abby can see a rooftop terrace with Chinese lanterns strewn across it, instantly reminding her of her beloved lightning bugs back home, casually fluttering around the yard for back porch revelers to enjoy. That flash of happy memory pretty much seals the deal for her. This is her backyard now. She moves into the other room and takes note of the rather eclectic wallpaper—dramatic, eye-popping, and rebelliously dark red. Every piece in this apartment seems to have an unusual backstory. Each unique piece has its place, and they make it a cultural playground for her to experience.

"I'll take it, Justine. This is the one," Abby says, with a mix of determination and relief in her voice.

"C'est bon! So, you will take it for a month, correct?"

"Yes, I will. Do you live here when you're in Paris?" Abby looks over at the letters.

"Non, non, I live in Neuilly-sur-Seine, as that's where my grandmother lives. My mother and I, we take care of her, but I come here sometimes when I need to get what I call 'a punch of *Par-ee*,' and I take care of things."

"'A punch of *Par-ee* . . .' I like that. I feel like I've been getting one punch after another since I arrived." Abby laughs.

"I don't know if François told you, but Paris is a city that will take hold of you and force you to fall in love with it. Like a captive. You need to pace yourself."

"He just told me Paris is always a good idea, and to be careful because I'm a walking target for thieves." Abby shrugs.

"C'est vrai. He's right. You must be careful, there are thieves everywhere, but I think in some strange way it adds to the charm. Maybe it's a little, how do you say, dysfunctional?"

"I can agree with that."

"Shall I give you the keys?" Justine shows her the many keys to the many locks and gives her the key ring with a metal Eiffel Tower hanging from it. Abby takes it, and her eyes fill with tears. Now she can finally settle in a bit.

"Please take care of her. She means a lot to us," Justine implores, looking Abby in the eyes.

"I will take good care of her. I promise." Abby smiles.

"You have a nice vibe, Abby. I'm glad you will live here," Justine says as she leaves.

Abby starts to walk cautiously around the rest of the apartment. She takes off her ballet flats and puts on the cute house slippers with gems across the toes that she brought with her in her bag, just in case it all worked out. The kitchen is a vivid yellow with a white subway tile backsplash. There must be twenty different paintings of sunflowers all around the walls. There's an old gas stove with vintage knobs and many different sizes of copper pans hanging along the wall. Abby takes one off and sees the inscription *D. Hellerin* engraved on it. She makes a note to look that up. The drawers and cabinets are filled with old ceramic pans and plates. Everything is colorful, eclectic, and fun. The yellow kitchen is reminiscent of her mama's kitchen. She puts her hand to her heart. She misses her mama. She grabs her phone to FaceTime her, but just at that moment, another call comes in. It's François. She clicks to accept.

"Bonjour, Abby! Ça va?"

"Très bien, merci, monsieur!" Abby is grinning like a Cheshire cat. She's so happy to be talking to him and to finally be in a good place, both internally and externally.

"Justine just left. She's beautiful and regal."

"Are you describing the apartment or Justine?" François winks.

"Maybe I'm describing both!" Abby smiles.

"So you like the place?" François shifts the focus.

"I love it."

"Not so bad a view, right?"

"It's okay. I love all the rooftops and the little terrace lanterns. Strangely, they remind me of home." Abby shrugs.

"I think you missed a room. Take me on a tour, and I'll show you."

Abby starts to walk around and shows him the rooms and comes upon a door she's not yet opened.

"Oh, I missed this door." Abby starts to open it.

"Wait. Make sure I can see your face when you open the door and go in," François says, propping his phone on the counter and leaning in toward the screen for a better view.

"Okay, okay. I mean, what's in this room, the *Mona Lisa*? And I'm not letting you off the hook on the bigger questions of who exactly Justine is to you and what your history is exactly . . ." Abby pushes the door wide open and gasps. François is watching, and his face softens into a big smile. Before her is a huge window, framing the Sacré-Coeur. It almost looks unreal, as it's so beautifully framed and proportioned. It is exquisite, and Abby is entranced, as is François as he sees her reaction to it.

"Merci, *Par-ee*," François says quietly under his breath.

"François, this is the most beautiful thing I've ever seen! I can't even comprehend what I'm looking at. It's as if I can reach out and touch it—it's so close and big, like a full moon."

"Oui, ma chérie. And it's all yours now. Or at least for a little while. Now turn around." Abby turns around with the phone, and there is an old brass bed with a fluffy duvet and hot-pink pillows. She runs over and leaps on it, then sits back up to take in the magnificent view once again.

"Time for me to go, Abby. Customers are coming in now. Enjoy. Make sure to go inside your masterpiece. Don't just look at it through a window, okay? That's where you'll really feel the magic. Au revoir." François hangs up.

"Wait! François . . ." Abby puts the phone to her heart and grabs one of the hot-pink pillows, made of chenille. She strokes it back and forth and sees how far she's come since that session with Charlene. She holds the pillow close and screams with glee. She's ready for all the whimsical wonderment that Paris can offer! She has finally arrived.

⁘ ⁛ + ✦ + ⁘ ⁚

As Abby was walking to meet Justine to look at the apartment, she noticed a gorgeous merry-go-round that was so magical with all its mirrors and ornately painted horses that she took note of it for a Plus-Size Real post. She's decided to head back to it to take some pics. Nearing it, she can see small, impeccably dressed children bumbling to it from the line and their parents gently placing them on the horse they've picked out during their wait. She snaps a few pics of those scenes, and then from the line she heads to her own horse. She positions herself next to it for a selfie. She takes a few shots and then does a video of the ride. This is so fun for her. She decides that with the older look of the carousel she can put something about it on Femme Fatale to match the vintage looks she organized and brought with her today for one of her first posts from Paris.

She takes out the items, an old Hermès silk scarf, a string of pearls, and on her arm a stack of gold bracelets she's brought with her to highlight. She wraps the scarf around the horse's neck with the pearls daintily hanging from it and then places her hand and wrist on it, as if she's petting it softly. With her other hand, she takes the photo. It's a good position, so she takes a few other shots just to be safe. Once done with that, she prepares the post for Femme Fatale with a caption: "Life can sometimes feel like a merry-go-round, but why not be elegantly accessorized along the way?" She links all the items for sale. Done. All uploaded. The carousel ride ends, and she hops off with all the kids and parents and exits through the gate. She pulls out her *Secret Paris* travel book and reads about the six most beautiful carousels in Paris. She wants to find another vintage-looking carousel. There's one at Luxembourg Gardens, not too far away, dating back to 1879. Abby reads, with great curiosity, that the old animals—still in working condition—were sketched by Charles Garnier, the architect of the opera house in Paris. She dog-ears the page so as not to forget.

TEN

Enchantée

The Claudette fashion house evokes a feeling of deep, rich artistic history. The building is a soft grayish stone color that seems to perfectly match the sparkling gray of the Seine. *Claudette* is written in sophisticated script horizontally down the side of the building, and there is a satin flag hanging above from the door, a proud standard-bearer of the home of high fashion.

Abby has only seen pictures of the fashion house in articles or online. Seeing it in person with all its beautiful decorative sconces and massive entry doors adorned with ornate golden door knockers just confirms for her why it is so highly revered, and she hasn't even entered the building yet. She takes a breath, and, looking down at her silver Birkenstocks, flowy skirt, and white blouse, she can't help but feel a little out of place.

Onward! she thinks. She didn't come all this way to turn back now. *Let's break down that door.* She firmly adjusts her tote bag, full of every item she could think of that she might need, and then approaches the doorman, who's the size of Schwarzenegger. He opens the door and stops her.

"Bonjour, madame. *Puis-je vous aider?*"

"Bonjour, monsieur, I'm here for the behind-the-scenes influencer event. Where can I find Madame Sophie Dubois?"

"Une minute, madame." The bodyguard checks his iPad.

"Or *mademoiselle*?" Abby smiles.

"Non, je voulais dire madame," the bodyguard says dryly.

"Parlez-vous anglais, monsieur?" Abby asks.

"*Un petit peu.* Yes, a little," he replies.

"I'm with Femme Fatale, and I have the emails and messages from Sophie. The bodyguard keeps scrolling and finds Femme Fatale's listing and then clicks over to the profile.

"Une minute." He gives her the now-accepted French once-over. He scrolls through and clicks on something. "Alors, oui. Okay." He opens the door for her.

"Can you please show me where I need to go?" Abby looks up at him.

"Up the stairs and to the right. Jeannette will direct you from there." He then whispers something in his earpiece. Abby can only make out "pour Sophie," which makes her nerves heighten. The impending doom is palpable.

The staircase is made of ornate marble, and Abby slides her hand across the polished oak banisters as she slowly makes her way up. Lining the walls are dramatic tapestries depicting scenes of eighteenth-century courtesans, their powdered wigs and elaborate gowns decorated with flowers and ribbons. It is gorgeous and visually stimulating in the most dramatic way. It is just what you would expect from a fashion house of this caliber. Abby is looking at every mural, drinking in all the details of the costumes and wigs. The dresses look so real, like a toddler's touch-and-feel book, so the temptation to touch is enormous. She puts out her hand to feel the skirt of one of the embellished dresses, her index finger hovering and about to touch it ever so carefully when . . .

"*ALLÔ! Non, ne touchez pas!* DO NOT TOUCH!" yells a voice from the levels above. A low-volume alarm starts to sound, which startles Abby, who almost loses her balance as she catches her clunky Birkenstock on the last stair. She catches herself and asks the lady approaching her, "Bonjour, parlez-vouz anglais?"

"Non," comes the robotic response from the standoffish lady. She stares Abby down.

"Okay. Um, je m'appelle Abby Allerton. Je suis ici pour the influencer event." Abby pulls up the invite on her phone to show her. Again, no reaction.

"Madame Sampson is here," the lady says into her little earpiece. Abby looks at her in astonishment. She does speak English. Not cool. Shit. She said her own name. Of course, the invitation has got Heather's name on it. The lady of *non* directs her to the next set of doors, farther down the corridor. Abby goes in and sits down on the chenille Louis XVI sofa. Curiously, the sofa has a built-in side table, complete with carved intertwining snakes and glass on top. She strokes the cushion beside her to ground herself. It's a good thing there's loads of chenille in this country. She's going to need it.

"Heather Sampson?" A different lady is now shouting the wrong name from the corridor. Abby rushes over to her.

"Oui, c'est moi. I mean, non, non c'est pas moi. C'est compliqué. Parlez-vous anglais?" Abby is out in the corridor.

"Non," is the curt reply. Abby, now that she's a bit savvier, has gotten in on the little secret since arriving in Paris that many Parisians do, in fact, speak decent English, but they don't own up to it. They seem to like to watch tourists squirm, to see the disappointment and dread in their eyes when they get that first *non*. Therefore, Abby's decided to respectfully decline and push back on this one.

"Non, no English? Or non, I'm not Heather Sampson? Because I'm not, and that's going to be kind of a thing. I'm prepared to explain why and clear this all up." She's going for the cute and funny approach. Maybe that will jog this lady's memory, and she'll remember that she does in fact speak some English, and that being difficult is only adding to the long-standing and perhaps unfair stereotype that *all* French people are rude.

"Both," the lady answers matter-of-factly.

"Well, je suis Abby Allerton, not Heather Sampson. And you are?" Abby walks up to her as the woman gives her the once-over, extending her hand for a handshake. She is not doing the kiss-on-the-cheek thing with this one. No way. The lady looks down at her hand, does not reciprocate, and looks back at her square on.

"Follow me." Like a soldier doing a drill call, she turns around. Her short, sleek ankle boots tap across the floor as she marches on. Abby follows in her wake and takes a deep breath. They enter a final room that's filled with cubicles, boxes, shelves, fabric rolls, mannequins, books, and a . . . fridge? Finally, Abby finds herself in an adjacent conference room, where five people are seated around a table so large it barely fits in the room.

"Here, you go here." The lady waves her in. Abby hesitantly enters and looks around and says, "Bonjour," then moves toward the only empty seat at the opposite end of the conference table. As she makes her way through, she must try to slide behind the two people who are literally sitting with their backs against the wall. There is maybe one foot of space.

"Pardonnez-moi," she says as she tries to wriggle in behind them. As she pushes herself onward, holding her bag up in front of her like a shield, she accidentally hits one guy on the head, and her bag knocks his glasses off. He's not pleased; in fact, he's perturbed. One down, one more to go. She wriggles in again, this time behind a woman who makes no effort to budge. Instead, she deliberately drops her pen at the exact moment that Abby is trying to get past, then pushes herself dramatically back, pinning Abby against the wall.

"Owww! *PARDON!*" Abby puffs her chest out, like a wrestler sizing up his opponent. The lady smirks, then daintily picks up her pen and scoots her chair back under the table, as if nothing happened. Abby reaches her seat at last and plops down with a loud sigh.

"Victory!" She puts up her fist in defiance. The others look at her with blank, glazed-over eyes. The lady at the opposite end of the table slides a folder across the table to Abby.

"And you are?" says the lady speaking to the group.

"Bonjour, je suis . . ."

"You can speak English. It will save us all a lot of time and trouble," the lady says.

"Okay. I'm Abby Allerton, and I'm here for Femme Fatale," Abby says, feigning confidence and trying to catch her breath after that entrance.

"Femme Fatale?" The lady looks and checks her list on her iPad.

"I have a Heather Sampson." She continues to scroll through her documents with pictures of the group's profiles and lists of attendees.

"Oui, that's me. See what I did there? That rhymed," Abby says, trying to lighten the mood yet again.

"I'm confused. It is you or not you?" asks the lady as she presses one of her palms onto the table.

"She wasn't able to attend, so I've come in her place."

"And who are you? Her sister, her friend, her what?"

"I'm the influencer that runs Femme Fatale, and frankly I did/do most of the work on it, so I feel just as worthy to be here as she would be to be here." Abby smiles. "Here in Paris at this amazing event with all you amazing people. I mean, I haven't met you all yet, but I'm confident you are all amazing." Abby smiles.

"But do you think you yourself represent the brand of Femme Fatale? Because I can't really see it," the lady says as she waves her hand dismissively in Abby's direction. "We will investigate this further at a later time, as we are on a tight schedule today," she says with a slightly clenched jaw.

"Ah, pardon. Why investigate? It's not like it's a case of murder," Abby jokes back. The others are watching intensely. This boring meeting just perked up.

"Non, you are right, but you may feel worse than murdered after Sophie finds out about you being some kind of imposter." The lady regroups and starts again. "So, as I was saying before our Madame Sampson—or, I mean, Madame Allerton—interrupted, this is the first time we are doing this event, seminar, whatever you want to call it. The head of the Paris Fashion Week is trying to make the event more accessible, reachable to the common people that couldn't or wouldn't normally attend. We chose each of you due to your impressive number of followers and influence on social media and the quality of your photos and posts. We looked for influencers who are tasteful and understand what real fashion is to the masses. You were all chosen because your online presence showed us that. So, congratulations, you won the fashion lottery. Yay!" The lady waves her hands, feigning enthusiasm.

"That's the exact same thing I said when I got the invite. I said to my friend that I felt like I had won the lottery or won a contest that I didn't enter. That's so funny you said the same."

Abby smiles big, looking around the room. They all look at her with zero reaction.

Abby then pulls out her phone to look at her agreement, then she looks through the reading material in the folder.

"*Excusez-moi*, Madame Sampson, is it? Am I boring you?" The lady at the other end of the table knocks the table with her knuckle to get Abby's attention and then smiles to save face. Abby shoves her phone back in her bag and concentrates on the folder with the schedule.

"Désolée, madame. I'm listening, and once again only to clarify I'm not Madame Sampson, I'm Mademoiselle Allerton," Abby says with a soft tone but sitting up straight and smiling. "And I'm really excited to be here! So excited."

"*Oui*, we all heard that." The lady once again feigns a smile. Abby knows full well she came here under false pretenses. She knew this was coming, and she's determined to make this work. She doesn't want to lie about this anymore. She's done. It will be hard to do a full-on promotional plan when she can't even pull on a pair of the most-liked jeans any farther than her knees, which is the exact reason she's slowly progressed to adding vintage items. This profile is not her, and it's not who she wants to be now. She will find a way out of this.

"So, as I was saying, we chose you all for your unique way of influencing. A cut above the rest," the lady continues.

"Pardonnez-moi, une question." Abby puts her hand up, like at elementary school.

"You don't have to raise your hand here. We are not *écoliers*. We are all adults. What is your question?" She leans in to hear.

"When you said, 'your unique way of influencing,' what do you mean, exactly?"

"We mean that you were all identified due to your ability to create content that is unique and has a different, elegant touch."

"Got it. Merci."

"Is there anything else?"

"Um, yes. I was wondering why you chose Femme Fatale in particular. I'm only asking so I know how to make sure I continue that look and content for you during the event."

"Just a second, I'll check the notes on it." The woman scrolls down on her iPad. "It says, 'Nice use of vintage and elegant looks together. Nice models with slim and sleek clothes, as well as interesting settings with relevant comments that thread it all together.' She looks up at Abby. "Is that clear?"

"Crystal. Merci," Abby says, nodding side to side, biting her lower lip a bit.

"Would anyone else like the notes as to why we chose you?" the lady asks, looking around the table. Everyone shakes their head and says, "Non, merci."

The room remains silent. They all look at each other. Abby thinks of Charlene and how often she's held silence in a space of truth for her. So, she sits and waits.

"Thank you, madame. Ally, is it?" the lady asks.

"It's Abby. Two *b*'s and then Allerton," Abby answers.

"Noted. Merci." She starts to type something in her iPad quickly. "Shall we do some introductions while we are here? Abby and Femme Fatale, we know intimately now. How about the rest of you?" A man with a linen suit jacket and Warby Parker–type glasses sits up straight.

"I'll go. My profile is Gays for Days, and I'm really excited to be here. I've been to Paris loads of times, thanks to my mother's knock-off fashion business, but I'm happy to be here just for me this time. It's important that I'm here on my own merit. Thank you for letting me share."

"C'est bon." The lady moves on.

"I'll go next. My profile is French Market—Forever French. It's all about everything French—from the lavender soap from Provence to the market scarves, to the *très élégant chapeaux* with *un petit peu de lingerie*—all in one place."

"Oh, I love your accent. It reminds me of *Downton Abbey*. Are you British?" Abby asks.

"Indeed. I'm guessing you are American by the way you barreled in here and made yourself known from the second you came through the door."

Abby blanches in shock.

"Whoa. Uh, yes, I am American. I'm getting the vibe that you may not be a fan," Abby jokes back.

"I'm Muriel. Muriel Lancaster," says the Brit, stylishly shifting her hip bangs away from her forehead.

"Nice to meet you, Muriel. I'm Abby." They both nod in agreement. They turn to the next influencer.

"Je m'appelle Mélodie, and I am French. My profile is Mélodie's Melodies. I am a concert pianist, so I have threaded together my music with my fashion, and I do scenes from all over Paris. I especially love polka dots—they are *très* simple, and they look like the bottom part of many musical notes, so I try to incorporate both music and fashion in that way."

"Mmm, très bien. We look forward to your musical contribution. Alors! Now that you all know each other, I will introduce myself, too. Je m'appelle Juliette. Enchantée." She nods from across the table and relaxes her body a bit.

"Enchantée, Juliette," they all say in almost perfect unison.

"Perhaps we should go over the expectations and what we are asking you to do, exactly." Juliette scrolls down on her iPad to the right spot. Abby is hoping that she will be able to find out as much as she can before she must deal with Sophie.

She knows that'll be coming soon. Very soon. Juliette picks up her folder.

"I think it's important that you take these folders and read through them. We have outlined things for you, and we expect you all to adhere to those items listed. Make us feel that you understand why we brought you here. Why we chose you. We want to feel that you all were worth the expense. You all were not cheap, not cheap at all." She half laughs and lifts one of her perfectly plucked eyebrows when making that point and zeroes in on Abby across the table. Abby gets the message.

"You will be meeting with Sophie very soon to go over details and present your ideas for how you will be influencing during the week. Nothing happens without Sophie's approval, so you need to impress her—*a lot.*" Juliette looks squarely at Abby.

And with that warning, Juliette leaves. Dramatically.

Abby takes her black Sharpie and scrawls *Merde* on her notes page and puts it in the folder. She looks over at Gays for Days, and he smiles at her knowingly. She smiles back at him.

ELEVEN

The Point of *NON* Return

Coming up the stairs carrying her bags of groceries and a bouquet of flowers, Abby runs into Claire, the intriguing neighbor. Abby again notices that Claire has a distinct vibe that is both daring and friendly. She's wearing a colorful brocade cropped jacket with wide-leg jeans and a white T-shirt.

"Bonjour!" Abby says, hoping it will lead to more.

"Hi, yeah, I speak English. So, you decided to live here?" Claire asks.

"Yes, I really like it. I detect an accent, but it's not British." Abby treads lightly this time, based on her unfortunate experience with Muriel.

"No, not British. I'm Irish mostly, but my mom is from Ghana. Don't need to guess that you are American, am I right?" Claire looks straight at her.

"Yes, I'm American, and I'm getting the message that it may not be a good thing in these parts. Would you like to come in for a bit? I could use some company. It's been a grueling day—well, more like a grueling couple of weeks. I can't seem to get my bearings, and I feel like I should have gotten them by now, and these bags are heavy, and I'm sweating, and I . . ."

"Sure, I'd love to." Claire grabs one of the bags as Abby starts to unlock the many locks on the door. Once inside the kitchen, they unpack the groceries.

"How long have you been here? You seem so settled and cool," Abby asks.

"I've been here nearly six years already. I came for a summer and never left. I teach English at one of the English schools down near the Louvre. I love it. It's good money, and it beats being in Ireland or Ghana, even though I spent most of my summers there and it is beautiful."

"Is Ireland or Ghana that bad?" Abby's curious.

"Ireland is a lot better than when I grew up there, but I still feel closed in living there. My parents met here in Paris, and the rest, as they say, is history. Ireland is a small country, and everyone knows everything about everyone. Ghana is the same, but I feel like I only visited there and didn't really live there, so it's a little different for me. I like a little more anonymity in my life than my little section of Dublin offered me when I finished school, so here I am, getting more." Claire smiles. Abby sees that when Claire smiles, her whole look becomes vibrant. She hopes she can make a friend for life here.

"How long did it take you to feel good here? Feel comfortable?" Abby asks, searching for an adjustment recipe where she can mix all the ingredients together and make it happen.

"It took a while. But we came to France a lot during school breaks when I was a kid, so I had some practice with the language and could get by, so that certainly helped. You speak some French, right?" Claire looks for some glasses to pour them some Badoit.

"You are so interesting. All the places you've lived and seen. I love it. I hope to do the same."

"Paris is a good stepping-stone for that. It's a real melting pot. Don't they say that about the US?"

"I suppose they do. I have had limited experience with it being that way just because of where I've lived my whole life. I'm seeing how much of a bubble it really is."

"Any place can be a bubble. I guess it's all about perspective and what you can see. I don't know. We'll have to dissect that later over wine, not sparkling water." Claire winks. "Now back to your French. You speak some, right? That will help you a ton."

"Yes, but since I arrived, I see how crappy my French is, and I'm afraid to try it on fully and put it out there to the French. They are so blunt and rigid in their responses—it's almost a hostile environment trying it out." Abby laughs.

Claire gestures for them to clink their glasses and says a toast: "Welcome to Paris!"

"Do you speak English in Ireland?" Abby asks after she takes a drink. Claire almost spits out her water.

"Oh my god, Abby. Yes, we speak English *and* Irish, which is shoved down our throats from the age of three. I hate it, and I dropped it as fast as I could, using my dual heritage as an excuse. *C'est la vie!* I'll stick with French."

"So, what's the word for *cheers* in Irish?" Abby asks, aware of this newfound feeling of curiosity coming up in her. Meeting someone from a different country in a country that is different from their own is fun and stimulating. It's helping to normalize the varying degrees of experiences she's had here, and she recognizes that she needs more of it.

"It's *sláinte*. Which means 'good health.'"

"I love that. Jeez, what's it in French?" Abby draws a blank.

"It's *santé*. Very similar. Now that that's out of the way, why don't you come out with me this weekend? I'll introduce you to some of my friends. We'll do what I call the Parisian pub crawl." Claire heads to the door.

"I'd love to. Thank you. I'll just knock on your door or . . ."

"I'll text you the place. See you there." Claire leaves after they exchange numbers.

What a relief to have a friendly neighbor! She was worried she was going to have to suck it up and deal with the *Fuck Off* floor mat alone.

. .+ . + + . . .

Game on now. Here we go. Abby, with her promotional plan in hand, is walking back into the Claudette headquarters. Today the influencers are to bring their first round of proposals on how they will "influence" during the event. Abby has been busy going through the guidelines they were given in the folder now marked *WTF* by Abby's black Sharpie.

She heads to the large notice board for the event, and there it is again, proof in black and white that, for better or worse, Heather's picture on Femme Fatale is what got Abby here. Her whole promotional plan is based on breaking the brand that Femme Fatale has built and making it something it's currently not. She's decided she's going to maneuver this in her favor and do what she wants to do—create change with something real, as she has done back home so successfully with Plus-Size Real. She walks into the massively big hall where the other influencers are also waiting, along with a huge crowd and what looks like a row of press with their big cameras and headsets. She goes up to say hello. Ice-cold responses from them make it clear that at least today this is not the place where lifelong friendships will be made. As she moves to her spot and pretends to be studiously looking through the material, in walk three people: a tall, rigid woman who's immaculately dressed and maneuvering a sleek microphone in front of her face, followed by her entourage of two men giving off the complex vibe of sexy yet emotionally unavailable.

"Attention, influencers. Welcome to #BTS of Paris Fashion Week. We are looking forward to having you do what you do best—influence on the worldwide *weeb*. There is free *wee-fee*, of course, throughout the building for you to work your magic, but first let us get down to business. I will call your name and the profile associated with it, and you will come forward. You will then be paired with the person you will shadow and pre-pare your content. Based on your profile, one of you will be paired with Jacqueline, the head of Claudette's haute couture atelier. So, with that we will commence."

Abby throws the folder and her phone in her bag. At that very moment, a group of long-legged supermodels strides purposefully into the room. They are wearing vertiginous stilettos and carrying see-through plastic cups filled with unappetizing-looking, sludge-green smoothies. Abby steps back to let them pass, but in her desire to respect their space, she accidently trips on a model's never-ending leg, causing her to fall. Like a stack of dominos, three more models stumble and then tumble onto each other, with Abby landing unceremoniously on the top. Green goo and long legs are everywhere, like an octopus covered in algae. Absurdly enough, no one has noticed because this all takes place behind a huge group of people, who now have little light-green splats sprayed across their backs. Abby has drops of green goo dripping from her hair, her face, her shirt. The models all regain their compo-sure seamlessly, pulling themselves back up and retaking their stances. They've simply gained a new accessory to sell—green goo—and the show must go on; one would expect nothing less from high-priced legs that cost more than a car. Abby, however, is not faring so well. She feels like Princess Fiona from *Shrek* standing next to them.

"And now the choice for Claudette: Heather Sampson with Femme Fatale, please come forward," the woman calls out.

"Oh no!" Abby exclaims, looking up at the model next to her as if they've been BFFs their whole life. Still somewhat dripping with green and frantically searching for something to wipe herself with, Abby can only find the Evian water spray. She sprays her face, thinking it will make it better, but all it does is make it more goopy. The BFF supermodel empathetically tells her she loves her hot-pink neon flats and gives Abby a couple of wipes from her Claudette bag. Abby smiles and wipes off the worst of the green goo. This comment and gesture from the BFF supermodel bring Abby back to her room in high school with Heather. Instantly she sees a kind of slow-motion memory of Heather always complimenting and encouraging her. The feeling of remorse makes her want to cry. The group parts, and Abby begins what she considers to be her heroic walk up to the front. It appears Gays for Days and Muriel are loving every second of this show.

"I'm—je suis—Abby Allerton, not Heather Sampson. I've informed Juliette of that already. Hi, it's me, Abby," she says nervously.

"*Ce n'est pas possible,*" the lady responds.

"*Si, c'est possible,* because I am. I'm Abby Allerton for Femme Fatale."

"*Vous* for Femme Fatale?" The woman is giving her the once-over of champions, up and down, all around. Abby has been standing there the whole time, frozen, waiting for this woman she's guessing is Sophie to say more. Finally, she does.

"*Vous*, Femme Fatale? *Ce n'est pas possible! Vous?!* The clothes on your profile wouldn't even go past your knees."

"That's so weird, I thought the same thing. Great minds think alike," Abby says back.

"It is some kind of internet deception, *non?*"

"Yes and no. What I mean to say is, I own the profile and I manage the profile. I literally just did a post this morning. I can show it to you. Are you Sophie?" Abby asks, trying to get back on track as she wipes more green muck from her face and chest.

"Am I? Maybe I should pretend to be something I'm not, too, non? Just for fun? To see how far it can get me. A trip to the USA, a fancy place to stay in Miami, a nice stipend while I'm there. Do you think I could get away with it?" The lady's face is red, and some veins appear to be close to popping. Gays for Days and French Market—Forever French are following all this, their mouths hanging open.

Abby watches Gays for Days lean over to French Market, and she can hear him whisper, "W-T-F? How did *she* get all those perks? Did you get all those perks?" She listens intently for French Market's response.

"Non, I did not. This is clearly a case of influencer discrimination. It's always the Americans with their ballsy way of doing things. No pun intended."

Abby sees Gays for Days pull back and look at her with disdain, saying, "What does that even mean?!"

Sophie, getting louder, continues and they all turn back to the ongoing drama playing out in front of them.

"Ms. Sampson, or whatever your name is, I will speak to you after you have cleaned yourself up *en privé*. You may leave now. My assistant will contact you."

"Oh boy, she is *sooo* out, like 2018 fall fashion out." Gays for Days looks around as he says it, waiting for a reaction. To his surprise, no one seems to care.

"Are you the Sophie I've been dealing with via email and text? If you are, do you have that kind of authority, to just kick me out like that? I'm so excited to be here. Truly. I'll do a fantastic job for you."

"Which we paid for, non?" Sophie snidely interrupts.

"Well, to be fair, I still don't have my plane ticket reimbursement, but I have my proposal here that I've worked all night on," Abby says as she holds up her folder. The note paper inside is sticking out of it with *Merde* written on it.

Sophie looks at the folder and says, "Is that your proposal? Excellent title. Most eloquent and very clear."

Abby quickly smashes the paper down into the folder and then puts the folder back in her bag. She then moves her body into a kind of superhero stance and says, "Well, if I may be so bold, you could be living proof of the stereotype that all French people are mean and rude and thrive on humiliating others." Abby looks at her straight in the eye, which entails looking up, because Sophie is tall and has some legs on her, much like Abby's BFF model, who is proving to be trusty by attempting to hand her another wipe. Abby takes it and wipes purposefully, once again being reminded of Heather. The combination of that memory and being touched that a massively gorgeous model is standing next to her in an assistant-like role, handing out wipes as she tries to figure this out, gives her purpose. Everyone is riveted.

"I can assure you I have the authority. I am the Sophie you speak of. Oh, such deception. This will not be accepted. And as far as stereotypes go, you are certainly a living representation of one from your own country, are you not? It shouldn't be hard to guess the one I'm speaking about," Sophie says, seething and rigid as steel.

"That all Americans only eat fast food and are chubby or fat, is it that one?" French Market—Forever French Muriel calls out in a tone that's way too gleeful. Everyone gasps.

"Oh, I would never say that, as that would be rude, right, Ms. Allerton?" Sophie smirks.

"But you certainly let others do the dirty work for you," Abby says quietly back. That one hurt.

"*ARRÊTEZ! J'en ai fini avec vous!* I'm done with you! *Hors de ma vue! Partez!* My assistant will text you, and we will meet to discuss your fate."

"Your fashion fate . . . ," Gays for Days says dramatically and looks around for consensus. Again, no one cares. Tough crowd.

Sophie leaves abruptly, and her entourage follows. Abby's left standing there until the bouncer/doorman comes to her to guide her out. She's gutted. Completely. The six sets of gangly legs disperse into the next room. The empathetic model gives her another wipe and points out some other areas of green to clean up, then sashays out the door.

"Time for you to go, madame," he says mercifully.

"Yeah, I got that. And it's mademoiselle," she says softly.

"Whatever you say, you've had a really bad day of terrible." He leads her out. Out on the street, she turns to him and stands firmly.

"I'll be back," Abby says in her best Schwarzenegger impression.

"I get off at nine tonight. I can show you the real Paris you'll never see," he says, deadpan, emotionless, not even a smile.

"Uh, non, merci, au revoir." She heads off in the direction of the Métro station with tears in her eyes. A corner café at the next block catches her eye with its little terrace tables and chairs and checkerboard tablecloths. She turns and heads toward it.

As she stands waiting to be seated, still holding back tears, she notices the fifth waiter who walks by without even a glance her way. What the hell is she going to do now? She looks in her bag and sees her journal. It's been a while since she's written in it, but now, she feels that all that she's experienced since arriving is starting to seriously swell up in her chest, and there is a huge, ugly sob needing to get out. As if dog poo, green goo, and Sophie weren't enough, she feels shaken inside, like those cheesy Parisian snow globes. She can't seem to let the snowflakes settle where they may because they don't seem to make it back to the ground. The ground that she knows and has relied on her whole life.

Thoughts start spinning. Damn Femme Fatale! Why did she start that stupid thing? It's not her. Half the things she puts up she hates, except for the vintage items. That's fun. Initially she thought it was what everyone would want. But now she understands it's not what they necessarily needed. Isn't that Instagram's purpose? To showcase the uniqueness of others and encourage them to be proud of it?

She takes out her phone and starts to prep a Story to save for a post later. She finds a picture she took of Heather a few years back and takes a screenshot. Then she starts to prepare a post. She wants to prepare a Story with a post where she addresses all this. Her heart can't help but feel the sting once again of how she handled the Heather situation. All this ruminating makes her aware that she's still waiting for one of those apparently oblivious waiters to notice her and show her to one of the many tables that are free in the back.

There goes another one. Shuffling by without even a once-over. She feels sadder and sadder with each waiter that shuffles by leaving her unseen, ignored, and dismissed. Why is this a thing here? The dismissiveness. It hurts. She starts to type on the Story shots, "Time for me to fess up. Time for me to say, 'I'm done being something I'm not online, and I don't want to lie to anyone, most of all myself.'" She puts the phone down just as she sees a waiter flutter by with a tray in his hand.

"*Pardonnez-moi, s'il vous plaît. Je voudrais manger,*" she says.

"*Un moment, madame.*" He shimmies away. This is an authentic old café on a busy corner down in the heart of touristic Paris. They don't need to care about service, as they make a good living and they have a union, so take that, impatient American customers who demand fast service and ice in their drinks. You may have to wait a little bit for a table.

He returns with a menu the size of *Le Monde*'s Sunday edition. He motions for her to follow him. Abby follows and starts to squirm her way through the tightly packed tables outside on the terrace, saying "Pardon" every step of the way as her body pushes up against the chairs and the people. It's impossible to get through. The waiter pulls out the small table and motions for her to sit down at a back wall decorated with strategically cut hedges that act as a lovely buffer to the neighboring terrace. Before she can make herself comfortable, he shoves the table right up against her, trapping her in with another couple to her left. She's relieved to see a way out to her right, if needed. The tables are dressed in stiff white tablecloths and perfect place settings. She loves that it feels fancy even when it's not. If this is considered everyday, what do the three-star Michelin restaurants look and feel like? She thinks of Wholly Crêpe, which feels so far away now, both in distance and relatability. Her thoughts are all over the place. She pulls the little stool next to her toward her and puts her bag on it so she can reach into it when she needs it.

"Bonjour, madame."

The waiter is there and ready. Abby notes that it took about fifteen minutes to get noticed and seated, but in 3.5 seconds someone is there ready to take her order. Go figure.

"Is it madame or still mademoiselle?" Abby says, giving it one last shot.

"Definitely madame, madame," he says with conviction.

"We'll have to agree to disagree." Abby holds her ground, kind of.

"Are you eating, or do you want to continue challenging the deferential parts of the French language?" he says, tapping his black-shined shoe.

"I would like to have lunch. Maybe my last lunch," she says sullenly.

"Are you going to die?" he asks matter-of-factly.

"Uh, non. It's more complicated than that," she says, shrinking behind the enormous menu to shield herself from his view.

"There is nothing more uncomplicated than dying. You just die. That's it, life is over," he says. Abby looks at him wistfully, wishing he were a Parisian François, but alas he is not.

As she's intently deciding, the waiter rolls his eyes and looks over at the customer who's just sat down next to the stool with her bag. The customer has an eerily similar vibe to Saul in *Ocean's Eleven*.

"Where did you go?" Abby's waiter moves to the other side of the menu so Abby can see him. "I will have the *soupe à l'oignon* and a Diet Coke, s'il vous plaît."

"How original. You are really living the life in *Par-ee*." He grabs the menu out of her hands and saunters off. Passing him is another waiter who's bringing a couple to sit down to Abby's right. It hits her that she needs to pee and that this is not a good situation. Why is peeing such an ordeal in this city?! It will be the maneuver of a lifetime to get out of this spot and then get back in to eat. She decides to hold it.

After she's enjoyed her soupe à l'oignon and Diet Coke, she's in a bit of a pickle. The *Ocean's Eleven* Saul customer and the couple to her right are deep into their lunches. She turns to her Goyard bag, unzips it, and pulls out her journal. She's hoping she can once again distract her bladder. She can't help but overhear the couple go on and on about what constitutes a truly fresh fruit and the state of France under Macron, respectively. But she really needs to go. She decides to try to get out to hit the toilets, which are only a few feet away down a steep spiral staircase. She starts to slowly push her table out. She looks to the left, and Saul is smiling big at her. The same type of smile as John the Baptist on the plane. She quickly looks down at her bag. It's zipped up, so all is good. She shifts to the right to give the couple a hint that she needs to move. Nothing. No response. They are immersed and fully swimming in a debate over what wine pairs better with mango. She pushes the table out, causing her bag to fall on the floor, as apparently it was hanging slightly over the edge of the stool and she didn't realize it. She bends down to pick it up and notices Saul quickly leaving the café. She gathers her bag and sits back up and wants to use this opportunity of an empty seat to get the hell out of dodge, or at least out of this cage of a café. No such luck. The waiter hurriedly puts another couple next to her. She's about to burst. She motions for her waiter. He comes up to the table, and she motions him to come closer so she can whisper something to him.

"About how long are these people going to stay here? I mean, how long can a person drink one glass of wine and eat a small salad?"

"It is an art, madame. And it is lunchtime," he says.

"And how long does this art form last here in Paris?" Now she's really dying.

"Until *quatorze heures*—14h00," he says, then leaves.

Abby looks at her watch. It's only 1:15. She can't wait here another forty-five minutes. She starts to tap her feet anxiously. The two people at the table next to her on her left get up to go smoke a cigarette outside. Thank god for smokers! Abby sees her chance at an escape. She stands up in such a hurry that a loose thread on the side of the tablecloth catches her bracelet, and everything flies off the table. The waiter runs over.

"What is happening? You are like a deer in a china shop," he says angrily.

"I think you mean a bull. But I've got to go." Abby, with her bag on her arm, darts for the staircase of relief.

"I was being kind!" the waiter yells after her. "And your check? You still must pay, madame!"

Abby nods and says, "*Oui, oui,* after the toilet! *Une minute.*"

After finishing her toilet time, Abby confidently and with much relief walks over to the cupboard where the waiters are standing and looks in her bag to pull out her wallet. Her Goyard is truly just an overpriced sack without any dividing pockets or divisions, so she must always rummage through it to find anything. She continues to rummage, throwing too many Pilot pens, her makeup bag, Post-it notes, a journal, three Evian spray cans, her phone, and a half-eaten *pain au chocolat* onto the counter. Where the hell is her wallet?

"Désolée, I don't know what happened. I have no wallet. It's completely gone. It was just here. I was sitting over there, and it was all fine. What is going on?" Abby is frantic.

"Madame, maybe you left it in the toilet?" her waiter says to her with growing impatience.

"I'll go check." Abby rushes down again and looks every-where. Nothing. She comes back up the stairs, frantic. "My wallet is gone! I don't have any cards or money or anything. Who would do such a thing?" She looks to the three waiters for an answer.

"All of Paris," they answer in unison.

Abby stands there blankly. "I don't know how to pay you. Do you take PayPal?" she asks.

They all laugh. "Non, we do not. Carte Bleue or Visa, Mastercard."

"I can't do those options because—I just told you—my wallet with the cards has been stolen. Wait a second. Do you know that old, kind of suave man that was sitting next to my bag?" Abby says with the determination of a detective who's just solved the biggest crime of her career. The waiters look at each other. It's clear they know him.

"You guys know him, don't you? Is he a regular? You must help me. I must get those cards back. Oh no. I need to cancel those cards, like right now." Abby moves to a table that is right next to the bar and plops down. She pulls out her phone to go on all the card apps and cancel the cards. The café barman has been watching this all play out, and he leans over the bar.

"Mademoiselle, are you new to Paris?"

Abby looks up at him with a WTF face.

"Isn't it obvious?" she says back.

"In fact, it is. Can I help in some way?" He leans over the bar at her. He's handsome, with deep-brown eyes and the standard hipster Parisian stubble. Abby looks at him and then continues canceling.

"Do you know that guy that was sitting next to me?" she asks without looking up.

"He's in here sometimes, but we don't know much about him. He's a little reclusive."

"You speak English well and without hesitation," Abby replies.

"Merci, I studied in New York for a year. Went to bartender school there. What drink can I do for you? It's on the house," he says with a smile.

"I better not, as I'm pretty sure my lunch is going to have to be on the house, too," Abby says, still not looking up from her phone.

"I'll make you a cosmopolitan. I get off in thirty minutes. I can take you to the police station so you can file a report. Not that it will do much good, but it may make you feel better," he says as he's preparing the cocktail.

"Merci, that would be really nice, as I haven't a clue how to deal with this." She finishes her stolen credit card tasks and moves up to the bar. The other waiters are watching this play out.

"What's your name?" the barman asks.

"My name is Abby," she answers as she starts a text to François. She really needs him right now.

"My name is Jean-Louis. Enchanté."

"Oh, another two-name guy. I met another one of you on the plane over here. Maybe it's an omen," Abby says.

He extends his hand to her to make it official. Abby shakes his hand and catches the way he's looking at her. Feels like the look of a marksman. She daintily takes a sip of the cocktail he put down in front of her and smiles. They chitchat a bit and continue commiserating about her wallet, and he tells her it will be okay. She keeps checking her phone, hoping François will answer, but nothing yet. The other waiter comes up to the bar and asks the barman in French what the status is. They speak French to each other at record speed, and Abby can only track some of it. Just then, her phone rings. It's François on FaceTime. She quickly answers it.

"Oh my god. François. It happened. It happened," she says in a heightened state.

"What, ma chérie?" François asks, concerned.

"My wallet was stolen! By some old guy that looked so freaking harmless, and it was right under my nose, like right next to me. I also had the most awful day at Claudette. This is just icing on my crappy cake today, François. I want to go home," Abby says assertively. She notices the barman continuing to nonchalantly clean the bar in her vicinity. She looks over at him as she continues to speak to François.

"But there's this barman here at the café where I was eating lunch, and when he's off, he said he's going to take me to the police to file a report that will apparently mean nothing. But I appreciate the gesture." Abby takes another sip of the cosmopolitan.

"Who is the barman? Do you think he could have stolen your wallet?" François says with one eyebrow up.

"Non, non, it was the old man with no socks and boat shoes. I know it was," Abby says, taking another sip. Just then, a couple of transactions come through on her bank account apps. She's being asked to identify and confirm them. One is for seven hundred euros at a boulangerie, and the other is for eight hundred euros at a wine shop.

"Oh my god. He's using my cards right now. How much bread can you buy for seven hundred euros? Wait, let me correct that and say, here, you could buy a lot of bread because it's truly magnificent, but seven hundred euros worth? That's a dedication I do not have, and I love bread," Abby exclaims.

She sees the barman, François, and the rest of the waiters are now laughing.

"Abby, he's not buying bread. He's getting cash from the bakery. There's definitely some kind of fief ring going on where he gets cash from the cards he steals. I'm so sorry this happened to you, but I will say it is a kind of rite of passage in Paris. *Félicitations!*" François smiles.

"What's a fief ring?" Abby asks.

"You know, a FIEF! A guy who steals stuff," he says, irritated.

"Oh, you mean a *thief*! No *f* but a *th*. Different sound." Abby grabs her cosmopolitan for another drink.

"You can't hear the difference? Doesn't matter!" François answers.

"This completely sucks. Totally sucks. I've never felt so violated," Abby says to him sincerely.

"I'm sorry, I know it sucks. Let me speak to this Mother Teresa barman," François says. Abby calls for Jean-Louis and gives the phone to him. They speak French and make a couple of jokes like they are old friends, and then Jean-Louis hands the phone back to Abby.

"What did you say?" Abby asks, cocking her head a bit.

"Oh, nothing you need to worry about. He'll help you to the police station and then home, but call me when you get home, okay?"

Abby smiles. "I will, of course." And hangs up the phone. Jean-Louis moves back over to show her that he's paid for her lunch, and they head off together out of the café in the direction of the nearest police station.

* + +

Abby and Jean-Louis are now outside Abby's apartment door giving each other "su-PEAR" sexy signals that they are both ready to take this further. Abby is ready for anything after the day she's had, and their adventure to and at the police station was filled with flirty sexual tension. They stopped and had a few more cocktails before getting to her door. This feeling of urgency to grab hold of this weird, surreal moment is beaming off them both, but for Abby there's an element of uncertainty and worry, compared to what she feels is Jean-Louis's steady, suave, and debonair way. He seems cool—been there, done that. She's still hedging but getting there. As she's unlocking the many locks, he leans in and kisses her. She manages to get the door open, and she leads him to the bedroom with the killer view of Sacré-Coeur but not without a stop by the kitchen first. He stops at the doorway.

"Nice view," Jean-Louis says with a sweet whistle and fluttering of the hand. Abby gets loud and clear that this must mean the apartment is astronomically expensive. "Where did you find this place?" he stops to ask.

"Through that French waiter François you spoke to on the phone. What did he say to you, anyway?"

Jean-Louis dismisses the question. "Nothing. It was a Frenchman to Frenchman chat. We don't tell." He walks over to Abby, who is across the kitchen by the fridge, taking out a bottle of Badoit.

"Wow, we are really partying tonight, non?" He smiles.

"I know, it's sad, but I'm afraid it's all I've got. I haven't been able to properly stock up on any alcohol. Not that I would anyway, as I'm not much of a boozer." She laughs, in complete denial that she is in fact very tipsy after all those cocktail stops on the way home.

"Could've fooled me . . . ," Jean-Louis says under his breath.

"I do have a question. Do you—aka, the French—drink, I mean, like, really drink to the point of falling down drunk?"

"Non. That would be unbecoming and sloppy. Two attributes that we don't tolerate in France. Plus, we've been drinking since we were thirteen. It's about education with us. Elegant education." Jean-Louis moves in closer to her, and the little button gape on Abby's shirt catches his eye. In the center of it, there's a blush-pink bra showing through with a dainty crystal in the middle. He looks straight at it and then up at her. As if on autopilot, she pulls it down to try and smooth it out. Damn button gapes. He stops her. He leans in for another kiss. Abby intentionally closes her eyes and gently kisses back, still holding the neck of the Badoit with the fridge door still open. The kiss is so seductive and so entrancing that she drops the full bottle on Jean-Louis's foot.

"OW!" he yells and jumps up and grabs his foot.

"Oh my god. Jean the Baptist, I'm so sorry. I'm so stupid. I got so carried away with that kiss. Wow, I mean you can really kiss. I mean *really* kiss. Like, you've been kissing me this whole time, but that one beamed me right up."

"Jean the Baptist?" Jean-Louis asks. Abby starts laughing.

"The other two-name guy. From the plane. I told you."

"Oh, did you ah . . ." Jean-Louis makes a gesture that seems to be asking if Abby had sex with him or not.

"Ah, that's a big old non, monsieur. He was not my type."

"It is an evening of casualties for us—your wallet, my foot," Jean-Louis says, still hopping around the kitchen with an agreeable shrug. Abby, still laughing, grabs an eye mask made of ice from the freezer. She directs him to the bedroom to sit on the brass bed. Now sitting on the bed with his leg on her lap, he lets her apply the eye mask to his foot. He lies back on the bed with her still holding his foot. She starts to massage it a little.

"You can keep doing that. That's nice."

Abby keeps stroking, putting a little more pressure, and moves her hand up. His leg is strong and muscular, and she surmises that he works out. He sits up, and one leg and foot are still on her lap, but the other is dangling off the side of the bed, touching the floor. The eye mask falls off. Abby reaches down to grab it. Jean-Louis stops her.

They are both now sitting across from each other. Both with one leg long off the side and one leg in front in a triangle shape. Abby's shirt is still button-gaping. She can still see that Jean-Louis keeps focusing on that dainty, cute rhinestone hanging in the middle of her bra, visible in the heart of the gape. He puts his finger in the gape again and flicks it. Abby starts to laugh at the irony of how she ranted about button gapes online before she left for Paris, and now she's here bene-fitting from them.

"What is so funny, ma chérie? You never stop laughing. Your joie de vivre, it's so intoxicating," he says quietly.

"You're flicking it like my cat would," she says to him as he leans over to kiss her neck.

"I want to play. Do you want to play?"

Abby nods, smiling a definite *yes*.

He moves off the bed and shifts her so that she's sitting on the edge, then starts to kiss her neck gently, slowly, and then sets his eye on the first button. As he unbuttons it, he kisses the spot directly underneath. Abby's breathing becomes more intense, and for some reason she keeps slipping off the bed and trying to get herself back up, so she won't ruin this moment. This is romance overload for her—in this setting, with this view, with this guy and the way he kisses. Again, is she being filmed by some show that's going to come busting in to tell her it's all a sham and a dream? Jean-Louis has now moved on to button number two. He gently undoes the button and kisses her cleavage right in the middle spot.

"There's the spot." He moves down and bites the little crystal on her bra.

"Is it? I always thought 'the spot' was a little lower," Abby answers assertively.

"Oui, it is, ma chérie, but relax and enjoy the journey. You Americans are so quick to finish everything and forget to enjoy the fun of getting to the destination. This is the time to enjoy the journey." The way he says it makes her instantly think of François. It's something he would say.

As if on cue, she asks, "Did you get that from the @MeaningfulQuotes account."

"What?" Jean-Louis asks as he continues to kiss her slowly, lower again, and very carefully unbuttons her shirt all the way down. He pulls her up, and they are both standing, facing each other.

"Your turn," he says sweetly. Abby starts to unbutton his shirt and kisses him all the way down his chest, just as he kissed her, but this time, she takes it further and grabs his soft brown leather belt and starts to unbuckle it. Her fingers are fumbling, and she can't smoothly get the belt undone.

"Allow me." Jean-Louis masterfully unbuckles it and rips it off in one fell swoop. Abby, impressed, pushes him on the bed. Jean-Louis stops.

"Wait. This is not right. We need to make this more romantic. What about some music?"

"Let's make our own music." Abby continues to kiss him. Forget the music. She wants to get it on.

Jean-Louis looks at her straight on. "I cannot fight you. Let's do this." With the mutual green light, a go, they both let go and start to ravishingly enjoy each other.

.· ·.+· ✦ · ✦ · ·.

"I've got to go, mon monsieur, or I mean, Jean-Louis." Abby catches herself calling him her nickname for François and feels instantly guilty. She is smartly dressed and ready to go. She leans over to Jean-Louis, who looks just splendid in her big brass bed.

"Me too, but I'm still lying here in your bed." Jean-Louis smiles at her.

"It's not my bed. I'm borrowing it." She kisses him again.

"Technicalities. What do I do now? Stay here and wait for you or go back to my life?" He mimics the thinking emoji. He's cute, but she really wants him to go.

They both leave the apartment, and Abby starts to work her way through the locks. She turns to head down the stairs.

"Just one more kiss . . . ," Jean-Louis says and grabs her. At that moment, Claire opens her door to head out. She notices them.

"Jesus! That was quick. Where did you find him, at a club?" Claire asks and winks at Jean-Louis.

"No, at a café where my wallet was stolen," Abby answers.

"Oh boy," Claire says.

"I will leave you two to talk further. It is not good etiquette if I'm listening to this discussion that will no doubt involve me and last night." Jean-Louis smiles.

"Au revoir," he says, bowing to both ladies. Once he's out of earshot and eye shot, Abby turns to Claire.

"He thinks a lot of himself, doesn't he?" Claire says. "Maybe we're going to talk about the latest football game," she quips.

"Should I be worried?" Abby asks. "Do they pick up women at cafés after their wallets are stolen?"

"What does your gut say?" Claire asks as they head down the stairs.

"It says he's really dreamy and so sexy, and I'm wondering why in the world I actually left my bed with him in it at all today," Abby says, smiling from ear to ear.

"I'd say your gut is in sexual overdrive, so you might want to do some more normal fact-finding on this Frenchman. They are masters at making women swoon. And you were a definite damsel in distress, so I'm pretty sure you may be one of many."

"Mmm, I get it." Abby smiles.

They reach the Métro station and go their separate ways. As Abby heads down the stairs, she suddenly realizes she never texted or did a FT call with François when she got back home last night.

TWELVE

Just Give Me the Cranberry Pills

It's another day in Paris, nearing the end, and Abby's had a full day of exploring with the book *Secrets of Paris* as her guide. She's been trying out the role of being a *flâneuse* as she tries to piece together how she can get back in Sophie's good graces and back on track with what she wants to do here. The sky on this gorgeous Parisian evening is a beautiful magenta and purple, but she's struggling with a horrible sensation in her side. At every café stop, she's felt the urge to pee, and when she does pee, it stings as much as she would feel a bee sting back home—it's burning, uncomfortable, and painful. As she's walking, she sees a pharmacy sign blinking neon green. She's lost track of where she is right now, but has grown to love that in this city; getting lost and discovering all the little streets and corners is a real pleasure, even if you are in pain. Hoping for a simple solution, she walks into the pharmacy, which is empty except for the owl-eyed pharmacy worker behind the counter. The place is an Aladdin's cave of lotions and potions, products promising eternal youth, and remedies for every known ailment.

"Bonsoir, madame!" the pharmacy worker greets Abby, cheerfully.

"Parlez-vous anglais?"

"Un petit peu. Just a little."

"Super! Do you have anything for a UTI?" Abby asks hopefully, holding her side.

"A UTI? What is it?" She cocks her head questioningly to one side, owl eyes behind stylish glasses focusing in on what's coming next.

"It's a urinary tract infection," Abby replies.

Miss Owl Eyes looks horrified. "Mais non, mademoiselle! We don't have toilets here." She waves Abby outside to the street, in the general direction of the public toilets, the ones with the sliding door. Been there, done that.

"Yes, I know. I'm not asking for a toilet. I haven't been able to pee properly for days, and now I think I have an infection," Abby says pleadingly, gesturing to her nether region.

"How do they happen?"

"The infections?" Abby is confused by the question.

"Of course, I know how it happens. I mean *your* infection," Miss Owl Eyes answers. Abby can see that she's now invested, for better or worse.

"It's a long, *horrible* story involving tables, no decent toilets in the city, snarky waiters, French people, and wine . . ." Abby trails off, having emphasized *horrible* with the biggest French accent she can possibly produce.

"Can you speak slowly? My English is again un petit peu," she replies.

Abby, frustrated with the language barrier, and herself because she keeps asking if they know English rather than just coming out with it and speaking French, understands now that she's in France, not America, and if the situation were reversed, how many Americans could reply in French there? So, really the onus is on her to speak as much French as she possibly can, because she is in France, and that's all there is to it. But today, jeez, just today, she could have really used *une exception* and gotten a pharmacy worker who speaks perfect English to get her through dealing with this unwelcome situation.

"I. Had. To. Pee." Abby begins to mime sitting on a toilet and pulls a painful face to show what it's like when she's peeing. The great mime performer Marcel Marceau would have been proud.

She continues her description. "The. Tables. Were. Sooo. Small. *Les toilettes* . . ." She makes a little sign with her fingers and tries to mime getting out of a tight spot. When she sees that this isn't working, she jabs her index finger at herself, as if she's about to start a round of charades, indicating that she'll be miming a person and that the woman's team should get ready. Abby can see that Miss Owl Eyes is quite engaged.

Out the window, there's an elderly Parisian couple watching, too. Even their dog is engrossed. Miss Owl Eyes shrugs at them. They are all agog. Abby continues to work hard to get through, posturing, gesturing over her imaginary toilet, and mimicking the flow out of her nether region, then back to the tiny tables, bursting out with things breaking and spilling all around her as she finally breaks free. It's become so intense that Abby feels she might break out into a sweat. Then a miracle happens.

"*Mais bien sûr! Alors!* Now I understand! Of course!" Miss Owl Eyes, proud of herself, points to shelves on the back wall. Abby follows her, relieved and breathing hard. Surely that masterful mime portrayal of a UTI has finally sunk in.

"Vous—you—will need A LOT." She turns to the shelves. It's full of weight-loss remedies and pills. All promising instant weight loss. Miracle pills, water pills, herbal pills to suppress appetite, and an abundance of cellulite creams. You name it. It's there.

"What the . . . ? Weight-loss pills? Again, it's about the weight? I came in here to get help with something not related to weight whatsoever, and yet I find myself in front of a shelf of weight-management products. WTF? And I don't mean 'Welcome to France' on this one! I'm allowed to take up space, you know. It's my birthright. I have a right to be here in Paris, in the whole of effing France, for that matter, and just *be here* without judgment, without criticism, and yet here I am, standing in front of weight-loss solutions when I desperately need something for a urinary tract infection. It hurts when I pee, *not when I eat*! It's not okay that from day one I've been given the message that I have to be a perfectly sized woman to exist here. What is perfectly sized, anyway? The perfect size doesn't exist. It's not right, and it sure as hell isn't fair!" Abby stops her rant to take a breath and spots a life-size cardboard poster showing a beaming, slender woman holding one of the products and exclaiming how happy she is with their supposed effect. "I mean, seriously," she continues, "do you think she even actually takes these things?"

"Without a doubt, madame," comes the immediate reply, without even a pause for thought.

"Well, that's sad, very sad, because she looks great just the way she is . . . dammit." Abby knows full well that she's lost her audience due to a massive language barrier and maybe an even more embedded cultural belief. She's lost the battle on this one. Can she win the war?

"You can, too, madame—non, mademoiselle—if you do something about it. Try them. What can it hurt? It can only help." Miss Owl Eyes is selling it as best she can.

"I don't need help! I don't need to change. I do, however, need to pee without pain. I am who I am, and that's okay. Do you understand what I'm saying?" Abby asks, looking for a light at the end of the dark tunnel of culturally imposed thinness. Another Gallic shrug in reply.

"Fine, I'll just take the cranberry pills, s'il vous plaît." They both walk back toward the counter. As Miss Owl Eyes taps Abby's purchases into the till, Abby looks back over at the cardboard woman, all smiles and joy, then back over at Miss Owl Eyes. She thinks about the influencer event and the mess-up and Femme Fatale and how that's what got her here, not Plus-Size Real. Maybe she's got it all wrong? She goes and grabs one pack of the product advertised on the poster and brings it to the counter. Miss Owl Eyes smiles.

"You won't regret it," she says as she puts it into the bag. Then, in a rare moment of sympathy, she adds a box of antibiotics with instructions, even though Abby doesn't have the required prescription. It looks like those comical charades were worth it.

"You'll need these, too. Follow the instructions. You'll feel better in two days," she says and hands the cute little sack across the counter.

"Merci beaucoup, madame." Abby smiles sweetly. She leaves the pharmacy asking herself what is happening to her that she bought those stupid, gimmicky French "get thin" pills? She knows they aren't going to work, and why does she want them to work?

As she leaves the pharmacy and turns right, she sees the Eiffel Tower in front of her. It's eight o'clock on the dot, and right on schedule *la dame de fer* starts to sparkle. It's only the second time since arriving that she's seen it right when it begins to sparkle, and she can't help but say, "Magnifique." Each twinkling light perfectly complements the other as they flash in a series of shimmering patterns across Paris's grand old iron lady. She slowly walks toward it, eyes upward, jaw hanging open in wonderment. "If you, my lady, can take up space and sparkle here, then surely I can, too . . . ," she says to herself.

·᠂ ᠂+· ✦ + ᠂ ᠂᠊·.

Abby's officially ready to lie in bed and bring on a "big ole ugly sob," as her mama calls it. The sob's in there, waiting to come out, but she hasn't given it permission yet. She wants to get through her FaceTime session with Charlene today. The WTF, or "Welcome to France," is getting to her now on a level she didn't anticipate. It's a great acronym to live by and helps to level out the frustration when it arises, but Abby hates that this is the case. She keeps trying to hold on to the excitement and anticipation she felt before she arrived, but it's a struggle. She's got some time before her session, so she pulls out her *BIG IDEAS* notebook and scrolls through what she's written down thus far for her IG posts. This reminds her that she needs to resolve the major *désastre* that she brought upon herself that's surely still brewing over at Claudette. She keeps scrolling, keeping herself in denial a little bit longer . . .

- French flight attendants from hell with size biases the size of the Eiffel Tower.
- John the Baptiste, or Jean-Baptiste. Oh la la! That was fun and weird.
- The Parisian tenant elevator police and his evil little Toto dog.
- The rats, oh my god, the rats and their "discerning taste."
- The boulangeries full of bountiful, tempting goodies. What's not to love? But what lies beneath those treasures of human troughs?

- The elegance and beauty of Claudette's HQ—the murals, the columns, and the back room, comically, with none of the above. Is there something there about false pretense and the reality of what's behind the beauty?
- Being perceived as a *grande* or *grosse américaine*, in Paris or Plus-Size in Paris (*Genius. MUST do something with that title.)
- The constant contrast of experiences, a never-ending roller coaster, up and down, high and low, all the way around we go.

As she runs through her list, it occurs to her that there is indeed a pattern. For every horrible, hard thing, there is a good one (or, at least, for every two horrible hard things, there is one good one) to counterbalance it. Her FaceTime rings. It's Charlene.

"Bonjour, Charlene!" Abby says cutely as she sits up on her bed. She is cuddling a pillow that Charlene can see through her phone screen.

"Well, bonjour, Abby! It's so good to see you. I'm so glad you reached out. I was wondering how you were getting along," Charlene says genuinely.

"I'm hanging in there. Wait. What am I saying? I'm drowning, Charlene. Drowning in gorgeous pastries, people, fashion, and architecture. I've hit a wall here. I can't seem to get grounded, and there's this whole thing going on at Claudette, the fashion house I'm supposed to be working at. I've been sent home, like that time I got checked for lice and had to go home, only this time it's not lice, it's completely on me. I did this. I made the conscious decision to screw my friend—not friend, whatever we are now—and I thought I could do this. Deceit or not," Abby says fast, without breathing, but not forgetting to say *deceit* with a French accent, which she sees gets a smile out of Charlene. At the end of it, Abby takes a deep breath.

"Okay, well, let's start with a deep breath." Charlene smiles. Abby takes three deep breaths. "From where I'm sitting, Abby, I'm not sure where to start—the beautiful architecture, the delicious pastries—so you tell me."

Abby pauses. "That. Right there. Because I'm in Paris, I feel I've lost the right to complain or be unhappy here. It's a weird vibe I get when I call home, from people I've met. It's weird and infuriating. It's not easy here. It's not easy for *me* here. I mean, who I am."

"I hear that. I'm sorry. I did not want to minimize or dismiss. You said, 'who I am.' What does that mean?" Charlene says.

"I want to say it's because I'm not a size six or under. I'm not stick thin. I'm getting that I'm too thick for here. I'd say I need to start there, as that's where most of the difficulty seems to be coming up."

"Okay, then. Tell me more about that. What's coming up?"

"It brings up that I'm not worthy enough to be here because my body isn't what it's supposed to be by the standards here. I thought the US was bad, but I'd have to say we are a little more progressive in this area." Abby takes a drink of Badoit from one of the pretty glasses.

"Well, you've played a major role in that culture shifting in the US, right?" Charlene asks.

"Yes, I think I have, and I'm proud of it."

"Would you like to work on that?" Charlene coaxes gently.

"Sure." Abby settles down a bit. She moves from her bed to the desk and props her phone up against a stack of her Paris books and puts the glass of Badoit next to her.

"So, your worthiness is being triggered? Is that correct?"

"Yep," Abby replies.

"Talk to me about the deceit part," Charlene says.

"I came here under false pretenses. I didn't tell them I was coming in place of Heather. I was in this place of *dammit, I'm doing this, and I don't care how,* and I was in the break-down-doors mode after our session. And they have a problem with it. I mean, it's the same account—I do *all* the work, and I've handled Heather, I think," Abby says, running her hands through her hair and looking away from the phone.

"Who says they have a problem with it?" Charlene asks.

"Sophie, the lady that yelled at me."

"Do you think it's an issue yourself?" Charlene asks. "To do the job they wanted Femme Fatale to do?"

"Not really, because who cares if it's Heather or me—it's about the account and the influencing I can do, and I'm really good at it."

"So, what are you worried about?"

"Well, I'm not sure if I'm going to be sent home. I'm in this weird holding place until they contact me," Abby says as she doodles on her notebook at the desk.

"Since when do you let other people dictate to you what's going to happen, French or not?" Charlene says, warmly smiling.

"Well, I don't. I mean, I haven't—well, that's not true. I have, because I've let Heather dictate by paying her to not be me, and then I had Mama and her illness. I mean, I had no choice but . . ."

"Are you at home now?" Charlene asks.

"No, I'm not," Abby says as she writes an exclamation point in her notebook next to her on her desk. "I see where you are going with this, Charlene, but they feel I lied to them, and they're right. That's exactly what I did. Most importantly, I've been lying to myself. I've been lying to myself for years," Abby says clearly with tears filling her eyes. "I'm tired of being something I'm not. I'm tired of having this dysfunctional pay-off relationship for the sake of not being found out, or maybe it was to keep a friendship that no longer exists. I don't know. It's so stupid that I've been so insecure about it all. And now I'm in this amazing place, in Paris, and it's still here. I wish I would've been invited for Plus-Size Real, not Femme Fatale."

"Let's turn this on its head a bit. What if you would've been invited for Plus-Size Real and *not* Femme Fatale? What would it be like? How would you hold yourself, and what would you do? Have some fun with it. What would it be like if you got that invite?" Charlene says.

"I would be writing posts nonstop about how Paris is missing out on women like me and what we offer and what we bring to this gorgeous city's table full of dreamy design with powerful tradition. I would proudly walk these quaint, small streets believing that I can offer an alternative, a way of being here that is *real*," Abby says with a renewed enthusiasm. Charlene takes a drink from a mug that says, *Fuck off until I've had coffee*. Abby laughs when she sees it.

"What's so funny?" Charlene asks.

"Your mug." Abby points to it on the screen.

"Oh yes, it's very true." Charlene smiles. "You're doing great. So where are you now, what's coming up?"

"Mmm, I don't really know. It's a lot to think about. I did feel that shift a bit inside."

"I can see it. It seems, though, by the sound of it that you've been thinking about it a lot. What about showing them they are wrong and that you didn't come there under false pretenses—meaning *you* belong there as much as anyone else. Because you do, you do. There's room for everyone, including you."

"It's not really about my body, is it?"

"What do you think?"

"Partly but not much."

"I'd tend to agree. Your body is yours, and just because it's not what you are seeing on the street or at this design house . . . I mean, come on, you aren't a model, although you could be if you wanted to—that's up to you. You are there to give *yourself* a magical time in Paris, living out a dream you've had for years. That's a lot of self-love, and it's wonderful. Your body is yours, and it's one part of that equation of making your dream come true, but just because they can't see it and see you because of their own limitations doesn't mean you don't have a place. I see you. Your followers see you. Go get it. Make your place. Sit at that table. Make it happen, whatever it is you feel you want to do in Paris."

Abby looks at her and pauses, putting her hand to her heart. "Easier said than done." Charlene looks at her intently.

"Do you remember what we worked on before you left? That hard piece of work that happened to you in middle school. I'm wondering how that middle-school girl is doing with all this, or that freshly graduated high schooler inside that's off to a gap year of travel and adventure she never got to take. Have you checked in with them recently? I'm wondering if you have taken time to hear *their* perspective. It sounds like they're struggling and need you to listen. They're awesome from what I remember."

"Yeah, they are kind of awesome," Abby says. "I haven't really written since I got on the plane, with the exception of a post on Plus-Size Real that was so full of angst after my journey getting here." Abby looks down.

"Do you think it's time?"

"I do. I'm miserable not doing it," Abby says as she writes down the word *misérable*.

"I think it may be time to do some cultural shifting through your writing and posting there, Abby. I think Paris might be ready for it. Seems like you're getting a lot of signs that it is."

"I think you're right. It's funny you mentioned it as I was just looking through my list of ideas I've compiled since I arrived." Abby holds up the list for Charlene to see on the screen.

"Good stuff, Abby. Don't forget to check in with those younger versions of you. They are willing and ready to inspire and help. I can feel it. And I think they want to play in Paris, too. They've come a very long way to already be dismissed," Charlene says as she takes another drink of her coffee.

"Thank you, Charlene. For everything."

"It's my absolute pleasure, Abby. Oh, and one more thing! Go get yourself a Parisian playmate. Have fun!" Just then, there's a knock at Abby's door.

"I think I already have. Gotta go."

"Take loads of care, Abby. Bye bye now."

They both hang up. Abby heads to the door. She opens it. It's Claire.

"Hiya. Did you get your wallet back or that Jean-Louis back? Somehow, I feel they are both gone for good. Am I right?" she asks happily.

"Ah, non and *oui*. I'm okay with the latter, not so much the prior. What's up?" Abby asks.

"Remember I told you about that night out coming up? Well, it's tonight. You in?" Claire says, smiling.

"Sure! What are we doing?" Abby's intrigued.

"Oh, you are going to love it! It'll be great craic." Claire hands her a card with the time, 20h00, written on it.

"Wait, what is 20h00 again? Sorry, I can't keep it straight. And what's a 'crack'?" Abby bites her lip.

"Listen, you'd better get with the program over here, or you'll look like a daft américaine, and that's not a good thing. It means eight o'clock. And I'll explain what craic is later. Here's the address. Dress sexy. You never know who you might meet at these things. Later!"

"Merci beaucoup, Claire." Abby smiles gratefully. Just then, her phone dings inside the apartment. A text has come through. Abby runs back to her room, as she's been waiting to hear from Claudette on her status.

> Bonjour Ms. Sampson/Allerton, Sophie Dubois would like to meet with you the day after tomorrow to discuss your deception and immediate plans for releasing you from the contract you signed under false pretenses. She will see you at 15h00.
> Regards, Emilie (assistant to Ms. Dubois)

Abby reads it over. Blanches back at the rudeness and then pauses. She looks out at Sacré-Coeur, picks up her list of things to write about that she showed Charlene, and turns to an empty page. She writes at the top, *Parisian Plus-Size Real aka Plus-Size in Paris* and firmly presses the Pilot pen as she puts the period at the end.

THIRTEEN

Not Feeling the French Love

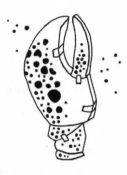

The way to the address Claire wrote down is through the Jardin des Tuileries. Abby has some extra time, so she decides to roam a little through this central Parisian park and see the sights. She notices heads bobbing up and down over to the right and a gorgeous vintage carousel to the left and then a big pond with distinctive green chairs all around it. People are lounging together, watching the ducks swim back and forth across the pond. The color of the water perfectly reflects the color of the sky above. It's a lively yet calm place, and as she walks along the paths, she feels the urge to take a jump on those trampolines where she can see the heads bobbing. That would be so silly, but it would be such fun. Charlene did encourage her to "play" more. That's it, then. She heads over to the trampolines and waits in line with the most put-together children she's ever seen. Up next, she prepares her five euros for her fifteen minutes of bouncing. Seems a bit steep, but the kids on the trampolines make it look worth it, and then it occurs to her that she is in fact the only adult in line to jump. *This is so ridiculous and silly. Hand on the heart. It needs to be*

done. Here we go. She takes off her shoes and puts them in the little cubicle.

"Aren't you too big for these?" asks the boy in front of her in the queue.

She responds with, "*Non,* I'm the perfect size. I'll get a higher bounce. Care to wager?"

"*Vager?* What is it?" he responds.

"Nothing. Let's just jump. Let's jump to the sky!" And she turns and heads to her assigned spot. She puts her AirPods in her ears and gets a blast of Meghan Trainor's "Me Too" and queues up "Made You Look." Meghan's songs have been her mantras for a few years, and she needs them now more than ever. Once on the trampoline, she just goes for it, up and down, shouting out on cue with Meghan. With each jump, she can see higher and higher above the fence and out into the park beyond. She catches a quick glimpse of a man with his dog. She jumps again to catch another. Then another. He's so gentle with his round, solid bulldog. It's an endearing scene, and she keeps jumping to see more of it. Finally, he starts to turn toward her to move along the path, and he catches her eye as she's jumping up and down over the fence. They smile at each other, and he moves on. She's disappointed that he's left, but she keeps jumping in rhythm with the song. She hasn't had this much fun since she arrived. Before she knows it, the whistle blows. Time to stop. She jumps off. The little boy next to her is impressed.

"You jumped high. Very high," he says, admiringly.

"I sure did," she responds, swaggering off confidently as she takes out her now trustworthy Evian spray bottle for a quick spritz to pat off the glisten of sweat on her face.

Now, as she nears the destination address, Abby notices a small black Peugeot pull up on the opposite side of the street.

It bumps first the car in front, then the car behind, then the car in front again, before finally fitting into the rather narrow Parisian parking space. The theme from *Rocky* is blaring from the speakers. Two middle-aged men jump out and open the small trunk. They zip open their leather duffle bags with gusto. Clearly, they have done this before and are both looking forward to what happens next. They whip out two crisp white linen shirts and strip off the T-shirts they were wearing. They pull out some deodorant and spray generously. As their image starts improving, they assist each other with their respective buttons. Next the cologne bottles come out. They spray each other and test to make sure it's not too much. One sprays, then steps in, then steps out, and the other pretends to casually walk by to see if it's too strong. The precision with which they act this out is something worth watching. Satisfied that they are sufficiently aromatic, they give themselves a thumbs-up and high five each other. Abby is fully aware that she is witnessing not only the ultimate male primping session but a very clear indication of their intentions for the evening as well. If this process had an instruction manual, it would be titled *Get women!*

Abby is rooted to the spot, watching the spectacle with great interest. With their chest hair perfectly in place and on display above the second button, and their perfectly measured cologne, they recall her admirer from the plane, "John the Baptist," and her barman, Jean-Louis.

"Lord, what is it with the male primping here? They are doing more primping than Mama and me combined in a month of Sunday brunches," she says to herself.

After much deliberation on whether to keep the top two buttons done up or undone, one of them, now holding a hand mirror so the other one can admire himself, decides to keep it open. At this point, they notice that Abby is watching them, but they continue undeterred. They must finish this ritual. They throw the mirror back and forth like jugglers until they both seem to arrive at the necessary level of groomed greatness. Swiveling toward Abby, they gesture for her approval in full synchronization, like a boy band on stage. Will she give them a thumbs-up or down? She's caught off guard. They keep at it, insisting she feed their narcissism one final time. Still amazed at what she's witnessing, she gives them two thumbs-up.

"Merci, mademoiselle!" they shout in unison. They shut the trunk, put on their very chic sunglasses, and head up the street to the very swanky and posh café on the corner with the all-white décor.

"Finally! A spontaneous *mademoiselle*! I knew it," she says, smiling from ear to ear.

Abby continues her search for the place on Claire's card. She almost misses it but at the last moment notices the drawing of a butterfly beside the entrance, the same butterfly that's on the card. It's all very mysterious and intriguing. She knocks on the door.

"Surname?" a person calls from the other side of the door through a little window.

"Allerton," Abby replies firmly. The door opens, and she enters a dimly lit room with white string lights, old vintage carousel horses, and bench seating. Everyone is wearing full-body animal onesies with masks in what appears to be a jungle masquerade ball. She's quickly handed a onesie by the concierge. "Oh, wow. I'm so into this," she says to herself quietly. She pulls the onesie out of the bag, and it's a lobster with huge red velvet claws and an antenna headband that's at least two meters tall. She pulls it on and looks in the mirror. Completely ridiculous and so fun. She gives herself a high five with her claws and heads out to the party. She slowly walks around, and as her eyes get used to the dim lighting, she sees that there are little cups filled with pieces of cheese, berries, and some type of candy. Champagne is offered by waiters dressed in waiter suits but with papier-mâché heads. *Where is Claire?* Abby keeps roaming around as she gulps the champagne, which is an adventure due to the claws. She is already on her second cup of dainty snacks, which she must throw into her mouth because her aim is off due to the claws.

"Bonjour, mademoiselle," a man whispers in her hair from behind. She turns quickly, startled, as his breath on her neck is a little too close for comfort. She steps back.

"Bonjour, monsieur," she responds. They are looking at each other through the onesie hoods and masks, eye to eye, laser focused and intense—him a lion, she a lobster.

"Parlez-vous anglais?" Abby asks.

"Oui, but of course. But why do you deny the most romantic language in the world?" he answers, still intensely watching her eyes.

"Not denying it. I love French. I'm just not feeling the French love tonight," Abby says. The man steps back, opens his arms wide, and starts to belt out the theme from *The Lion King* in full bravado with his French accent.

He's immersed in his artistic interpretation and has an audience now. Abby's mortified.

"Care to join me out on the terrace?" he asks.

"Okay. Do you know my friend Claire? She's Irish, gorgeous . . . ," she asks hopefully.

"Claire? Yes. Of course. She's the hot-pink flamingo out on the terrace. *Après vous.*"

"Thank god." Abby follows him into the elevator. Thankfully, it's a bigger elevator than some she's experienced.

She almost gets her antenna caught in the elevator door, but the king of the jungle quickly grabs it with a swift maneuver of his big paw. Abby smiles big and laughs. He's growing on her. They get out on the terrace floor. Just then, Claire sees her. Abby sees her, too, and is taken with how gorgeous she looks. Her hair is big with sparkles sprayed through it, and her skin is glistening with a hot-pink shimmer, and her flamingo onesie seems to have been bejeweled a bit more than Abby's lobster. She is laughing, full of life, and heads toward Abby.

"Abby! Hi! I am so glad you made it!" Claire does the bisous-bisous thing on both cheeks. Abby obliges because, well, they are neighbors, and she really wants this friendship to keep.

"Hi! I was looking for you. You look amazing. What is this place, and what are we doing here?"

"This is a soirée, Abby, and we are here because my friend Maxim has just graduated from Le Cordon Bleu! Isn't it great, this crazy animal theme? The French are so fun with their parties. You'll get used to it," Claire says, smiling.

"Isn't that the fancy chef school? Is he a chef?" Abby asks, trying to figure out the connection between the animal onesies and masks, and the potpourri of snacks in the cups. Well, the snacks make some sense now—it's clear he's experimenting with his newfound skills to find the most creative appetizer mix possible.

"Yes, he's worked so hard. Come meet him." Claire grabs one of Abby's claws and drags her over. Abby follows, half-committed.

"Maxim?" Claire grabs the shoulders of a man in a caterpillar suit.

"Eh, Claire. My Irish lady. Ça va?" He does the bisous-bisous thing and waits.

"Maxim, this is my new neighbor, Abby. She's moved to Paris for a couple of months, and I invited her here tonight to make some friends." Claire puts her arm around Abby's shoulders.

"Abby, it is a pleasure." Maxim pushes back her velvet claw and takes her hand and kisses it. This makes Abby swoon. He's handsome *and* charming, plus he's a chef. So much to love.

"The pleasure is all mine," Abby replies, matching his charm tenfold. She notes this evening just got a whole lot better.

French Lion King is back, and he moves in for the kill.

"Are you feeling the love yet, ma chérie?" he asks. "If not, how can I help?"

"Maybe by not singing that song ever again?" Abby replies, waspishly.

"Okay, what song shall I sing? I have an impressive repertoire. Maybe some Elvis Presley?" he says as he does the King's infamous move.

"That was strangely impressive, Lion King. Did you ever work in Vegas?" Abby asks.

"Oh no, should I?" he says as he does another move.

"Well, you do resemble the King." Abby smiles and takes a drink.

"If you are trying to make friends and make it work here in Paris, you are winning." He smiles.

"I would think Paris would be a lonely place without friends," Abby states.

"It is, which is why I'm asking once again if you CAN FEEL THE LOVE TONIGHT?" He's at it again, only this time louder than before. Abby succumbs to the lion and the many glasses of champagne she's had and takes a photo of him and then a selfie with him. She turns to say thank you, and he plants her with a kiss as her long antennae bobble back and forth.

"Wow," Abby says as she pulls herself away.

"I bet you can feel the love now, can you not?" the Lion King says, smiling.

"I can. Merci. Oh look, there's Claire. I'm going to head over," she says, trying to let him down gently. She takes herself in the lobster suit, big claws and all, over to the flaming-hot flamingo.

"I'm so sorry, Claire. I just don't have it for Lion King tonight. Not a bad kisser, though. Goodness me. I have been kissed more here in Paris than I have in my whole life!" Abby says, laughing. "What is that?" she says, still laughing.

Claire laughs. "It's Paris," she says, looking Abby right in the eye. "Do you wanna dance?" Claire starts to shimmy.

"Yes! I'd love to."

They both go inside to the room where there is dancing. There's a cool French song playing with a slick, unique beat. They both start to dance with the other animals. One of the lyrics in French hits Abby in a humorous way. She leans into Claire.

"Did she just say something about not being a downer with a magic marker?"

"Yeah, it's Christine and the Queens. You've never heard of her? She's amazing. You should listen to her." Claire turns and keeps dancing. The caterpillar comes up behind her and joins her. They both start to dance more seductively. Abby can see there's something between them, but she can't help but watch for a second as the caterpillar and flamingo go at it in full swing. She decides to take her lobster off the floor and make a discreet exit from the soirée.

Back at her apartment a little while later, still in her lobster onesie, she's now listening to the same song, "Tilted," on repeat as she moves through her apartment.

Move over, Meghan, you've got some French competition now. She smiles to herself and can't stop laughing about that crazy nonsense "magic marker" lyric but thinks maybe somehow it fits? As bizarre as it is to her, it makes sense. Maybe that's what this is all about. Not being able to make sense of the change but letting it in, embracing it, and finding her place in it. That could be nice and a kind of fun.

With that, she falls on her bed. Holding her chenille pillow to her chest, she strokes it as she continues to sing along with Christine. She closes her eyes, singing the parts of the song that speak to her, which are many. Music has always been a comfort, a friend, a partner in getting her through hard times. Now she's got a nice theme song for her time in Paris, and it's a good one.

FOURTEEN

La Grande Exception

After her shot-in-the-arm session with Charlene and listening to the song "Tilted" about a hundred times, she approaches the door of Maison Claudette once again. She spots the same bouncer who asked her out on that dismal first day and realizes that she feels like a different person this time around. It feels as if months have gone by since she was last here, not days or weeks. Wearing a more French girl look today, she's in straight-leg jeans with Mary Jane flats, an oversized navy blazer with gold buttons, a white T-shirt, and her Laflore Paris bebebark backpack with big gold hoop earrings to top it off. Basic. Classic. French.

"Bonjour, madame." He smiles slightly.

"*Pas moi,*" Abby says.

"*Bienvenue, mademoiselle,*" the guard says, smiling.

"Told you I'd be back," she says triumphantly, emphasizing the last part in full Arnold Schwarzenegger fashion. He opens the door for her and gestures her in.

With her Goyard portfolio case full of event tricks, she's ready. She's got her ducks in a row, ready to deal with whatever Sophie throws at her during their "discussion of deception." She wrote the first draft in her limited French, detailing a progressive plan for the event and what she wants to offer #BTSPFW by possibly running Femme Fatale and Plus-Size Real parallel, maybe even joining the two. She then sent it to François for his review, and he put his su-PEAR French twist on it, asking for *une grande exception*. He emphasizes with humor that it would be the proper thing to do for such a clumsy, green (no pun intended after that incident with the models) américaine.

She enters the same conference room she'd been in earlier and starts to nervously pull out her proposal and her notes. She wants to set herself up from a position of strength. Can't break down doors without a solid stance to begin with. She can see catty-corner to her through the glass walls that Sophie and two other people are talking expressively with hands flying and voices raised. It's crystal clear they are talking about her and her "deception," so she keeps her head down and reviews her notes even more.

"Bonjour, Ms. Allerton," Sophie says as she and the other two people step into the room. Abby takes a deep breath.

"Bonjour, Sophie, it's nice to see you," Abby says, keeping it positive. Sophie doesn't respond. She sits down across from Abby with the two other individuals on either side of her. Abby moves her proposal and notes to the side. Her "game on" vibe is waning. This is daunting, and the vibe across the table is feeling dire.

"To my left is the event social media manager, who was responsible for researching all the influencers and invites, and to my right is the *layer* that did the contracts." Abby tries not to laugh. She knows she means *lawyer*. The social media manager seems uncomfortable, both in her clothes, based on all the adjusting and pulling she's doing, and with her place in this tribunal atmosphere.

"Enchantée. I'm grateful you all are meeting with me. I have what I think are good ideas on how to bring this back around to where it's real and authentic for all of us—"

"*Stop.* This is not a brainstorming meeting, Ms. Allerton. This is a meeting to discuss your overall fate at this event, given your decision to be deceitful coming here," Sophie says as she leans back in her chair, crosses her legs, and rests her arm on the back of the chair. Oof. This isn't going to be easy.

"I did come here under false pretenses—"

"You mean you lied, were deceitful, and are a fake?" Sophie interrupts.

"Yes, yes, and no. I'm not a fake. I'm me. That's what I'm trying to tell you," Abby answers.

"Well, at least you can be honest about your deceit. That is progress," Sophie says, adjusting her watch and bangles. The other two people sitting on either side are watching, waiting, ready for cues on what to do next. Sophie nods to the social media manager that it's her turn.

"Ms. Allerton, we have reviewed your situation and your two accounts. We found your account, Plus-Size Real, is it? We reviewed it. It's about being fashionable and fat, correct? It's not bad. In general, we respect the quality of your work, and in fact that is why you or the other one that you pretended to be were invited here—because of that quality of images, content, etc. And believe me when I say this, we know good work when we see it. I mean, we are French, and having an eye for good fashion and good looks is in our blood." The event social media manager looks to Sophie for approval. She nods and flicks her hand to continue.

"Alors, after reviewing the contract, which I will let my colleague address in une seconde, we are here to tell you that we release you from the digital event, and you are no longer a part of it." The social media person puts her pen down without looking Abby in the eye. She looks over to Sophie and the lawyer. Abby takes her hand from her heart, which was helping her stay focused and breathe, and pulls out her printed contract from her pile of proposal materials.

"Can you please show me where in the contract it says that you can just throw me out like this?" She looks straight at the lawyer.

The lawyer looks back at her and states, "It is inferred. And you are not that person we invited."

"Where is it inferred? I run Femme Fatale. Because with all the time I had waiting to hear back from you all and preparing for this meeting and dealing with my wallet getting stolen, I didn't quite find where it is inferred." Abby holds her ground.

The lawyer leans over and whispers something into Sophie's ear. She looks at him in amazement. Then stands up. "We will be back in a few minutes." They all file out of the room and go back into the office that Abby can see catty-corner to her. She watches a round two of all of them talking, puckering their lips with much exasperation and waving their hands. This is the best silent theater Abby's seen in ages. She sits and waits. She takes a few deep breaths, and then the trio files back in. Their energy is different this time. Less righteous, more nervous. Abby sits back and waits for them to speak. She's got a feeling their perspective may have been swayed due to the social media element and how this could go very wrong if put online.

"Ms. Allerton, we have decided that we will allow you to stay at the digital event on the one condition that you not post from your fat fashion account, you only post from Femme Fatale, and you do not reveal that you are the one behind Femme Fatale until a certain period of time we determine after the event and the fashion week have concluded and you are back home in the United States, well out of France and whatever implications there may be of you doing that to the event and Maison Claudette. These are our requirements, take it or leave it. And I mean really leave." Sophie says all of this with intermittent taps of her chic gold pen on the table, tapping twice as hard as she finishes what seems like a very long-winded manifesto. Abby looks across the table. Her eyes are big and holding the space. She looks down at her well-prepared solution, which she hopes will bring her salvation and this event some true body inclusivity. She's hit another big-ass door that's tightly closed.

"I understand. I brought this proposal that I've worked on and would love to share it with you all. I think it could really work and make this event even better, showcasing Claudette's commitment to body inclusivity." She waits to see their reaction.

"Ms. Allerton, we are not here to discuss your proposal, as I said. We are not here to look at grand plans for your latest cause. What is it with influencers and causes? Now, take our offer, or we will make your arrangements to return home. Also, we will need a written apology for your deceitful ways, plus an agreement that you will not engage in any posts that aren't in line with the original guidelines you received in your first meeting with Juliette. You can address that to me," Sophie says, looking over at the lawyer. "After all, we thought a completely different person and brand were coming to this event."

"But the brand is the same. I will give you that you thought I was someone else, but Femme Fatale itself hasn't changed. I have and I promise to do better. I owe you that."

Sophie stands up. The other two follow suit. The trio are on the move again.

With Sophie refusing to even look at Abby's grand plan of parallel posting from both accounts, Abby agrees to continue the superficial surface shit and nothing else. She writes the letter, signs it, and delivers it to Sophie's assistant, Emilie. Abby has gotten what she wanted, which was to be back in the good graces of the event. In her heart she knew Sophie was a lost cause, but she gave it her best shot. She's back in, and now it's time to get busy. First item done on her project list for Plus-Size in Paris.

She walks out of the back conference room area and into the main hall and stops for a moment to take in the splendor of the place once again—the murals, the activity of beautifully dressed people flitting around—then walks back to where all the influencers are being held, because it is like an influencer prison, with everyone all kept together, with each person in their own small cubicle. She missed adjusting to this configuration because she was on her "deception hiatus" while Sophie thought about what to do with her. She walks toward the table clearly marked with her name. She's pleased to see an elegant bag of swag attached to it. Just then, Gays for Days walks up.

"Well, if it isn't *not-so Femme Fatale*. Off your suspension?"

"Oh, hello. Yes, I'm back. Did I miss anything?" Abby asks, smiling.

"So much. You missed *so* much."

"Care to fill me in? On what I missed so much?"

"Nope, not really. Oh, but there is one thing. They put me with your assigned première atelier of haute couture because, well, you were on your fashion suspension, so . . . ," he says, trying to contain his glee.

"There is no such thing as a fashion suspension, you do know that, right?" Abby says cautiously, silently wondering if in fact there *is* such a thing in this culture and she missed it.

"Well, this has been fun," he says and moves on. Abby starts to look inside her swag bag, which is ornate, gorgeous, and filled with so much beauty that each piece is like a piece of art. It reminds her of when she would visit her grandmother's house when she was little. She would pick up each one of her grandmother's glass pieces so carefully and speak to them in gentle tones because she knew that they were precious and deserved her full attention. The contents of this bag—including a scarf with an artistic rendition of the five main Parisian monuments, a makeup bag filled to the brim with all their latest and greatest products, a hair piece, and costume jewelry—strangely evoke the same feelings. She knows it's ridiculous, but they seem to her to deserve that same respect.

"Eh. Non!" A female voice comes up from behind her. It's Sophie, again. She's moving briskly with her assistant in tow.

"Bonjour, Sophie. Merci beaucoup again for letting me come back to the event. I'm very grateful to you," Abby says warmly, hoping to take down just one stone from that very solid French fortress of a woman. Kill them with kindness, her mama always said.

"We will see if you will thank me later. But that bag, *you* cannot have." Sophie swipes it from her, even though a few items are out on the desk in perfect order.

She keeps walking and shoves the bag to her assistant Emilie, who scoots backward quickly and gives it back to Abby, making the "shh" sign, saying, "J'adore everything you are. Let's do coffee? Oui?"

Abby smiles big and says, "Oui! I'd love that. Merci, Emilie!" Then she rushes back up to Sophie, and they walk out of the room. Sophie, in her state of vengeance, is oblivious to the fact that the bag went right back to Abby, accompanied by a future café au lait date now on the books. Abby gathers the items on the desk and puts them back in the bag and shoves the swag into her own bag so it's no longer visible. Phew. Swag is back. What's next?

"*Vous êtes* Abby Allerton? Oui?" A woman is approaching her cubicle with Gays for Days in tow. She is medium height, dressed in black capri pants, gold loafers, and a crisp white button-down shirt that's open just enough to showcase a gorgeous pendant made of a slice of crystal rock encased in gold. She has a Claudette fanny pack full of pins, measuring tapes, extra flowers, and trimmings, and a second, smaller fanny pack around her midsection. She's not stick-thin but a little curvy. Her hair is a warm brown, with lighter ends. She's elegant and serious.

"Oui, c'est moi. Et vous?" Abby puts her hand out. The woman looks down at it and then looks back up. "Parlez-vous anglais?" Abby asks, smiling hopefully.

"Non," comes the curt reply, in the same sort of tone she might use to command her little dog if she had one. She points to Gays for Days for him to make the introduction.

"Soooo, meet Jacqueline. She is one of the three premières of haute couture here at Claudette. It is her responsibility to oversee you during the event, and it is your—our—job to come up with evocative and interesting posts about what they do here at Claudette." He looks at Jacqueline to see if he's missed anything.

"*Processus d'approbation!*" Jacqueline scolds him in response.

"Oh yeah, and there's an approval process that we must go through before we can post *anything*. It's a level of strictness I've never encountered before, and this is from someone who went to Catholic school his whole life, so that tells you something."

"You went to Catholic school? Lord!" Abby says in amazement.

"I know, right? Hard to believe. True story." Abby gets that he desperately wants to expand but knows it's for another time and place. He looks over to Jacqueline for affirmation that he's done his job. Abby can see that Jacqueline doesn't approve of his dismissiveness and hasn't warmed to him.

"Comprenez-vous?" She bows her head slightly, showing a hint of a double chin, and like an old-fashioned schoolmarm looks up at Abby through her black-rimmed, silver-point-tipped glasses, waiting for Abby's consent. Her expression feels eerily familiar for some reason. This whole time Abby has been thinking of a polite way to ask if Gays for Days will be a part of this, or if he'll be asked to move on—please, for the love of god, let him move on—but nothing comes to mind. She's made too many enemies already, so she decides to let that one go for now. She's relieved that Jacqueline seems to be a normal woman, competent and serious, but there seems to be a level of sadness underneath, too.

"Oui! C'est bon. I'm looking forward to it." Abby looks Jacqueline straight in the eye and again feels like she's seen those eyes somewhere before. Abby shrugs it off, chalking it up to meeting too many new people in such a short time.

"Su-PEAR!" Jacqueline exclaims and turns around, waving for Abby to follow, which she does after grabbing her bag. They all three speed-walk through what seem like ten different adjoining rooms into the haute couture room full of fabrics, tables, and oh so many feathers. With the feathers, there are also silk flowers and linen-covered cloth mannequins strewn everywhere, but even in its disorderly state, the room looks perfectly put together, as if every single item is in its rightful place. Abby starts to walk around and look at the different tables with the patterns and notes and sketches. They are amazing. Works of art not yet finished and a feast for the eyes. It's

just fashion, it's just clothes, but she sees the depth and commitment these people are putting into each piece. She can see the love and inner work they have all invested into each piece they are handling.

"Wow! This is something I've never seen before and never thought I'd ever see. It is a level I can't describe. I can see why Claudette holds itself above the rest. You have earned every bit of this reputation. With every chiffon flower and feather, I'm in complete awe." She looks over at Jacqueline with an expression of complete astonishment. What a day to be brought into the inner workings of this place filled with such elegance and beauty.

"Yes, we have earned it. But there is more to do," Jacqueline responds in a thick French accent. Once again, she knows more English than she let on.

"I am at your service. What do you want me to do?" Abby says, matching her intensity.

"Revenez demain, et écrivez votre première article. Oui? Understand?" Jacqueline says.

"*Compris!*" Abby gives her an enthusiastic two thumbs-up.

"*Nous n'imposons pas*—we don't . . ." Jacqueline mimics Abby's thumbs-up and shakes her head with a big *non*. "Ce n'est pas dans nos habitudes! Not our style," Jacqueline says, then she turns on her heel and leaves.

"Alrighty then," Abby says to herself. Abby turns and glares at Gays for Days, feeling the sting of her faux pas. "You could've told me that."

"Are you serious? I've been dealing with her the whole time you've been on your fashion suspension. It's time *you* got some of her wrath. I'm out. I'm being reassigned to an up-and-coming designer, so she's all yours, *not-so* Femme Fatale! *Bonne chance!*" He gestures like he's wiping his hands clean and leaves.

"Yeeesss, win-win," Abby says softly to herself and smiles.

··+·+ + ··

Back in the apartment that she's grown to love even more, she steps out onto her balcony, taking a break from preparing her latest Story and Reel with a link to the event blog for Jacqueline. She's been at it for a few hours now, and it's bothering her. She put together something very stylish and chic and was truly overwhelmed with the beauty of what she witnessed today, shadowing Jacqueline's work and seeing her team's amazing commitment. It is still surface shit; they aren't curing cancer or ending wars, but there's nothing wrong with a little beauty that brings you up a level or two from what you are used to.

She steps back into her kitchen and grabs her phone. She starts a Story on Plus-Size Real: "I'm not a *parisienne* yet, but I've been here long enough to be inspired by this amazing skyline. Look . . ." She turns the phone around and shows the staggering rooftops, and then she positions herself with them in the background. "Back to me. So, one of the things I've noticed, my plus-size friends, is that I'm in the minority here and it's hard. Très hard. But—and there's a big butt, no pun intended—love to all my big-butt ladies out there!" Abby blows a kiss. "I'm learning that there's room for me here, and there's room here for us. So, stay tuned. I'll take you along on this journey of making space for those of us that are sized in a way Paris hasn't seen yet." She preps the Story and saves it.

As she looks out at the Paris skyline, she sees the apartments across the way with their lit terraces that remind her of front porches back home. She lets her eyes move across the different scenes and indulges in some "good ole nosy neighbor watching," as her daddy says. This makes her miss him.

"Oh my," she says to herself and takes her phone back out to take a pic. Her eyes and phone camera have landed on a window with a shirtless man who is listening to music and dancing. Click. Got it. This is just for her and her camera roll. No consent—no post.

Her eyes move to the next window, where there's a party going on inside the big room and people smoking out on the balcony. A woman at the party kisses a man on the balcony, then drops his hand and moves into the other part of the apartment and onto the next balcony, where she turns another man around and starts to kiss him. She's thin, wearing a silk halter-neck top and ripped jeans and a long wooden beaded necklace resembling a rosary tumbling down her flat chest.

Abby moves on to the next apartment. In the next window, there's a lady in matching lingerie looking at herself in the mirror, twisting and turning, smoking a cigarette. She's dancing to the neighboring apartment's party music like she should be there, but she's not been invited. There's a sadness about her, and watching her trying to psych herself up all alone makes Abby's eyes well up. The girl reminds her of her cousin, whom she only saw once, when she was on TV competing in the Miss America pageant. For some reason, Betty Lou was estranged from that side of the family, so Abby never saw them, and she wouldn't have even known it was her cousin had her mama not walked through, casually pointed to the TV, and said, "Oh, that's Stacey, your cousin." Abby can still remember vividly the disbelief she felt. As it turned out, Stacey was eliminated after the swimsuit round. Hips too wide. The way this neighbor is twisting and turning in her lingerie reminds Abby of the disbelief she felt that her cousin, a stranger, too, by all accounts, was cast off because of body measurements, something she could do nothing about, something that was inherited and that she couldn't change. Even at the age of eight or nine, watching that, she knew that it was so unfair, as does this woman, who is clearly picking herself apart in the mirror in a rooftop apartment in Paris. Two different countries, two different women, both torturing themselves inside. Why? She's got some of the answers but not all, but she knows for damn sure there shouldn't even be a question.

She sits down and looks at her screen. She pulls up the saved Story on her phone and then puts it back down.

"Let's do this surface shit. But hold on a second. Maybe it's not all surface shit?" she says and starts to click, drag, and type on her MacBook until she has a post that is quite lovely. It has no value other than to say that Claudette is the most amazing fashion house ever, which everyone in the whole world already knows ten times over, but it is the truth. It's not a lie. It is beautiful design. She gets up, grabs her phone, walks to her bedroom, and looks at the gorgeous view through that picture-frame window. She lies down on the bed and grabs her pillow and starts to stroke it. The last session with Charlene comes to mind and so does that date at Wholly Crêpe with François. She types a text.

> Abby: Bonjour, mon monsieur!

> François: Bonjour, ma chérie! How are you? Lonely tonight?

> Abby: A little. I need to tell you something.

> François: This sounds scary. Have you been to the catacombs?

Abby: Non, pourquoi?

François: Because they are scary, very.
And a tourist trap.

Abby: Okay. Note taken.

François: What is it?

Abby: I feel guilty about something that
happened after that date we had.

François: Oh. Did you kiss another man
at a crêpe shop? ☺

Abby stops. She lets the three dots linger and then puts her phone down. She looks at the view and remembers her time with Jean-Louis here in this room. Then picks it back up.

Abby: Would you be hurt if I did?

Now the dots are lingering on her end. She waits. Squeezes her pillow. Abby checks the Story she posted with the Lion King, Claire, and the caterpillar chef. She sees that François watched it and is active.

François: I must go. You know these
customers. ;) I'll text later. Don't be
lonely in Paris. Looks like you are having
a lot of fun! Bravo!

She puts the phone down, grabs one of the many books about Paris off her nightstand, and starts to read, but within minutes she falls asleep.

FIFTEEN

It Is Fantasy, and It Is French!

Abby watches as Jacqueline holds her MacBook in her hands, slowly looking through her first post and accompanying pics. As she quickly scans it, Jacqueline's lips are sticking out in a curled duck-lips fashion, bottom lip overlapping the top one for emphasis. She makes some strange noises. "Mmm, oui. Très jolie. Mmm, non. *Très moche.*" As she reads, she continues to say random, completely contradictory sentences—one second something is very pretty, the next it is very ugly. Abby is completely lost as to whether Jacqueline approves of the post or whether she's just not saying bluntly that she absolutely hates it. It seems to Abby that Jacqueline is walled off pretty good, much like Sophie, but she's not mean like Sophie. Jacqueline is a melancholy, can't-be-bothered type of woman. Abby can see there's heart there with her work, though, and it makes Abby curious to know more.

"Alors, c'est bon. You can post." Jacqueline hands the laptop back to Abby. Abby can't believe it. Her first post and it's approved. This is great! This is significant, especially coming from Jacqueline.

"Merci beaucoup, Jacqueline." Abby can't help but jump a bit with joy. She wonders if now is the right time to bring up what she was thinking about last night. She'd like to shift from producing only superficial shit to real, meaningful, and culture-shifting shit. Jacqueline continues to stand there, as it's clear Abby isn't done.

"Do you want to say something or just continue bouncing?" she says.

"Thanks for asking. I do have *une petite question*." Abby makes the "petite" sign with her fingers.

"Oui, I'm listening," Jacqueline says, looking over her thick, black-rimmed glasses in her signature schoolmarm way.

"Why does Claudette *not* make haute couture for curvy women?" Abby asks, gesturing with her hands outward to show larger sizes.

"Pardon?" asks Jacqueline, leaning back in shock and putting her hand on her décolletage to steady her no doubt fast-beating heart.

"Désolée. Sorry. I'm just wondering why Claudette only makes these exquisite dresses and ensembles for women who have thinner bodies. Why not make them for women of all sizes?" Abby continues, with much trepidation and relief that she's finally asking the question that's been burning inside her since she walked in this building on that fateful day of her fashion suspension.

"You mean these works of art on women who are bigger? Like you?" Jacqueline says again, wide-eyed and incredulous.

"Well, yes, why not?" Abby asks again. By this time, fellow influencers are hanging around to see how this convo will go. Jacqueline looks around; Abby can see that she is carefully formulating her response.

"This is not *une petite question* but rather a big one. No pun intended. And I will be happy to discuss this later. Is that acceptable?" Jacqueline zeroes in with those eyes again. Abby gets the message.

"Oui, very acceptable. Merci." Abby smiles warmly. She's proud of herself and of Jacqueline, who didn't answer abruptly or rudely, but respectfully. She'll take that as her green light to keep going, une petite question at a time.

On her way home after a most successful day, Abby walks past Angélique's house and sees the mermaid door knocker once again.

"Such a cool door knocker," she says to herself. She takes out her phone to take a picture once again, to post on Femme Fatale, as it's so elegant, but looking down this time to make sure there is no surprise dog poo there. Just then the door opens, and Angélique comes out. They meet face-to-face. Angélique, without hesitation, kisses Abby on both cheeks. Abby clumsily reciprocates.

"Ça va, Abby?"

"Believe it or not, I think I can say très bien!"

"I'm headed to the corner café. Care to join me?" Angélique asks.

"I only have a half hour or so, as I have work to do tonight, but I'll walk with you until my corner." Abby starts to walk along with her.

"My daughter always puts time limits on our talks, too. I always feel like she has somewhere more important to be. I wonder if, when I die, she'll put a time limit on how long she can stay at my funeral," Angélique says, laughing but with a twinge of hurt.

"I'm sorry. I'm sure your daughter doesn't mean to do that. I know I do lots of things that hurt my mama when I know I don't mean to. I guess it's just . . . ç'est compliqué, you know, the *maman*-daughter relationship." Abby shrugs.

"Let's change the topic. It's depressing, and I don't have the energy for it. Have you been to see the doctor I recommended?" Angélique asks. Abby thinks her accusatory tone might give some insight as to why her daughter distances herself from her.

"Ah, the prospect of me going to see that doctor is equally depressing. Maybe we should talk about your amazing suit. Is it Claudette? Is it vintage?" Abby jokes.

"I'm serious. She was waiting for your call. I told her all about you. And yes, it is a Claudette vintage suit, circa the 1970s."

"It's amazing, Angélique. Truly."

"I know it is. I designed it and made it," Angélique says dryly.

"Whoa. You were the one that came up with this iconic design?" Abby asks with her mouth hanging open.

"You can close your mouth, my dear. It is not a good look on you," Angélique says.

Abby closes her mouth and laughs a little.

"Oui, it's my creation. Although you'd never know it because the head designer took all the credit. C'est la vie. I know the truth," Angélique says, attempting to sound Zen about it after all these years. Abby's not convinced.

"It's beautiful. It's so simply elegant," Abby says.

"It's good design, which should always be simply elegant," Angélique responds.

"Absolutely." Abby smiles as she looks at Angélique with softness in her heart but knows she needs to be clear with her about her doctor recommendation.

"Well, Angélique, I'm sorry to disappoint you, but the likelihood of me going to that doctor is about as likely as all Parisians cleaning up after their dogs. It's apparently *never* going to happen," Abby says, attempting to keep it light.

"You are clever. I can see that." Angélique half-smiles.

"Someone else tells me that, too." She's thinking of François, and it gives her a pang in her heart.

"Go see the doctor. You won't regret it," Angélique says, firmly but nicely this time. The way she says, "You won't regret it" is just how the owl-eyed pharmacy worker said it when Abby went against everything in her and bought those stupid weight-loss pills. And look what she did with those. Nothing. It was stupid of her to even buy them. A moment of weakness.

"Your concern is touching, Angélique. I'll think about it," she says with respectful resignation. Abby reaches her corner. She does the obligatory parting bisous-bisous and starts to walk home toward her apartment.

·· ·+· ✦ ✦ ·· ·.

The next day with many Plus-Size Real posts and Stories saved on her Insta profile, Abby heads back to Claudette to see if she can't make some more inroads with Jacqueline. Her Parisian Plus-Size Real project is her focus now, and she's determined to triumph. Writing that draft after her cathartic sob and session with Charlene has helped her take on the mantra: "I will find my place in Paris." Slowly drinking her extra-hot chai latte (with her name correctly written on it this time) and walking into the back room, aka influencer prison, she hears determined footsteps coming toward her from behind.

"ABBY!" Jacqueline yells at her frantically.

"Oui! Madame!" Abby turns around, calm but a little afraid of what's coming.

"Come here now." Jacqueline summons her into her office. Abby quickly goes in and sits down in a chair across from her desk. Chenille fabric. Thank god. She starts to stroke it a bit. Jacqueline notices her stroking.

"It is a chair, *pas un chat*," she says, dismissively. Chastised, Abby abruptly stops.

"*Alors*, Sophie told me that you are to take down your fat fashion account to stay here. Is it true?"

"No, she said I couldn't post on it but didn't say I had to take it down. I don't think she can do that. Pourquoi?"

"They've done some further research and see that you posted." Jacqueline shoves the phone in her face. "Plus-Size Real, yes that's it?"

"And?" Abby asks, holding strong.

"You must take it down. Sophie is insisting. It's a conflict to have both going from here." Jacqueline looks at her over her glasses.

"No, I won't. I posted that before our meeting when I had to sign my influencer life away," Abby replies, feeling that familiar sense of resignation, only this time, there is a conflicting new phrase—"I will find my place in Paris"—now sitting directly across from it in her mind. *Here goes nothing, or something—we shall see.*

"Jaqueline, can we talk more about my *petite question*? Maybe just revisit it a bit? Because you said it would be possible at another time, and maybe that another time could be right now?" Abby says, keeping her tone soft. Jacqueline puts the phone down on the desk and walks back around to her side and sits down.

"We do not make these dresses for large women because our haute couture is fantasy, and it is French. We do French, we do fantasy, we do what's unattainable by the average woman.

The French woman understands this. It gives her something to work toward, to look her best when she's preparing to walk out the door every day. It is luxury, something beautiful to look at. It makes people proud of what France is all about—tradition and elegance."

"But you are French, and you seem real, so why wouldn't you deserve to wear these dresses or be represented on the runway?"

"I have no interest in wearing these dresses. I make them, all day long and long into the nights before shows. I love them like my children, and then I'm sick of them by the time they show up on the models and in the show. Which is why I don't have children—because I can't give them away. So, no, I don't think I'm a good, how do you say, reference?" Jaqueline says with some annoyance.

"Okay, maybe it's a bad example, but don't you think it would be truly fashion forward to put real, normal-sized women in these exquisite outfits, dresses, and gowns on the runway? I mean, this year's show theme is Elegantly Empowered Women." Abby is still trying to strike while the iron is hot.

"You mean women like you? Would you like to be a model? On the runway? Is that it? Is that why you came to Paris?" Jacqueline asks.

"Well, why not? Why shouldn't women like me be allowed to show off and wear these amazing pieces of art? Why are we excluded? I don't want to model them, but I would love to see some great curvy, voluptuous models strutting them down the catwalk at Paris Fashion Week so I can then share it around the world." Abby is genuinely curious as to what her answer will be.

"To make a garment like this is expensive as it is, and to make it with more width and dimension will make it an over-the-top price. Making each one of these dresses costs as much as a nice car or a deposit on a flat here in Paris. When you add more fabric, more details, more layers to the design, it will become even more costly. Claudette will never agree to increase the cost of something that they don't need to or for some social movement or statement. After all, this is France, not America, and as I said, we work from a place of tradition coupled with high-level artistic ideas. Rooted in the history of making a woman feel like an out-of-this-world princess when they wear these designs. Last time I checked, the whole world tries to emulate our designs, they try to copy and replicate them, but they can't fully because it's inherent to who we are in this industry in France. The heart of beautiful fashion," Jacqueline answers, businesslike but with genuine emotion. Abby can see she has a deep love for her work.

"I love what you just said. I wish I would've recorded it. So, to be clear, it's about expense, not social stigma or keeping up an unattainable cultural message that all women need to be stick thin to enjoy it?" Abby prods further.

"I don't know the answers to your questions. I am not the CEO of Claudette. I work for the head of design, Pierre Peltier. I do what I'm told and do my job, and I think I do it well, non?" Jacqueline says as she waves toward the sewing room in front of her office. She notices that Abby has been taking notes the whole time. Abby can see that this is unnerving to her, most likely due to Sophie's wrath.

"Alors, Abby! What are you writing down?" She looks over her glasses for emphasis.

"Just some notes for any future posts, my followers."

"I will give you a *nooget* of advice."

"A *nooget*?"

"*Nooget.* A small piece of something. Chicken *noogets,*" Jacqueline, annoyed, responds.

"Ah, you mean nugget. Nugget. Different vowel sound," Abby corrects.

"My advice, whether it's nugget or *nooget,* is, do not cross the design house. You tried it once. Don't do it again. They will not be so understanding."

"I'm supposed to post what I see and what I think is relevant to my followers *only* on Femme Fatale," Abby says, putting her Pilot pen to her lips and looking off to the side as she decides what to write further. "I'm just wondering if my Femme Fatale followers wouldn't wonder, too, why these designs are made only for a certain body type," Abby says as she makes some notes.

"You will be crushed like a bad croissant if you don't follow my advice," Jacqueline says, irritated. Abby looks at her, cocks her head to the side, and puts her hand down slowly.

"Well, Jacqueline, I'm pretty sure there's no such thing as a bad croissant in Paris, or at least I haven't found one yet, and believe me, I've been trying *beaucoup de croissants* in this city," Abby retorts.

"Well, you do have a point," Jacqueline says, laughing a little.

SIXTEEN

Eau d'Urine

With French chanson classics playing through her AirPods, Abby is ambling slowly near Notre-Dame, in the heart of Paris. Her mind is full of wonderment and curiosity, a sensation she hasn't enjoyed since she first received the invitation from Sophie. Slowly licking a cone of famous Berthillon ice cream as she wanders, she decides to stop on the Archevêché Bridge, from where she can take in the majesty of the Gothic cathedral, still standing tall after all these centuries, proud and indestructible after a harrowing fire, a testament to a medieval man's building prowess and faith. Her eyes follow the flying buttresses around the cathedral to the garden behind, full of flowers and trees in full bloom. The garden is packed with people enjoying it, too.

She's happy to stay right where she is, as she's seen since arriving in Paris that there's nothing worse than trying to take in tourist destinations with all the tourists shoving each other with their backpacks and their smartphones and their selfie sticks. She spots a group of tourists crossing the bridge toward the boulevard Saint-Michel, and there is no mistaking, from their typical outfits, their sneakers, and their extra-loud conversations, that they are American. As they walk past her, curiosity gets the better of Abby, and she decides to follow them. She tosses what's left of her ice cream in a bin and starts to trail them, at a discreet distance, along the Seine for a few minutes until they come to a famous Anglophone bookstore, Shakespeare and Company, and the cute café smartly located next to it. Both places seem to exude historical significance and are very quaint. Abby stops and reads the painted saying on the store across the way, *Be not inhospitable to strangers lest they be angels in disguise*, and feels compelled to enter.

Without hesitating, Abby follows her pretend newfound friends inside and ends up sitting next to them as if she's known them her whole life. She hasn't felt very connected to her country lately, and that feels foreign to her, as foreign as she herself feels in Paris. It's a strange juxtaposition she finds herself living in, so this encounter is a welcome happenstance. She's sitting among a crew of Americans who would be complete strangers at home, but here they feel like the best of friends. She notes that it's odd to feel that way, but that is the reality of it. A man with a guitar sits down in front of the crowd and starts to play some songs he's written. His lyrics make no sense whatsoever, but he looks so into it and sings so convincingly that everyone acts as if they get it, if only out of the respect for his total commitment to his art. Abby watches, taking it all in. When it's over, they all get up and discuss where to go. She eavesdrops, hears that they are planning to go to the Latin Quarter, and decides to follow. She wonders if they would even notice that she's tagging along, or if they would take it for granted that she's one of them, a fellow American meeting up for an evening in Paris. Abby follows until they reach their destination, a hole-in-the-wall French bistro that looks like it could use a visit from the health inspector. The saying on the bookshop wall genuinely touched her and stayed with her since she left it. She decides to head back to the shop and maybe get a souvenir or two.

She slyly moves away from the Americans and does an about-face and heads back. She stops and takes out her note-book, quickly jotting down the most heartwarming phrase, and then steps into the bookstore, heading straight toward the back. She starts to look at all the titles, the old staircase to the upstairs, the different postcards, and the handwritten ads with requests for meetups or invitations to expat cookery courses, book clubs, and walking tours. It is an eclectic message board for people looking for a community in Paris. Reading the requests tugs at her heartstrings. She is also someone looking for community. Maybe she should hang an ad, too? But what would it say? She lets her mind have some fun and takes out her journal and jots down a few lines on the blank page:

> New to Paris, living with imperfection in this gorgeous city full of perfection. Apparently, I'm eating way too many pains au chocolat. C'est la vie! Vive l'imperfection! I would love to meet others that are trying to find their place here one cute Insta post at a time!

"Sure, that'll work," she says to herself out loud as she throws her journal and pen back in her bag.

"Pardon?" a masculine voice says behind her. She turns around. He is stunningly handsome. He's got brown hair in a perfectly cut style, a linen scarf, and eyeglasses that must have been chosen from those "best eyeglasses for your face shape" advertisements.

"Oh, uh, *je parlais à moi-même*," she answers, a little flustered. Somehow, she killed that phrase in perfect French. "Uh, *parlez-vous anglais*?" she asks hopefully. She knows that the odds are stacked against her, but she's feeling lucky tonight.

"Yes, mademoiselle, I do," he says, seeping with charm. And he called her *mademoiselle* without her attempting to correct. Promising.

"Wow. You are one of the first."

"To ever speak English?" he asks, smiling broadly.

"Ha, no, to say yes so confidently and to speak English confidently. I keep getting duped by others." She smiles back.

"What kind of book are you looking for tonight?" he asks, looking at the book in her hand called *French Women Don't Get Fat*. She quickly turns the front of the book toward her and hugs it to her chest.

"I'm browsing tonight. I love this bookstore." She looks up at all the shelves.

"Me too. It has so much history in it and makes a lonely night like tonight much more romantic, even when one is just browsing."

Abby takes that as intended, said for her benefit.

"I can definitely see why." Abby looks away. *Oh no!* She can feel the need to pee coming on again. Seriously? Again? Such a killjoy, this urinating situation in Paris. She puts her hand out to introduce herself, causing the book she has been clutching to her chest to drop to the floor. They both reach down to retrieve it, causing their heads to bang together.

"I'm so sorry. I'm so sorry." She's rubbing her head, and he's rubbing his.

"It's okay. What is the saying, great minds think alike?" he says, trying to keep it light.

"I'm not sure there is a saying when two heads knock together. Maybe there's one in French?"

"I can't think of one, but I'll let you know when I do."

He offers his hand to her this time. She takes it. He kisses her hand softly. Abby looks around again to see if this is real and to check that someone's not going to yell, "Cut!" in a strong French accent to stop this wonderful movie that she's found herself starring in.

"My name is Sylvain. It's a pleasure to knock heads with you," he says and smiles and taps his head, inferring that he's a genius.

"Very cute." Abby smiles back.

"Shall we?" he asks as he offers his arm for her to take.

"So sorry, I'm on my way to visit one place first. I'll be back in a flash." Abby goes to the bookstore clerk and asks where the toilet is. She points to the door and says, "It's a squat one, though." Abby smiles and shakes her head, not knowing what that means. Doesn't matter. She just wants to get this over with and get back to handsome Frenchman number *trois*. She opens the door into the cube-sized room, and there's a ceramic hole in the floor with a pipe to the top and the water basin near the ceiling. "Oh, my word. What the hell is this?" She closes the door and locks it. She takes out her phone and types in, "How to use squat toilets . . ." She's doing the pee dance, scrolling, and then just throws her phone in her bag. "Here goes nothing." She throws one leg over to the other side of the ceramic hole, almost like she would if she were mounting an imaginary horse, then she pulls down her pants, trying to make sure they are not in the way of the impending stream, which feels impossible at this point. She's squatting, holding steady, with one hand pulling the crotch of her pants forward tightly, and then releasing. All good so far. She looks around to grab some toilet paper, and there is none. Her bag is hanging on the door hook that is about to fall off, with one screw dangling about. "Good thing this is not a big room," she says out loud, straining to reach her bag. With one final hoist of her body, she gets her bag with the one free hand not holding her pants crotch and grabs the tissue pack she now carries with her religiously. In one synchronized superhero-like motion, she drops it in the floor hole, pops up on her legs from her squat, and pulls up her pants. She pulls the long chain, watches the dinosaur of a toilet do its job, and turns to the miniature sink, where she sees a lovely glass bottle of hand soap from Compagnie de Provence. She laughs as she washes her hands, thinking that, regardless of the hole in floor for a toilet, there is still a gorgeous finish, courtesy of the French. She gives herself a high five in the mirror and walks out.

Smiling big, she heads toward where Sylvain was supposed to be, but he is gone. Nowhere to be found. Disappeared. As the feeling of being dissed starts to grow inside her, a flicker of François's face comes to her. He always approaches her with genuine interest, and she realizes that she misses him once again. If this is why Paris is known as the City of Love, then she totally gets it. She grabs a free bookmark with the saying about not being inhospitable to strangers from the front counter and heads out to the riverbank.

There is something in the air on this (in)famous riverbank, and whatever it is, she wants in on it, one hundred percent! But with the right guy. A man selling cheesy light-up plastic roses approaches her, smiling. She buys one for herself and carries it along with her as she slowly walks the riverbank. She sees a sign depicting a man peeing on the stairs leading down to the riverbank with a huge forbidden sign circling over it. The smell of urine is ever present.

"Ah-ha! So that's why," Abby says out loud without realizing it as she takes out her phone to take a picture of the forbidden-peeing-man sign. An old man sitting on a bench not too far from her says, "The perfume of Paris is *Eau d'Urine.*" He stands up to leave, tipping his flat cap to her.

"Well, that certainly makes sense," she replies.

SEVENTEEN

Coudre et Découdre

"Jacqueline! Jacqueline!" A man's voice, manic, is scream-
ing out from the huge bolts of fabric. It sounds like he's
being smothered and can't get out.

"Oui! Je suis ici! De quoi avez-vous besoin?" Jacqueline
replies, hurriedly.

"Travail de merde! Quelle incompetence! C'est inaccept-
able! The way you have put together this dress. Why is this line
of flowers here and not over the waist, as I said to you many
times? We had this discussion. I want it diagonal across the
chest and then around the waist, not as a neckline. What are
you thinking? This is idiotic. Do you think we are designing
for Monoprix here? To sell 9.99-euro dresses?"

He extricates himself from the massive area of fabric bolts
and heads to the mannequin. In one fell swoop, he rips off
the ribbon of hand-sewn chiffon flowers that took one of
Jaqueline's seamstresses hours to make and Jaqueline hours
to finalize. He is like Cinderella's wicked stepmother, tearing
apart the dress that Cinderella made herself to go to the ball.
The whole place is frozen as they watch to see what Jacqueline's
response will be. Will she fold, or will she fight back and put

the very cocky head designer, who thinks he's god's gift to fashion, in his place? The whole place is riveted.

Jacqueline takes a deep sigh and says, "Most of Paris wears Monoprix's 9.99 specials, and most of Paris will *not* be wearing these dresses, nor will they care if these delicate flowers are around the neck or around the waist when they see them on the model on the runway. What *you* will care about is if your première of haute couture suddenly disappears when the show is only weeks away. Perhaps I should go work for Monoprix, then. I'm sure they are more congenial with their première seamstresses."

She takes a deep breath and looks around. There's a committed audience. Pierre walks to the massive fridge and opens it up. It is completely full of Badoit sparkling waters in all flavors, neatly organized according to the color of the bottles, as if a crew from the influencer organizers the Home Edit had come and worked their magic and Pierre was part of the big reveal.

"Huh, I guess it really is the best sparkling water . . . ," Abby says from the edge of her seat, watching this supercharged scene of fashion greats. Pierre, after some hesitation, chooses a mint-flavored water, aggressively opens the bottle, and takes a long drink, gulping dramatically, then abruptly stops. He walks over to Jacqueline and says, "Then I guess you'll be moving to China, my dear. In all their workshops, the seamstresses, if you can even call them that, have to wear masks and breathe horrible air." He throws the half-empty bottle in the chic recycling bin and puts his hands on his hips, looking like a defiant little boy trying to get candy from his maman. Jacqueline stares him down. Her stern look prompts him to turn around, retrieve the ribbon of flowers, and bring it back to her. He then drapes it around her neck.

"These flowers are to go where I said for them to go, per my designs. Do we understand each other?" he says firmly, maintaining his toddler stance. Jacqueline keeps staring directly back at him. She is still and keeping calm, with only a small bulging vein in her neck.

"Is she breathing?" Gays for Days says, leaning over to Abby. Abby nods slowly without looking at him. She's too keyed into Jacqueline, feeling protective of her and hating every entitled, obnoxious cell of Pierre right now. This is the first time she's seen Pierre, and what an introduction.

"Pierre. Did you do your meditation this morning?" Jacqueline starts in a measured tone.

Pierre takes a deep breath. "Non."

Jacqueline nods knowingly. "I will put the flowers where they are, per your designs, because I was raised to respect the art of good design. I will not, however, respect this behavior from you, whose designs I would say are mediocre at best and lack genius this season. *Cacher votre incompétence en se montrant impoli avec vos travailleurs.*"

Abby watches Jacqueline keep herself self-regulated. No doubt she's had to do this a lot with him; her red face is working alongside those protruding veins to keep in control. All mouths are hanging open in astonishment, and they all look over at Pierre for his response to this most direct and insulting serve from Jacqueline. Abby is still rooting for Jacqueline, as she's seeing a different side to her now, and it's très cool. Abby has her hands clenched in fists, as if she's ready to pounce on her behalf.

"*Arrêtez! J'en ai assez!* I'm done! Let us once again revisit the definition of haute couture, shall we? *Haute* means *high*, and *couture* means *fashion*. Your job is the dressmaking, the sewing, the bringing it all together, making sure that the *haute* and the *couture* are in fact respected and shown to the best effect in each of the pieces I design. *I design! I am the high fashion designer, and you are the seamstress, not the designer!* I work with class; you, however, are the working class. *Capisce?*" Pierre pauses for emphasis. "I await the flower fix by this evening, or else China is calling for you."

Jacqueline doesn't move a muscle. Pierre flounces out of the room, flamboyantly flinging his scarf—or big piece of fabric, no one is sure what it is, but he loves to use it dramatically whenever he makes an entrance or exit—over his shoulder.

"Abby?" Jacqueline calls out, looking around for her now.

"Oui, Jacqueline! *Je suis là!*"

"So, after that show you just witnessed, would you like to *really* see how things work?" Jacqueline says determinedly.

"I sure would," Abby says back.

"Follow me." Jacqueline turns and waves her hands. Abby follows. She's getting the vibe that there may be a major opening here with Jacqueline, courtesy of Pierre.

They head back to all the different sewing spaces, and as Jacqueline passes by the tables, she says to each of her seamstresses and one tattooed man, *"Coudre et découdre,"* and they all sigh in perfect synchronization, doing the "French pouf," that special sigh of theirs, in such unison and with such force that a pile of feathers blows off the table. Abby's tried to mimic this exasperated response in the mirror at home but has been lacking in just the right intensity and amount of air protruding from her upper and bottom lips for it to feel authentic. In the meantime, another question for Jacqueline has come up.

"Jacqueline?" Abby asks, tilting her head as she looks at all the designs on the tables. "What is *coudre et découdre?*" she asks.

Jacqueline blows her lips and says, "Oh, c'est compliqué."

"Of course, it is," Abby replies, smiling to herself.

After a full day of shadowing Jacqueline and her team of seam-stresses in action, Abby leaves Claudette, exhausted yet stim-ulated by all that she has seen. The process of watching them gently tear apart the dress all because of how a ribbon of flow-ers was placed made her feel protective and empathetic toward them. She's grown to respect these seamstresses and their heart-felt commitment to getting it right, producing a piece of art that may only be worn once and maybe not at all if Pierre pulls one of his hissy fits again. With the fabric pieces laid out on the table and calls made to the chiffon flower maker across Paris informing him that more are needed and *rapidement*, they are all quickly corralling their chic wagons to just get it done.

Abby, still processing all that's happened, stops for a sec-ond and takes in everything that's around her. She realizes that she is a part of something now. It feels good to her to walk up and down these streets, deep in her own thoughts, and to take in her fellow Parisians as they pass by. She hopes this feel-ing will remain, as up until this very second, she's felt like an outsider who really needs to go on a diet. It also occurs to her that she hasn't thought about being the *grande américaine* for a while now, and that feels so *su-PER! I'm finding my place*, she thinks to herself.

As she lingers with that thought, she's also aware that she's been walking through a land mine of dog poop. Just at that second, she sees an old man looking suspicious with his dog. The dog is squatting, obviously constipated, as it's taking way too long to offer its unique contribution. Feeling irritated that this part of Parisian life is constantly raining on her few and far between parades of positivity, Abby stops to see what in the world this old man will do about it. He looks over at her, and she pointedly does the "I'm watching you" signal with her two fingers. He laughs and shrugs. This makes her angry. With a newfound feeling of activism, she stomps over to him, leaving some distance between them. Closely holding her bag, she takes out her phone to show that she's about to take a picture and then says, "You are breaking the law, and now I have a photo!" in perfect French. She has officially amazed herself. He just shrugs again.

"What is it with you all, just shrugging every time you get caught red-handed doing something you shouldn't? Say *fromage*!" She takes a photo.

He curses her in French and then says, in French, "I don't have any poop bags. Do you have any, poop police?"

"Non! Why would I have poop bags?" she says, again in perfect French. She's on a roll. She shrugs back at him with emphasis, so he gets it. He does the pouf out of his lips and shrugs back. She adopts a full-on "clean up the dog poop or else" stance now, with not a solution in sight. Abby continues to hold her phone, like a cowboy ready to shoot. She looks down at the dog that's still squatting, still trying to poop.

"Are you kidding me?" Abby says. The man looks at her apathetically. It's obvious to Abby that he spends a lot of his time dealing with this. Finally, the dog is done and starts to walk away as if that's the usual drill—poop and walk away without any hesitation to allow his owner to clean up after him. Another sign that this guy is a repeat offender. He pulls the dog back, and it sits, tongue hanging out, looking at his owner and looking at Abby as if he's posing for the photo.

"Oh my god. So cute," Abby says as she takes in all his slobbering happiness. The dog seems completely oblivious to what's happening and just happy to have finished his own challenging bodily function. Once again Abby's not picking up that pile of crap, and the owner clearly isn't either, so it's a

Parisian poop stalemate. She puts her phone back in her bag and does the "I'm watching you" with her two fingers again and walks on. The man shrugs, laughs, and pulls the dog along with him, leaving the steaming pile behind.

As Abby moves up the street, she sees Angélique leaving a café table. She finds it interesting that every time she has an encounter with dog poop, she also has an encounter with Angélique. The ultimate pro and con. Angélique notices her and walks over to her. Abby has an official soft spot for Angélique, and for the first time she does the bisous-bisous greeting as if she's lived in Paris for years.

"Would you like to come up for a cup of the tea you don't like? Or some Badoit?" Angélique asks cutely.

"Oui! Merci. But did you not just have tea at the café, Angélique?" Abby asks.

"You can never have too much tea, my dear. Especially tea from Mariage Frères. You should send some to your maman. She will love it," Angélique says.

As she opens the door, Angélique is laughing so hard, she's crying. Abby has just finished telling her the green goo story, about the day she got covered with smoothie at Claudette. They are both laughing and enjoying the story for different reasons. Abby is finally able to laugh about it without feeling like the pile that dog left earlier. Angélique heads into the kitchen to prepare the fancy French tea she mentioned to Abby, and Abby finds what feels like her usual spot on the sofa. Then she watches Angélique walk in with her lovely silver tea tray in hand, making sure the perfectly placed teacups don't spill.

"Oh, it is so funny. You in that upscale, pristine environment, and then all those models . . . oh *mon dieu*. How did you manage?" Angélique says, patting her décolletage. Settled and sitting down, Angélique picks up her teacup.

"Claudette is an institution, a French institution. It is not an easy place to exist. I would ask you how you are finding it, but it seems not well, non?" Angélique asks as she takes a sip of tea, slowly looking over at Abby.

"It's been difficult, but today I was thinking that I'm starting to feel un petit peu that I'm finally finding my place." Abby smiles.

"C'est bien! And how do you find the head or première couturière? Is she open to you, or is she cold and distant?" Angélique asks.

"Well, she's difficult and very hard, but there's something about her I really like, and I sense that she's on the verge of something," Abby reflectively answers.

"A breakdown?"

"Maybe. It's funny you say that. Do you know some of the seamstresses there? I mean, you said before that you did designs, and those sketches are amazing," Abby says.

"Yes, I know some of the seamstresses, and I know what they go through. Every dress they make is as precious to them as their own child. It can be ridiculous. It is a piece of clothing, nothing more. It has no real meaning in life, and yet so much sweat and tears are caused because of it. People are hurt, relationships are ruined, and for what?" Angélique is getting emotional, almost dropping her teacup as she sets it down on the table. Abby can see that this goes way deeper than dressmaking.

"Were you a couturière?" Abby inquires, gently.

"That was a lifetime ago. Let's move on." Angélique adjusts her blazer and her perfectly coiffed all-gray French bob.

"Désolée. I didn't mean to . . . ," Abby says, trying to make amends.

"Oh! It wasn't you, ma chère, just bad memories, that's all. C'est la vie!"

Angélique stands up to shift the focus and goes to her gorgeous bookshelves. They are filled with books on all subjects, in many colors and sizes. The book she pulls out is an old Claudette coffee table book with black-and-white pictures from the late 1940s and 1950s. The book is a piece of art. She brings it to Abby. Abby takes it gently and politely as she knows from all those years antique shopping with her mama that pieces like this are sacred to those who have them. This book feels especially so. An old Post-it note is sticking out from one of the pages, and Angélique turns to that page. There is a young lady next to a mannequin covered in a dark fabric. The eyes give it away.

"*C'est vous?*" Abby asks, looking up at Angélique.

"*Oui, c'est moi,*" Angélique replies, with a twinge of sadness.

EIGHTEEN

Lanterns of Love

Claire was right when she said that French men are masters at making women swoon. Jean-Louis popped up again with an invite, and Abby, determined to enjoy her time in Paris as much as possible, decided to meet up with him again but no hookup, just a meetup. She doesn't want to be in that space with him again, or for that matter her bed. That last text from François is still hanging.

They walk up to each other outside the dark warehouse room behind obscure black doors at L'Atelier des Lumières and do the bisous-bisous when they greet. They are about to enter a unique take on Van Gogh's *Starry Night* with a special, visually artistic presentation called *Dreamed Japan*. It's a fine example of Parisian art and culture because it's all taking place in a simple black room with an ongoing tapestry of artwork rolling across the walls, telling the story of its featured artist. This interactive take on Van Gogh's work is mind-blowing. It's sure to impress anyone lucky enough to see it. Abby is thrilled to be here and lukewarm to be with Jean-Louis again. It's a strange, gritty part of Paris she's not yet explored.

Entering the dark room, they stand and wait. Suddenly, images of lines morph into trees, then into village houses, then a skyline forms on the walls around them. What was originally in black and white has now become full of color—yellow, blues, reds, and oranges. It's magical. Abby is spinning around, open-mouthed in wonder and delight. Jean-Louis watches her. Abby is filled with enthusiasm and wonder. They can't find a good place to sit, so they stand hand in hand for a bit until finally he stands behind her and puts his hands around her waist. Abby notes it. Doesn't reciprocate, and just then an amazing landscape starts to appear on the walls, and she moves closer to it to take it in. The crowd then starts to dissipate, and they move to a spot where they have more room.

"We'll have a better view from here," he says, lying down on the floor and crossing his legs to get comfortable. Abby stays standing.

"Care to join me?" he asks, patting the floor. Abby looks around, hoping there are other people on the floor, but alas there are not. She looks up to see if he does in fact have the best view and agrees the best vantage point would be from the floor. She lies down next to him. They lie next to each other like two childhood friends looking up at the night sky.

"Van Gogh is my favorite," Jean-Louis says.

"Pourquoi?" She turns to look at him, but he points for her to keep looking around at the masterpieces playing out around them rather than at him.

"There's something so interesting about his cutting his ear off."

"Okay. I was expecting more depth to that answer." They laugh.

"I think you'll find that I'm not so deep, but rather very simple and practical, though I do like what he said about Paris."

"And what's that?" Abby replies.

"He said, 'There is but one Paris, and however hard living may be here, and if it became worse and harder—the French air clears up the brain and does good—a world of good.' Nice, non?" Jean-Louis quickly turns to her to see if it registered and then turns back to the walls. "Do you agree?" he asks.

"I'm beginning to understand that now. I'm not sure if I'm fully there yet, but I'm getting there. This is certainly helping." Without realizing it, she takes his hand.

They end up lying there for almost thirty minutes, their heads touching, saying nothing as they take it all in. As each one of Abby's breaths rises from the floor, she feels enriched, in ways she can't explain. Lying on the floor in a warehouse in France with a Frenchman (still not the Frenchman she really wants to be here, but a Frenchman nonetheless), watching Van Gogh's masterpieces play out on the walls, is all she needs at this very moment. Her mind is open, her heart expansive, and she understands that saying her daddy told her once, "Art enables us to find ourselves and lose ourselves at the same time," which is so true. She wishes her daddy could be here to experience this, too.

"And now we go to Van Gogh's Japan," Jean-Louis says to her, taking care not to move his head in her direction in case they bump.

"Have you ever been to Japan?" Abby asks him, also not moving her head, keeping focused on what's around her.

"Oui! It's another world. I loved it," he says, pointing to the left as some Japanese ladies in traditional kimonos appear on the wall.

"Another stint at bartender school?" she asks.

"No, just a trip for a few months. Kind of like you here."

"It looks amazing. I have so much yet to see in the world. I'm only understanding that now. I thought I understood so much before I left home, like I had experienced so much with my mama's illness, but now, being here, I see I really didn't experience anything at all except a lot of fear, sadness, and relief when it was over. It makes me kind of sad," she says, trailing off.

Her eye is drawn toward a small lantern, beautifully lit, which is rising from one of the corners of the room. Another one starts to rise, and then another, until the whole room is filled with these lanterns in full glow, offering a kind of mystical and holy light to the experience. She looks around and sees that every single person is transfixed by the images that are moving across the room.

As Jean-Louis watches the images rise up the black warehouse walls toward what seems like the heavens, he says in a fading voice, "The Japanese lanterns symbolize joy, celebration, good fortune, and longevity . . ." This moves Abby to tears. The tears well up and slowly fall down her cheeks. There is no sobbing, just a soft rising, a deep welling, and tears slowly cascading down. Watching what seems like hundreds of lanterns light up the room and hearing their meaning as she lies on this floor, her soul swells in gratitude. For all of it. The difficulties, the disappointments, the trouble, the frustration, the feeling of lacking and insufficiency, and finally the feeling of unworthiness—she's grateful for all of it. It's brought her to a more expansive place inside, and that's what she wanted with this experience—a bigger place inside. That is something to celebrate. Jean-Louis is completely oblivious to all of this, but that doesn't matter to her. The person she wants to share this newfound awareness with is the one person who knew this instinctively would happen to her all along. That person is François.

NINETEEN

Threading Together

Claudette again is a flurry of fabric and threads. The seamstresses are all working together like violin players in an orchestra, only with custom-made silver thimbles on their fingers instead of bows in their hands. In an unplanned unison they poke in and pull out their needles in elegant swoops. The thimbles, all engraved with a capital C, are such a part of this process that they look like pieces of designer jewelry added to their outfits for a unique touch. Abby is watching, taking pics with her phone, trying to capture the gorgeous vibe in front of her. They all work together, smiling, happy, focused, and clear in their purpose of getting it done and doing it well. The thimbles remind her so much of her grandmother when she would sew quilts.

Abby still has one of those quilts. Grandma's thimbles weren't as sophisticated and didn't look as chic as they do here, but she knows that her grandmother put the same intensity and love into making her quilts as the women (and one token tattooed man) today do. Abby's trying to determine the best angle and approach to produce good photos to highlight more of the behind-the-scenes activities. She circles around one bigger table to see how she could do it from above and from the side. She wants to capture this scene of synchronized sewing to emphasize the amount of effort it takes to make just one piece, knowing that Claudette must make at least fifty original pieces annually to meet their quota as an haute couture house. A message from Sophie comes through.

Bonjour Ms. Allerton,

We've been reviewing your posts, and though we find them acceptable, we would like for you to highlight more the incredible effort it takes to put on a show of this caliber. As I said to you after your deceitful infraction of trust, you are being watched and given warning. We have more than enough raison de vous faire partir already.

Regards,
Sophie Dubois

"I'm on it, Sophie, I'm on it," Abby says to herself. This once again brings up her longing to post something on Plus-Size Real. She's proud of what she's written for Plus-Size Real, but she's not proud of what she's being forced to do on Femme Fatale except for the one post she's done about Jacqueline and the seamstresses. She's very proud of that.

Sophie's sinister reminder that they are "watching" is forcing her to continue living in her self-inflicted façade. Which she hates. She hopefully ended it with Heather, although she doesn't really know because she hasn't heard back after Heather's equally sinister text. So much has happened to her since arriving, like stepping stones of self-discovery, and she desperately wants to get back on track. Those posts she's written have depth and relevance to her and possibly so many others like her, yet her hands are tied, for now anyway. She's working on engaging Jacqueline in a little mischief, especially after seeing how Pierre treats her. *C'est horrible!* But it could mean the door to Jacqueline isn't shut so tightly. Maybe she could use that to her advantage, to get Jacqueline to join her in a kind of fashion coup d'etát? The thought makes her laugh to herself a bit.

"What are you laughing about?" Gays for Days appears out of nowhere.

"Bonjour, monsieur, ça va?" Abby asks, arching one eyebrow in preparation for his response.

"Look at you, embracing the local language. Stopping by to see if you'd like to have lunch with me," he responds, almost whispering to ensure no one can else can hear him.

"You okay?" Abby asks.

"Yes, I'm totally fine. Do you want to go or not?"

"Where are we going?"

"Just come," he responds and starts to walk out of the sewing room. Abby grabs her pile of notebooks and stuffs them in her bag.

"Why do you carry a library around with you? It's so geriatric," he asks. Abby turns around and doesn't realize she left her *BIG IDEAS* notebook on the sewing table.

"What is your name, anyway? I just keep calling you Gays for Days but I'm sure you have a name, right?" Abby asks as they walk down the stairs.

"My name is Albert."

"*Albert?* Oh boy, I can see why you prefer your profile name."

"Thanks, that's sweet," he says, oozing sarcasm. They leave the building and head to a café down the street. Abby is thrilled to be invited to lunch. She was told by François during one of their Parisian tutorial sessions that having an invite for lunch is paramount in Paris, especially in the workplace, so this is an unexpected treat today, not only because she was invited to lunch but because she was invited by Gays for Days . . . or, rather, Albert. She's one hundred percent sure she was his last resort, but she'll take it. It's lunchtime in Paris. The offices are completely empty, and the city's population has all descended on the many terrace cafés and restaurants, bringing a unique midday energy and flow outside in the city. Abby is thrilled to be a part of the masses of perfectly dressed Parisians headed out to lunch and not on her own just grabbing a quick sand-wich at the canteen. Another milestone. Albert starts to head toward the café where Abby lost her wallet and met Jean-Louis. She sees he's busy behind the bar talking to another woman intently. Abby notes it and is relieved she didn't sleep with him again after the Van Gogh exhibition and gently steers Albert away from the café.

"What are you doing?" Albert asks.

"Can we go somewhere else?" Abby asks.

"What's the story? Did you sleep with a waiter in there or something?" he asks, laughing.

Abby smiles and shrugs.

"OMG. You vixen." Albert laughs. "Fine, let's go to my usual, right down here. Not nearly as exciting because I didn't sleep with any waiters, but it'll have to do, and they do know me now."

Now seated at a small terrace table at a corner café, Abby and Albert are perusing the menu and giving each other awk-ward glances.

"You said you've been here before, Albert?" Abby asks.

"Oui, you could say I'm kind of a regular now," Albert says as he waves over to the small group of waiters. One comes over.

"Bonjour, Albert, ça va?" the waiter asks.

"Trés bien, merci," Albert answers without hesitation. Abby watches him with admiration. He seems very confident in his abilities.

"*C'est mon amie,* Abby," Albert says.

"Mon amie?" Abby leans forward. "Wow, I'm so flattered." She smiles.

"Oh, shut up," Albert says in return.

"Enchanté," the waiter says to Abby and does a little bow of acknowledgment. The waiter takes their order and moves on after giving them their glasses and filling them with Badoit. Abby takes a sip and looks at Albert.

"So, how are things, mon ami?" Abby asks, smiling.

"Now you're just being annoying," Albert says.

"I know, but this is so fun," Abby says. "How are things for you at the event? Let's do this. Let's bond and move this along. It's taken us long enough, as long as it takes these waiters to bring *l'addition* most days," Abby jokes.

"So, what did you think of that big spectacle with Jacqueline and Pierre? That was something, wasn't it?" Albert asks as he pulls out a cigarette to smoke. Abby watches with curiosity as she didn't realize he smoked. He lights it and takes a puff, then instantly starts to cough.

"Are you okay?" she asks. "Do you need me to pat your back?" She gets up to pat it and he stops her.

"No, Mom, I don't need you to pat my back." He puffs out more and then takes a drink of the water.

"So, what did you think?" he asks again as he holds the cigarette.

"You don't usually smoke, do you?" Abby asks.

"I do now," he answers and takes another drag, yet again coughing up a lung. This time Abby gives him the glass across the table. He takes a drink and then puts the cigarette on the ashtray.

"You're just going to leave that there while we eat?" Abby says, turning her nose up.

"We're friends, right?" he asks cutely.

"We are, and friends don't let friends continue bad habits when it doesn't suit them, and I'd say I'm witnessing a very unhealthy habit forming here, and it's my job as your *amie* to do an intervention and tell you, you will be just as dashing without the cigarette," Abby says.

"Note taken. We will revisit this later. Back to your question about the event. I have so much tea to spill it's unbelievable," Albert says.

The waiter brings a basket of baguette. Abby grabs a piece. "Do tell," she says.

"Well, from a source I have, Pierre was poached from one of the other fashion houses for his 'superior designs,' which I'm still honestly underwhelmed, aren't you?"

"I'm still in a mesmerized state of mind that I'm even here, so I'm probably not the best judge, *but* I will say I think the way the seamstresses are so undervalued really sucks. I mean, from what I've seen," Abby says, taking another bite of baguette.

"So, related to that," Albert says, chowing down on his second piece of baguette, "there's a rumor that he's having an affair with the CEO, but that's not been confirmed yet by someone au courant at Claudette."

"What's *au courant*?" Abby asks, leaning in.

"It means *in the know*. It's an old term they used back in the days of the royal court with, you know, Marie Antionette and Louis XVI—those times," Albert explains.

"Huh, au courant," Abby repeats. "I love it. It's so intriguing. So mysterious."

"I know, right?" Albert says.

"Since you shadowed her before, do you think Jacqueline is happy there? Or that she's showing signs of wear and tear, no pun intended?" Abby asks. Albert shakes his head again. Abby can see she's growing on him, whether he likes it or not.

"I heard that Pierre worked his way up the ranks of a competitor fashion house and was poached by the CEO here in one of the fashion world's biggest scandals. He's notorious for being the designer that won't quit. He works insane hours and is so driven he's gone through a total of twenty assistants in the years he's been at Claudette," Albert says, as if he's telling a scary story at a slumber party. He reaches for the cigarette. Abby gently shakes her head and puts her hand over it. He sits back. She smiles and gives him a thumbs-up.

"And he's known for his abusive fits—that we all saw," Albert says.

"Did that trigger you? You seemed very upset when it was happening," Abby asks, concerned.

"Weren't you?" he asks.

"I was, totally, but since we're friends, I'll tell you that I do therapy, so it helps me stay levelheaded, and it's clear there are some very dysfunctional dynamics at play." She smiles.

"Well, I've seen you in some bad situations here, and somehow you seem to come out of them and keep going. It's impressive."

"Merci, mon ami. That's very kind of you."

"Yeah, don't get used to it," Albert says sarcastically.

"Well, in that case I'd better overshare now because I may not get this opportunity again. It's been hard here. I realized the other day that I thought I would leave some emotional baggage behind, but I think I brought it all with me. Weird how that works."

"Yeah, my mom used to do that. She would use her trips over here to find stuff to sell as a way to deal with my dad. He's a real asshole. She called them the great geographical escapes."

"Oh, I'm so sorry, Albert. That's rough," Abby says as she puts her hand on his across the table. She makes eye contact with him, and she sees him hold it for a second but then he quickly pulls his hand away and takes a drink of Badoit.

"Too much?" Abby asks.

"Un petite peu."

"Got it. Switching gears! I may have some intriguing info for you." Abby takes another drink of her Badoit.

"Oh really? If it's about your fashion suspension, old news. We're all over it, and apparently you are, too, as you are still here, so . . ."

"Uh no, I'm thinking about something a little bigger than that." Abby smiles.

"I'm in. Whatcha got?" Albert picks up the cigarette and takes another drag. Coughs and puts it down. Abby shakes her head.

TWENTY

Non, Je Ne Regrette Rien

With everyone back from lunch, Jacqueline is walking through the seamstress tables, checking the dresses, which are now in their final stages. They are inching closer to their first fittings on the chosen models and will then be forced to endure Pierre's torturous first official inspection. Abby is watching, mesmerized as usual. This is her new norm, watching Jacqueline work, full of wonder, amazement, and admiration. Abby preps her phone for a Reel on Femme Fatale. She holds her phone out and starts to record. She gestures to Jacqueline that she's recording now.

"Jacqueline?" she asks.

"Oui?" Jacqueline responds as she pulls out a thread from one of the pieces of this particularly difficult dress, with its unlimited details in sequins and buttons.

"Did you always want to work in an atelier? Is it something you dreamed of or something you fell into?" Abby asks.

"It's a difficult question because I come from a long line of seamstresses. It's in my blood. I grew up with a mother who wore a thimble so much I thought it was an accessory, not a tool. I loved to watch her pull the threads in and out as I do now. She did it with such elegance. Maybe I felt that way about it because she was my mother, because, you know, when you watch your maman do anything as a child, you think it's the most amazing, most *jolie* thing you've ever seen. Do you understand?" Jacqueline asks, putting a pin in her mouth as she folds over a pleat.

"Oh yes, I totally get that. I feel that way when I watch my mama cook, especially when she's kneading biscuit dough. I love it when she balls it all up and then pats it with this kind of loving pat like you would a baby's bottom," Abby says, smiling.

"Patting a what?" Jacqueline asks.

"When you have dough, it's all one big heap . . ." Abby gestures to show her everything with hand motions on the table.

"*Sur la table . . . ,*" Jacqueline says. "Do you know this term in French?" she asks Abby.

"On the table, is that right?" Abby asks.

"Oui, but it means something else, too. It means to literally put things on the table, but also to put it out there, or be honest in a real way when speaking about something. I would've thought you would know this one as you seem to be a *sur-la-table* type of person." Jacqueline smiles.

"*Merci pour le compliment!*" Abby says happily. She stops the recording and saves it, as she'll prep and post later.

"Je t'en prie, mon amie," Jacqueline replies with an affirmative nod. Abby hesitates and makes sure she heard everything right. Not only did Jacqueline pay her a huge compliment, but she also said "my friend" to her in French and used the more familiar *tu* instead of *vous* when addressing her. Baby steps. Yet another milestone in Abby's eyes and for her experience in Paris. What a great day!

"Your English is very good, Jacqueline. Much better than my French."

"Mmm, well, I think we both may be hiding that ability. That's okay. You must hold something close to your chest." Jacqueline winks at Abby.

"Have you ever thought about doing this on your own?" Abby asks.

"Opening my own atelier?" Jacqueline asks, taking the iron to prepare a good pressing on yet another pleat. Abby gathers that Pierre went a little pleat crazy on this one, and it seems to be driving the seamstresses nuts.

"Yes, or maybe design your own clothes? Do you ever think about that? Doing something that's the creative side rather than the technical side of design? I mean, you could so easily do both," Abby says in an enthused tone with a twinge of selling as she continues to take pictures of the process.

Jaqueline does the "pouf" and puts the iron back on its stand. She looks at the pleat and carefully places it back on the table and then carefully folds the material again, takes the iron again, and presses down the point of the iron right along the crease as she moves it down the fold, this time with more force. Abby watches her intently and is a little scared she may have just lost her baby steps with Jacqueline, because she's not answering and seems to have pulled back.

"There was a time when I thought about this a lot. I thought about putting the two together, but as you can see, there is so much focus that must happen on this side that I don't know how I would keep my wits about me if I had to do the other side. I would be like a basket case, trying to make sure every stitch is done properly. There is a reason why Pierre sticks to designing—he'd kill someone with an iron like this, and he'd stick himself silly trying to sew anything. I don't know how you could combine the two in one brain. Not in a professional way. Of course, people make their clothes and create their own creations at home and wear them with pride, as they should, but I'm speaking strictly of this caliber of art, this caliber of clothing. It's art. Combining the two would cheapen it. It's what I think." Jacqueline shrugs and removes the dress from the table with such delicacy it's like she's carrying a newborn child. Then, gently but with precision, she puts it back on the mannequin.

"I understand. I guess I'm inspired by someone I met recently, an older lady who used to do this same job, and she wished she would've designed. It was a little sad to see it in her eyes—the regret of not trying something more. I wondered if you felt the same or had any regrets," Abby asks gently.

"*Je ne regrette rien.* There is nothing I can do about what's happened before, so I don't like to dwell there," Jacqueline says, half-convincingly.

"I understand. C'est la vie. Right?" Abby affirms.

"Mmm, not exactly. When you say *c'est la vie*, you are speaking of something more that you can't control, or it's happened and it's not a deep thing. I'm speaking of something I choose not to visit again. I don't want to waste my life on things that I know deep down would not work. Such is the case with my designing. Most importantly, it doesn't bring me the full joy as pulling these threads in and out of beautiful fabrics. It brings me joy," Jacqueline says as she looks intently at a stitch and pulls it through.

"That's funny. I got the same kind of response from the older lady I just told you about that I met, only I got the feeling she had some regrets."

"Maybe it's something we are both telling ourselves to get through the days. Who knows? *Et toi?* Are you a psychiatrist or an influencer? What do you think you will do with this life? You are young, bold, and have your opinions. You are also creative and clearly know how to sell yourself and your ideas. Those are strong, good qualities. What will you do with them? Just continue to be an internet influencer?" Jacqueline asks.

"I guess I hope it will evolve into something more meaningful. I mean, it has back home. I've created a strong community with my other account, and I would hope I could do the same here so that it would have an impact. I'm not sure what yet, but I feel like something's brewing, stirring inside," she says, looking off in the distance at the other seamstresses.

"For someone so young, you are so philosophical. Are you always this deep? You must be very fun at parties . . ." Jacqueline smiles and winks at Abby.

"Yeah, I've been known to dampen some good times, taking the conversations to a place of depth, but I like to have a good time, too. It just seems those are few and far between here in Paris." Abby shrugs.

"Mais oui . . . I'm sure your tendency to go deep is an enticing thing for François, or is it Jean-Louis? Frenchmen love to sit around and discuss life's big questions. It makes them feel like they are big and have a grip on the world when they do not. I mean, it's a worldwide fact that without women in every industry, the world would collapse. Right?"

"Wait, what? Do you know them? This is so weird. I didn't know you knew them," Abby responds, taking a step back.

"I don't. I may have seen something on your notebook that you left behind." Jacqueline stops what's she's doing completely and stands at the table.

"What notebook?" Abby asks.

"Your *BIG IDEAS* one with all the big splash of colors on it."

"Oh, you read it. How? When?" Abby is very confused. She puts her hair behind her ears, trying to understand how this could've taken place.

"You left it behind one day, and I may have taken a peek." Jacqueline makes the "petit" sign with her fingers.

"More than a peek. Those notes were three pages in and a part of a very personal list and a very *privé* project I'm working on." Abby is part angry and part confused.

"Did you find anything on the list that interests you? Did anything make you mad? I wrote some harsh things about Claudette and its 'traditions,' let alone the French. I'm so sorry. I was working through some things. Did that upset you?" Abby waits.

"Non, nothing made me mad, as it's only your opinions and not anyone else's, and I told you before to be careful with the design house. They are not so understanding," Jacqueline says, looking down through her glasses.

"Oui, I know. I just can't do superficial shit, Jacqueline."

"No offense, but Femme Fatale is hardly a deep initiative, and you've been doing it for some time, non?" Jacqueline quickly interjects.

"I know, I know. It's the biggest of surface shit. Believe me, I know. I'm miserable not being myself and doing these posts that are so surface and trivial, but now I'm boxed in because I'm here and came under 'deceitful pretenses,' which Sophie reminds me of regularly."

"You did come here under deceitful pretenses. I can see why she was angry," Jacqueline affirms.

"I know, and I'm sorry. It doesn't change how restricted I feel and how I can't do what I really want to do. Have you ever restricted yourself in a way that makes you feel miserable?" Abby asks genuinely.

Jacqueline looks down and mutters in French, "My whole life . . ."

"What?" Abby asks. "I couldn't hear you. What did you say?"

At that moment Pierre comes thrashing through.

"Jacqueline? Where are you?" he yells. He turns and she's right there. He jumps back in surprise. "Are we ready? Are you ready to show me the fixes and the next versions?" Jacqueline nods and gestures for him to follow her into the bigger room with the mannequins, where a couple of models are waiting to try on the designs. Abby watches her once again lead him somewhere with an almost regal level of professionalism. She can see that Jacqueline is the thread that keeps it all together. Without her, he's sunk.

TWENTY-ONE

Don't Mess with the Tour Guide . . .

Abby is walking through the 7th arrondissement, as it's one she hasn't been able to explore just yet. She's enjoying the abundance of florists with all the lovely, colorful flowers on display in a variety of heights and creative creations wrapped up in soft tissue papers. Just then, her phone rings. It's François calling on FaceTime.

"Allô, Abby! Bonjour! Ça va?" François is waving to her through the phone.

"Oh, François, you really do have impeccable timing. How are you?" Abby smiles big and is truly happy to talk to him. She's been worried since their last text.

"Je vais bien! Et toi? You see I'm speaking French with you," he says cutely.

"Indeed, you are. I'm having a lovely day exploring the 7th arrondissement." She turns the phone and does a pan shot for him to see what she's seeing.

"Did you get mugged yet?" he asks.

"No, François, so far so good in that department, but we can mark off *wallet stolen* on our Parisian bingo card, right?"

"Indeed, we can. Hasn't turned up yet?" he asks.

"Non, not yet. I'm doubtful," Abby says, melancholy.

"It's been a while since we've spoken. Are you booing me?"

"Booing? Do you mean ghosting?"

"Yes, I just put my own unique take on it."

"Cute, as always. No, I'm so sorry. I'm just really focused on something here, and I've been a little tunnel-visioned. Désolée, mon monsieur." Abby smiles.

"Then what, my friend, is happening with you? Tell me." François puts his face on his fist. Abby has the urge to jump through the phone and kiss it long and hard. If only there wasn't the obstacle of a whole ocean between them.

"François, how often do you come here?" Abby asks, trying to be nonchalant as she knows she asked him this before.

"You know, it's probably time, but I don't know when, no plans right now."

"Don't you miss it? It is your home," Abby asks.

"I do sometimes. Are you missing home?"

"I do sometimes, but mostly I miss certain things at home that I can't get here." She moves her eyes to what's ahead of her so she's not looking straight at him.

"Such as . . . ?"

"Chloe, my mama's biscuits, and . . ." She stops and sits on a bench between two small trees on the street.

Just then, a call from Jean-Louis comes in and distracts her. She hits Decline. Now *there's* someone she's ghosting. Oh, mon dieu!

"I would miss those, too. I miss the life there. Isn't it full of life?" François asks.

"It is indeed. A life I didn't expect, really, but yes, it's full of life, very busy. There's a tempo to this place. It's kind of invigorating in a way, but then it can kind of suck, too," she says, looking at him and then away.

"In what way?"

"Oh, I just felt that it would be more, I don't know, like a movie *all* the time. I mean, there are times when I feel like I'm in a movie, but then there are times when I'm like, *Whoa, this really sucks.* Does that make sense?" She smiles, shrugging.

"Totally. It's what I call the 'Parisian paradox.' It's hard, it's difficult, and then you turn a corner on some street in the center or you go for a walk through Luxembourg Gardens and take in the design of the garden and realize you are in a place like no other, and you get a nudge to keep going, keep moving until the next unexpected turn and experience."

"Parisian paradox? I love that, but I'm not sure you are using the word *paradox* in the correct way, although it kind of works. Well, look at you with all the meaningful mantras! Another one from that Insta account?" She smiles.

"No, ma chérie, that is all mine." He smiles back.

"I have a question for you."

"Hit me."

"You had to adjust to America, too, right?" Abby asks.

François makes the "pouf" and looks away, saying, "Oui, c'est vrai, and I can tell you it wasn't easy."

"I was wondering about that."

"And what wonderings do you have about this Frenchman in America?"

"I mean this architecture, it's something out of a fairy tale, and the strip mall where Wholly Crêpe is, well, it's . . ."

"'Merican?" François says with an American accent. Abby starts laughing. So cute.

"Yeah, that's 'Merica for you," she says in full southern drawl.

"Oh la la. I love it when you talk to me like that," François says.

"Well, I will let you go. I'm headed back to the design house, as I was on a break. They are so militant over there." She tucks her hair behind her ear.

"Well, it is French, and it is—"

"Fantasy, yes, I've been told," Abby interrupts him.

"I was going to say, very sarcastically, 'superior to all fashion in the world,' but I guess fantasy works, too." He winks at her. "Well, au revoir for now, ma chérie. Call me soon."

"I will, mon monsieur. Thank you for calling. This call was the turn of the corner in my Parisian paradox today." She waves to him and clicks End Call.

She takes a deep breath and attempts the "pouf" again, sitting on the bench. She looks at her watch and realizes she's not due back at Claudette for another hour or so. She continues to walk with her arms across her chest in a kind of self-love hug as she takes in all that's around her on the little street.

She finds herself outside the Musée Rodin. It looks intriguing to her, and it's on her must-see list, so in she goes and buys a ticket. When she enters the courtyard, immediately on her right is the infamous statue *The Thinker*, surrounded by shrubs. She rushes over there. She can't believe she's looking at the original. Then she moves into the building and takes in sculpture after sculpture, reveling in Rodin's talent and art. She devours all the information, handily posted in French and English next to every piece. Before long, she's standing in front of *The Cathedral*, a piece with two right hands seemingly floating in air, about to touch, but something is stopping them—air, space, time, or, as the placard says, "a loneliness."

This makes her stop and look at them more intently. She circles them a few times. The title *The Cathedral* intrigues her. The only thing she can equate it to is when her daddy taught her the hand movements and the rhyme:

This is the church, this is the steeple,
open the doors and see all the people.

Funny that such a simplistic association of hands evokes such a strong memory of her being close with her daddy. Once again, art is connecting the senses and emotions of her life. She remembers her loneliness at home wasn't because her daddy wasn't there; he was, so much. She wonders if he was lonely and if he was loved enough. She wants to ask him that the next time they talk. A female tour guide walks by with a tour group scurrying behind her and hits Abby with her huge courier bag full of papers and maps. She's moving the group to the next room. Abby follows them.

"And this is *Le Baiser*, or *The Kiss*. I challenge you to find me a more romantic, more sensual, more intimate sculpture than this one," the tour lady says. Abby notices that the tour is made up entirely of women, and they all "ooh" and "ahh" in their various accents. She hears some Americans in the mix, and this prompts her to follow them more.

"Rodin called this piece his 'huge knickknack' and wasn't as in love with it as everyone else. It was in his piece *The Gates*, but then he took it out because it was too obviously happy and sensual for the vast theme of being condemned to hell. He then exhibited it by itself, and that is when the name *Le Baiser*, or *The Kiss*, was aptly coined," the tour guide explains, with a smidge of pretension. Abby's completely enthralled with this piece of art. The lines, the softness of the body parts, and the way they are entwined with each other in the moment of a simple kiss makes her put her hand to her chest to grasp it all. This is one of the coolest things she's ever seen, and she's seeing it in person, in Paris at the artist's original home and workshop. This is one of those moments that she knows she needs to fully appreciate because it may never come again.

"There is another one of these in the Jardin des Tuileries, right in front of the Musée de l'Orangerie. I highly recommend you go see it. An interesting thing to notice on the one in the park is that there will be an original signature of Rodin and a No. 1 on it. Per French law, only the first twelve casts of sculptures can be classified as original. Taking in that one at the Jardin des Tuileries is a real treat," she says as she looks away from the sculpture.

"Are there any questions?" she asks.

"Oui, une question," Abby says, completely enthralled and forgetting the fact that she's not a participant of this tour. Abby sees the women all look at her with inquisitive looks.

"Yes, what is it?" the tour guide responds, irritated.

"I'm wondering about the twelve original editions. How do they keep track of each of them to make sure they are authentic when they are all over the world? It must be incredibly hard to make sure there aren't random copies." Abby is genuinely interested in the process of keeping something so special and delicate safe from insensitive and lowly practices.

"Well, I guess I could ask you. Aren't you doing the same?" asks the tour guide.

"I'm not sure what you mean." Abby is confused.

"Well, aren't you also trying to be an imposter in a space that's original?" she replies in a rather disciplinary tone.

"I don't know what you mean. I'm not a sculptor."

"Oh, I'm speaking of you trying to pretend you are a part of the original twelve ladies on this tour. This is a paid tour, my dear. It takes me weeks to put a list together and then create such interesting topics and destinations once a month."

Abby sees the ladies give each other knowing looks that inform her this has happened before, and they take out their phones and start texting.

"Right. I just followed along, as your tour was so intriguing, and I was overcome by so much in this museum. I'm sorry. Can I offer you cash to remain on the tour?" Abby pulls out a twenty-euro note to offer the annoyed tour guide. The tour guide doesn't move and doesn't take it.

"My tours are much more than twenty euros. I don't work for the tour kiosks down at the Eiffel Tower that take your money and offer you nothing of real substance in return. I have a doctorate in Fine Arts and a PhD in French History. I offer you the real Paris with a level of education that far surpasses twenty euros," she responds.

"I'm very sorry. I understand. I'll just back away then and review what I missed on my own." Abby backs up between the women slowly, and as one of the women is looking away, Abby catches a glimpse of her huge phone screen and sees the texting with these words: *freeloader*, *Madame Le Vot*, *American*, *fresh-faced*, *happy*, and *won't last long*. She continues to stand there for a second reading it, when another woman in the group gestures to her friend for her to turn around. She notices Abby and quickly puts the phone to her chest to conceal the screen.

Too late. Abby looks at her straight in the eye, then shakes her head in disbelief and makes her way out of the group.

Abby retraces her steps back through the museum and exits to the courtyard in the back where there is a lovely café and garden with lounge chairs to sit on. She chooses one and sits down to write in her journal.

I feel naïve saying this as I'm still so new here, but it does feel like Paris is a place that throws you in, and either you swim, sink, or, frankly, drown. Thrive or survive. Strengthen or weaken. Push or be pulled. Full of contrasts and extremes. It's hard to keep up, but I feel I'm on such an adventure, and that's what I came to do, be on an adventure, and that's not always easy. Nothing is, so why would this be, either? My mama having cancer was and is an adventure, too, a sad, depressing, but also deepening one, I guess. It's what got me here, or is it? Possibly a combination of those things.

Abby stops writing and then looks up at the sky peeking through the tree branches above her. At that moment, a butterfly flutters by and seems to hover over her. She follows it with her eyes, still holding the pen to the paper. It flutters right in front of her in its own rhythmic dance, unaware of its surroundings. Completely immersed in its own movement. Light, free, airy, and easy. Abby starts to write again with more intensity and purpose.

I'm here for a reason. I came for a reason. I can't forget that. I'm here to be in my own space and make my own place. I WILL find my place, and it will be just as lively and elegant as that butterfly that just danced in front of me at this gorgeous museum filled with solid pieces that ensure they can endure the test of time. Kind of like me and my mama. We've both withstood the test of time, beat all the odds, and are still here. Hell, it's just the beginning. With my project I've got in mind, I think I can make my mark, and if it all goes to hell in a handbasket, well, so what. It'll be worth it because I was brave. I also need to apologize to Heather, much to my chagrin. In a way she got me here, too, and I've been unfair to her. Just like those ladies inside.

Abby drops the pen. She stretches her arms out to the sky and sees the butterfly once again. *What are you trying to tell me?* she asks herself. She looks up and sees the tour group now at the café about to get lunch. She watches them as if she was watching a research control group, taking mental notes of them as they all chat away about the lunch on offer and whether to day drink and get a glass of rosé to go with it. As she gets up to leave, the butterfly is fluttering along the path, making its way to the exit. Abby gets up, grabs her bag, and follows it. They both flutter out together, freer from the perfect and a little more comfortable with the imperfect.

TWENTY-TWO

A Revolutionary Meeting

The Arc de Triomphe is lit up and looks imperious and strong, especially tonight with the French flag flying in the center of its arch. It's stunning, and Abby sits down on one of the empty benches facing it to watch the red, white, and blue French flag flutter in the wind. This has quickly become one of her favorite spots in Paris. All the traffic buzzing around like oversize bumper cars as they weave their way around the arc's crazy roundabout. Life in Paris is full, busy, and fun from this spot.

As Abby takes it all in, it occurs to her that things have been happening so fast since she arrived in Paris. She's been kicked out of an elite event and then let back in again, only because, according to François, there are two things that are impossible to do in France: fire someone and break a contract. *Guess those are two proven benefits of the French bureaucracy,* she thinks. She decides it's time to head back to the apartment she loves. Maybe she'll take the way that goes past Angélique's and stop by if it's not too late.

With that thought, she pops up off the bench, adjusts her cross-over bag, and heads in the direction of home. It's a nice night to walk home, much nicer than going by Métro or taxi. A good long stroll home through the heart of Paris is balm for the soul. That thought immediately makes her think of François and the list that Jacqueline saw. He's not here, and he told her recently he's not planning to come back to France any time soon. Maybe there's a possibility when she goes back home to the States? Will she go back? She can't believe she's even asking herself that question, that it is, in fact, an option for her in her mind and heart. She always thought she'd just head back home after the month, but right now, for the first time, she's wondering if she shouldn't think about staying, do a good ol' pros and cons list to see what she'll come up with. But then there's her project, and the outcome of that if she succeeds will most definitely impact her ability to stay or not, so first things first. Things have changed so much since her little flirty exchanges with François at Wholly Crêpe. Things feel so different, so much bigger than they felt when she would bustle into Wholly Crêpe to get a quick pick-me-up with crêpes and Diet Cokes. She continues to walk until she finds herself on the banks of the Seine, where she sees a crêpe truck.

"Well, that's serendipitous," she says to herself. She stops and orders one, just the way she does at Wholly Crêpe, and waits. As she's waiting, she watches the boats pass underneath the bridge and sees all the tourists waving to everyone on the riverbank. She waves back happily as she's handed her crêpe. She takes the first bite and savors its texture and delicate flavor. *So much better than Wholly Crêpe. Sorry, Philippe.*

As she continues to walk and enjoy her authentic Parisian crêpe, she looks up and sees the beautiful Russian cathedral with its shiny golden domes just off Pont de l'Alma. On one of the poles there is a flyer for an event happening that evening at the American Library in Paris, a talk about Marie

Antoinette and her place in fashion during the seventeenth century. This piques Abby's interest, as Albert mentioned her the other day at lunch. She continues to the library, pitching her gingham-patterned crêpe wrap in the garbage bin before she goes in.

She stops at the counter to pay her nonmember ten-euro fee, then heads into the bookshelf-lined hallway and slowly makes her way down through the shelves. On one of the tiny shelves, she sees a book called *French Women Don't Get Fat*. She takes it off the shelf, looks at the cover, and starts to read the back copy. Then she notices through the hole a man on the other side. He notices her, and their eyes meet. Judging by all the titles around her, she realizes she's in the French lifestyle section and connects the dots that he's most likely a Frenchman. For some reason, she's fumbling to put the book back on the shelf and accidentally drops the book she has as the neighboring books topple off the shelf too. The book-hole man comes around to help her. He's handsome, of course, with dark, longer hair meticulously brushed back this time, with an "Oh, did I forget to brush my hair, not a problem, I'll just casually run my hand through it to fix it" vibe. He's also broody and dressed impeccably. Abby's got *The French Woman's Guide to Sex* in her hands now. She quickly turns it around, hoping he didn't see. Nope. Not doing this again. She boldly turns it back around for the library hottie to see in full force. It bothers her that it's still her instant reaction, to hide what she's really doing or who she really is, with the French. Enough of that. She doesn't know him, and she's certainly not interested in getting to know him, so who cares what books she's looking at?

"Can I help you? I didn't mean to startle you," he says politely.

"Non, non. C'est bon. Thank you, I'm fine," she replies. She gathers up the books and starts to put them neatly back on the shelf. She used to play library when she was little, so she subconsciously lines them all up carefully and correctly. She notices the man watching this with interest.

"Interesting books. There should be one titled *French Women Can Be Overrated and Unfairly Stereotyped, Too*," he says jokingly, attempting to ease the tension.

"That would be interesting. They appear to be highly rated, both within themselves and worldwide," Abby quickly says.

"Mmm, I don't know. I can't figure them out, and I'm French." He smiles.

"That makes two of us."

"Are you a lesbian? I'm okay if you are."

"Uh no, I'm not. And even if I were, it's a) weird that you asked me that question, and b) even weirder that you just gave me your permission?!" Abby curls her face a little in disgust as she replies.

"That's not what I meant. Are you going to read those?" he asks.

"I don't know. I'm feeling that if I'm to stay in Paris, I might need to understand this part of the culture a little better."

"But why? You are not French," he says, stating the obvious.

"You are right. Clearly, I am not. However, the feeling to fit in this tiny, restrictive, annoying, misogynistic box is not lost on me," Abby says, again realizing that she needs to quit oversharing. She starts to position herself to move elsewhere. Just then, she sees Angélique approaching them. Abby says, "Excuse me" to the man and walks over to Angélique.

"Bonjour, this is so serendipitous seeing you here! Are you going to the event?" Abby asks as they do the bisous-bisous.

"Bonjour, I am. Are you also a fan of Marie Antionette?" Angélique asks.

"I don't know yet, but I saw the sign and was very intrigued." Abby smiles.

"Shall we sit together? Find a seat?" Angélique waves her hands toward the chairs all lined up. Once seated, they have a few minutes before the event is to start.

"What do you like about Marie Antionette?" Abby asks Angélique.

"In France, we are all about revolutions. This talk tonight is about Marie Antoinette and how she revolutionized fashion in her time. She created these magnificent wigs that no one had ever seen before, and her dresses were out of this world for that time. We, the French, are all about going against everything that is the norm. It is in our blood. Paris is the epicenter of that. Just look at all the strange little shops and cafés—all filled with hype and so-called 'uniqueness,' but then after all that initial hype is over and done with, only five regulars continue to show up. They will still call it a success because it was *originale*." She says *originale* in her broad French accent.

"It's funny we ran into each other here, as I was thinking about you the other day in relation to this. I thought about inviting you but thought a young woman like yourself would be off doing something more jovial than this. I guess I was wrong."

Abby shrugs. "Caught me. I'm a sucker for the library crowd."

"Apparently. Not sure you will find love in the library, but maybe that's not what you are looking for?" Angélique asks.

"No, I'm okay for now," Abby says, looking over at the man that flirted with her. He smiles at her. She smiles back but then turns her attention back to Angélique.

The lecturer starts her talk, illustrating it with slides of Marie Antoinette in her many dresses and wigs. Then she shows some scenes from Sofia Coppola's *Marie Antoinette* and explains how, being the fashion icon that she was, Marie Antoinette was able to influence politics and all those who were au courant, or "in the know," to bring her vision to life. Her lack of "Frenchness" worked to her advantage in this way. Abby's ears perk up, as once again she knows that term from Albert. How fun! She zeroes in to listen even more intently. Marie Antoinette's way of doing things brought enthusiasm and fun back to a court where life was dreary and dull, stifled by old traditions and an outdated culture. Abby pulls out her *BIG IDEAS* notebook and starts to scribble notes as fast as she hears them. Marie Antionette wasn't French—she was an outsider, an Austrian princess, who with her own mark made France a place of class and style in a fresh new way. This take on what Marie Antoinette did for fashion, her risk-taking and her strength to be herself, keeps Abby writing note after note with her own side thoughts in the margins. This has sparked her curiosity, and she's all-in. It also fits in nicely with her project plan for Parisian Plus-Size Real.

After the lecture, she quickly gets up.

"Where are you off to, my dear?" Angélique says.

"I'll be back. I just want to get some books," Abby says as she heads back to the shelves and finds books on Marie Antoinette with as many paintings of her as she can find. They all remind her of Claudette's entrance with its extravagant murals. She's piecing together now where they came from and why they are so prominently gorgeous in that hallway. This is all helping her to understand Claudette and its brand and why it's so important for them to keep their "traditions." She gets it now but wonders if there's still an opportunity there to shake things up, just as Marie Antoinette did from the inside with those au courant all those centuries ago.

Abby is in line now waiting to check out, as she's already done the paperwork for her library card. Angélique is elegantly sitting in the chair near the checkout counter waiting, and the book-hole hottie is standing in front of Abby in line.

"So, do you come here often?" Abby asks. She knows he's there because of her, so why not take charge and start the inevitable? Why not have some fun?

"Oui, I love it here. So peaceful, so light, and so many great books and lectures." He's holding a copy of Dr. Seuss's *Green Eggs and Ham.* Abby looks at it.

"Dr. Seuss, huh?" She smiles.

"Without a doubt the best way to learn English, especially those pesky articles. 'Do you like green eggs and ham? Yes, I do. I like it in a box, with a fox, in a car, in a bath.'"

"There's no bath." She smiles. They finally reach the two librarians. One is a man, and one is a woman who seems to take her job seriously, based on how thorough she is with scanning books and taking names. They hand their books over at the exact same moment.

"Thank you, Miss Librarian," the book-hole man says, laying it on thick. The librarian blushes. He winks at her.

"Are we interrupting something?" Abby teases him. The book-hole man's librarian gives her the stink eye.

"Don't be silly," he says.

"Now I know why you come here, 'Sam I am.'" Abby gathers her things and pats his arm, then goes over to Angélique.

"Well, look at you. You have mastered the art of the Frenchwoman's flirt. It was quite fun to watch," she says, smiling.

"Really? I have to say it was fun." Abby laughs and takes her arm.

"You know, Abby, I saw something in you tonight. The way you were listening to that lecture. It was like you were building something in your mind, first on the paper and then in you. Let's talk more about revolution and rebellion. Come over soon, yes?" Angélique says with a determined look in her eye.

"Yes, of course. I'd love to!" Abby excitedly says. Abby walks her out of the library and onto the street and helps her into her Uber.

"Su-PEAR!" she says. "Au revoir, mademoiselle."

Abby salutes her, turns around, and walks down the street lined with gorgeous Haussmannian buildings. After the Uber is out of view, she turns to go the other way, and right there in front of her through the trees, she once again sees Madame Tour Eiffel herself. She is twinkling and sparkling bright in all her glory.

"Whoa. You always seem to sparkle just when I need it." She's had enough walking for tonight, and she's exhausted. She heads to the next busy street. While she waits to hail a taxi, she starts to pull her phone out of her bag to take a picture. On top of it is a small leather sketchbook with the monogram *A* on it. She takes it out, and it's chock-full of sketch designs on gorgeous parchment paper done in sleek lines by black felt-tip pen with soft lines of charcoal and a precision-sharpened pencil. She thumbs through it until the end and sees what's written:

Angélique des Places
Head of Creative Acquisitions—Claudette Fashion House

TWENTY-THREE

Let's Coup d'État

With the little leather book in hand and all things Marie Antoinette filling her brain, Abby is heading over to Angélique's. It's a Sunday, and it feels like a good time to drop by with some market flowers and a couple of fresh pains au chocolat in her bag. She can't wait to discuss the gem that "mysteriously" found its way into her bag.

Abby now carries a straw market bag with the long leather straps as well as her cute little Laflore bebebark bag. A little touch of *Par-ee* on a Sunday morning. She knows she'll be the only one eating the pains au chocolat, as Angélique won't touch them. She's told Abby that they are too rich for her. Abby can't understand how this city is full of these flaky, delicious *pâtisseries* and all these women who claim not to eat them. The thought sparks a theory that there is some underground pâtisserie place where they all go and eat them secretly. A dark, underground, secret meeting place with trays and trays of warm, freshly baked pâtisseries for those who secretly adore devouring them. She giggles once again at the fun thought as she takes a bite.

As she's nearing the mermaid door knocker that she adores and has come to revere with fondness because of its association with Angélique, a Deliveroo scooter honks at her and almost hits her. As she's repositioning herself a few feet away, she sees Jacqueline coming from the opposite direction. She's hurrying with a bunch of bags and looks stressed. Abby's never seen her show this much stress so openly. She starts to approach her but then sees she's going through the mermaid-knocker door, too. Abby stops and waits. It's strange and oddly coincidental that they are headed to the same building, the same door, and at the same time. She decides to give Jacqueline a minute to enter. Jacqueline quickly punches in the code to enter, and she goes in. After a good amount of people-watching on the street, Abby heads back to the door, punches in the code herself, and heads to the second door to buzz Angélique's apartment.

"Oui?" Angélique answers over the buzzer.

"Bonjour, Angélique, c'est Abby."

"Bonjour, Abby. Is everything okay?"

"Oui, c'est bon. Merci. I was in the neighborhood and thought I'd stop by with some treats from the market. Can I come up?" Abby asks hesitantly because Angélique usually buzzes her straight in. Today something feels amiss.

"Oh, Abby. Merci beaucoup. Désolée. I'm not feeling very well today. Perhaps another time?" Angélique says, her voice sounding strained.

"Oh, I understand. I'm so sorry you are feeling bad. If you need anything, please let me know. I'd be happy to help," Abby says through the buzzer.

"That's very kind. I'll be fine. Do please come by another time."

Abby slowly leaves the building, and as she steps out of the mermaid door knocker door onto the street again, she's almost run over by a second Deliveroo scooter. The driver honks at her all the way down the street just for added emphasis. She laughs. Parisians in transit—a definite con.

Dammit. She's disappointed that she can't get the skinny on that leatherbound book that she's 99 percent sure Angélique placed there on purpose. So many ideas have sprung from it and the lecture they both attended. She also wants to tell her that she's contemplating staying longer and wants to pick her brain on her petit projet, a turn of events she knows Angélique will appreciate. News, news, and more news, and, of course, all these treats. And no one to share them with. Claire, her neighbor, is away this weekend. She could call her mama or François, but they aren't here, and they wouldn't understand why it's such a big thing for her. For the first time, she realizes that she now has experiences that people back home are not a part of. She's always had the same people being privy to the happenings of her life, but now it's just her and some people she doesn't really know but seems to like and admire. It's a strange realization that her circle of (dare she call them?) friends or her support system has changed so much and become so different from what she's had her whole life. It's another one of those confirming moments that, had she not gotten on that plane, her life would be so different. Something sparked inside her at that lecture, the same spark she got when the event invite landed in the Femme Fatale inbox—a spark of risk, a spark of the unknown, and a spark of curious excitement that was clearly already percolating but waiting for its moment to shine. She got on that plane, and here she is walking down this beautiful street taking a bite out of the best pain au chocolat on the planet.

"Manna from heaven, manna from heaven . . . ," she says to herself.

It's a new week now. Hanging out in Claudette's open-air terrarium-type hallway that's especially for smokers, Abby feels a part of the crowd. She doesn't smoke but likes that she can be somewhere in the building that is still outside, so she goes there frequently. It's also just outside Claudette's canteen—the one for the lowly workers, not the one for the higher-ups upstairs that has a nice terrace and a bird's-eye view of all the Parisian monuments. She's leafing through the leatherbound book, staring at it. "I'm going to call her," she says to herself out loud.

"Call whom?" Albert comes up from behind, startling her.

"Oh, hi! No one. I'm just talking to myself again. What's up with you? How's the new designer? I loved your shots of his prep. Very cool," she says, trying to be supportive.

"They sucked. You know it, I know it, and Sophie didn't hesitate to say so, so it's unanimous." Abby can see he's trying to be stoic. "Why do you hang out here, anyway? Did you bring your geriatric bag of books with you, too?" he says, smiling.

"Very funny. As you can see, I am with un petit book this time. I just like it out here. I can think." Just then, a whole smoke ring passes by, blown with expertise by the smoker to their left. They both let out a series of coughs.

"Maybe we should go in?" Albert asks. "I've quit smoking."

"Good for you. It didn't really fit your brand, did it?" Abby asks.

"No, I just kept coughing and coughing and couldn't get the rhythm right. It was a whole thing, so I bagged it."

"Well, I'm sure I filled my quota for secondhand smoke today," Abby says. They go back inside and part ways, as they are stationed on different floors. Abby heads back to her space and wants to grab her phone to call Angélique to make another stop-over date.

"Abby?" Jacqueline calls. "Can you come to my office, please?" She ushers Abby in frantically, and Abby obediently sits down. Jacqueline looks outside both ways and then shuts the door. She looks stressed again, like when Abby saw her on the street the day before.

"Abby, I need to fill you in on something personal. It is okay? I feel we have that kind of rapport, almost. If not, I'm risking a lot," she says.

"Yes, of course Jacqueline. Is everything okay?" Abby is genuinely concerned.

"I'm not sure. This is top secret I mean top, top. Understood?" She laser-beams her eyes at Abby over her glasses. Abby gets the message loud and clear and slowly nods.

"I'm getting rumblings that the whole team in my atelier, including *moi-même*, may be replaced because Pierre wants to bring in a whole new guard for his new, ridiculous *grande idée* of using only one hundred percent recycled materials. He wants to make clothes from discarded cartons and materials that are then made into clothing. Can you believe it?" She's pacing behind her desk.

"Funnily enough, I can, and in general it's what all fashion houses should be moving towards, but I can see you don't agree?" Abby says. Jacqueline pauses and looks at her.

"You are right. Why am I surprised? He's an imbecile. Of course he would do something so stupid."

Abby's going for it. "I think his idea is kind of cool and the way fashion needs to move to a more earth-conscious way, but why does he need to get rid of you and your team?" Abby asks.

"That's my point," Jacqueline says.

"So, on a scale of one to ten, how much worse is this compared to my idea of Claudette putting real women on the runway in his 'works of art'?" Abby throws a curveball. It's worth a shot, and she's thinking about her next play, which is to meet up with Angélique and see what that little book can offer. Jacqueline looks at her and does the "pouf" and throws herself down in her chair. She's a mess in the same way Abby saw her on the street that day. She kind of likes this side of Jacqueline. It makes her real.

"Where did you hear this?" Abby asks.

"Out in the smokers' fishbowl. It's where everyone knows everything," Jacqueline says dismissively.

"I was just out there. I didn't hear a thing about that," Abby responds, surprised.

"Abby, you would not hear this. You are not au courant, as we say. However, that is the exact reason I am sharing it with you. There is no risk to me as you are not—I'm going to be blunt, you are simply a no one in this organization. You are a visitor. You would not be privy to this, so I can tell you things such as this with no risk to myself," Jacqueline says. Abby is watching her and wondering how to play this next. Jacqueline has told her that she's a no one, but what Jacqueline doesn't know is that she's very much got a potential someone in her hands she can call. To tell her or not to tell her. Mon dieu! So many dilemmas and plot twists here in Paris. It feels like the old soap opera her mama used to watch on weekday mornings, only with uppity French characters.

"Does that make sense?" Jacqueline asks.

"Oui, su-PER sense. I'm no one. I get it. But can I get philosophical for a moment?" Abby asks.

"Really? Now? Sure, why not, it seems to be something you cannot control," Jacqueline says.

"How many amazing, unique, wonderful things were started by someone who was thought of as 'no one' by others? Let me answer that for you: many, Jacqueline, so many. And I'm wondering if this isn't an opportunity for that here, too." Abby is now standing behind her chair, stroking the top of it. Jacqueline watches her.

"Why do you always do that? Stroke the chairs like *les chats* or, I mean, cats? Is it a condition you have or something?"

"It's a security thing. The fabric calms me. It's soft and smooth. I do it when I need inner security. Not that huge-guy-outside-the-main-doors-on-the-street type of security."

Jacqueline looks at her. She then sees the little leather-bound book in Abby's hand with the monogram *A* on it.

"What is that book you have? Where did you get it?" she asks, alarmed. Abby feels a little protective hearing Jacqueline's tone and puts it behind her back.

"Oh, it's just something a friend gave me with my initial on it," she says and smiles.

"Uh-huh. A friend, you say?"

"Yes, a friend back home. Not here in Paris," Abby says.

"So, as I was saying. I may be fired and all of them, too, and I'm stressed. Why am I telling you this?" She stands up again and looks out of the window behind her desk space.

"I thought it's impossible to fire people in France. I mean, I'm still here after my so-called "fashion suspension" or whatever the hell it was," Abby says.

"It is indeed. I would receive a very generous separation package, it's true. Much more generous than the other girls and . . ."

"The one tattooed man?" Abby interjects.

"Oui, him," Jacqueline answers.

"So, what do you want to do?" Abby asks, as she's not sure where this is going, but she knows where she would love it to go—to a major f'ing fashion coup d'état with all the markings of real women wearing those dresses and strutting their stuff down the runway to amazing, pulsing music and the crowd going wild, with posts and Stories and Reels flying across the internet, blowing up, going viral, and daily newspapers running the pictures and Jacqueline and Abby being praised and admired for their never wavering inclusivity. She's smiling at the thought of it and can almost reach out and touch it, like a kid wearing virtual reality goggles. She's right there and can see it so clearly. It's just a matter of getting this stressed-out seamstress on board and perhaps the one token tattooed man because they are, after all, principled, and it would be total equality for all.

"What are you smiling about? This is not a happy occasion," Jacqueline says, frustrated.

"I just had a vision," Abby replies, still in a kind of transcendental state.

"Are you some kind of prophetess now?" Jacqueline says. She slumps back down in her desk chair. "Désolée, Abby. I can see that I shouldn't have shared this with you. It's way over your head and concern. It's my problem, and I will fix it as I always do."

Now out of her daydream trance, Abby says firmly and with a determined nod, "Jacqueline, leave this to me. I have an idea." The little leather book in her hand, she leaves the office with a newfound determination.

"All right, former Madame Head of Creative Acquisitions. I've got one helluva acquisition for you, or at least one helluva revolution. Yeah, that sounds better," Abby says to herself, as she heads out back to the smokers' fishbowl for some privacy and to see if it is indeed true that all business is done here in this polluted, carcinogenic atmosphere.

TWENTY-FOUR

Un Petit Espionnage

Sitting on the terrace at Café La Belle Ferronnière near the Conciergerie, where Marie Antoinette spent the last weeks of her life, Abby is processing all that she's just learned about Marie Antoinette's last days. She's officially obsessed. She's already bought way too many books on Marie Antoinette and checked out even more from the American Library. She's been a bit of a hermit, curling up in her brass bed with her rooftop view out of her window, reading until she falls asleep. She's even dreamed that she met Marie Antoinette and asked if she could take a selfie with her to post on her profile. She feels connected to her story for some reason. Marie Antoinette being different in this society, even though she was a royal, trying to make her way in the culture and gain respect and alliances with the people who thought of her as an outsider—all those aspects feel relatable to Abby (minus the royal part, of course). She's far from royalty, but that's a part of the story she's choosing to disregard. Marie Antoinette's story is a universal one of staying true to yourself in a place that's far from your home. Even up to the day your head is chopped off.

She hired the same somewhat snippy tour guide she encountered at the Rodin Museum. She wasn't cheap, but Abby thoroughly enjoyed knowing that this lady had to work hard to keep her exclusive audience of one interested and that Abby could ask as many questions as she wanted. Abby ended up really liking her, appreciating her commitment to telling the stories of these remarkable buildings and who built them and finally those that took residence in them. Let's just say the lady earned her pay in spades.

Abby takes a sip of her new favorite café drink, *chocolat viennois*. She's grown to love this decadent, extravagant drink because so far she's found that Starbucks is the only place in Paris to get a chai latte. Still basking in the afterglow of her amazing tour with the sad yet insightful stories of how Marie Antoinette lived out her last days, Abby starts to people-watch, a pastime she's picked up with full commitment and focus since arriving in Paris. Many elegant, slim ladies walk by in what feel like uniforms to Abby now. She's noting out loud as she jots down what she sees: "Chanel small pillow bag across hip. Check. Straight-leg jeans. Check. White button-down or white T-shirt. Check. Oversized blazer. Check. Chic sunglasses. Ballet flats or cool platform boots. Check. Check." All the same. But damn, if they don't look amazing wearing that same outfit!

"Hey!" Albert runs up.

"Hey you!" Abby stands to do the bisous-bisous, and then they both sit down.

"How was the tour?" Albert asks.

"So good, I'm still in its afterglow. I can't get enough of her." Abby folds her arms across her chest and leans on the table.

"Of the tour guide?" Albert smiles.

"No, silly. Marie Antionette," Abby says in a French accent.

"You are really obsessed. You've sent me so many pics of her. What's the story?" Albert asks.

"I need your help." Abby looks around to make sure no one is listening.

"Uh-oh. I see that look in your eye. You are up to something that's most likely going to lead to Sophie issuing fashion suspensions all over again and you taking that big bird in the sky back home to your mama." Albert orders a café au lait and turns back to Abby. "Don't do it," he says to her.

"I won't without you," she says back, smiling. "I promise that I only need you for this one part, and then you can just wash your hands of me with the rest. Absolutely no risk to you, I promise. Except maybe some espionage activity that I know you'll be in for—you can wear a whole getup if you want," Abby says.

"What the eff are you talking about? Espionage?" Albert says merci to the waiter and takes a drink of his café au lait.

"I need help getting some info and then taking that info and making something happen with the info," Abby says.

"What office? What info? And you've said the word *info* way too many times. Your level of intrigue is going down by the second," Albert says as he adjusts his sleeves under his linen overcoat.

"Nice jacket," Abby says as she takes another sip of her drink.

"Merci, mademoiselle," he says, smiling and sitting up straight.

"You in?" she asks, rubbing her hands together.

"Hold on there, Agent A, if it's an in-and-out job, I'll do it. If it's all maps and flashlights and black turtlenecks, I'm not. They make my neck break out."

Abby laughs. She's so glad she and Albert have become friends.

"No black turtlenecks. I promise," Abby says as she offers her hand for a handshake.

"Oh god, no. My word is enough," Albert says.

Abby smiles and does a "YES!" with two arms. Albert shakes his head at her.

.· ·.+ · ✦ ✦ · ·.

Once back home, Abby kicks off her shoes and sits down at her little kitchen table, nicely nestled in her bright yellow kitchen with all the sunflower paintings smiling down at her from the walls. She peruses the stack of books she dropped there a couple of days before. One book catches her eye. It's the only one that's not about Marie Antoinette. She remembers that she grabbed this book quickly from the shelf at the English-language bookstore because she liked the title and the cover—a bright-red one with *TWENTY PERSPECTIVES OF PARIS* written in gold capital letters on the front and two beautifully contrasting photos on either side of the title. As she flips through it, she can see that each of Paris's twenty arrondissements is cleverly and carefully represented in the book, with uniquely characteristic photos highlighting what makes each arrondissement different and special. Each chapter has photographs, both vintage and modern, color and black and white, with descriptions of the history of the arrondissement as well as notable people who lived there and how their presence influenced the arrondissement's culture and status.

There are boutiques highlighted and words like *gritty, posh, unapproachable,* and *old money* used to describe each. Abby is devouring it all. She grabs her notebook and starts making notes about each of them, and then she takes some photos with her phone of the map on the inside cover, thinking she will do a Story in each arrondissement. She lists the words that stand out for her as being quick representations of the area. She can see that some have words that cross over into more than one, like *old money*, which can be found in the 16th and the 8th arrondissements, whereas the 18th, which is her arrondissement, and the neighboring 19th have words like *bohemian*, *artsy*, and *Picasso*. She's been so wrapped up in the digital event and its super micro perspective, as well as piecing together her Parisian Plus-Size Real project, that she's missed all these pretty pieces of Paris that this book is urging her to explore. Her phone rings. It's François once again on FaceTime.

"Bonjour, Abby, ça va?" François asks with a huge smile.

"Bonjour, mon monsieur, I am good. How about you?" Abby smiles back.

"Well, this is promising. You've not been so enthusiastic on one of our calls before. Did someone put something *su-PEAR* positive in the Parisian water?" he asks.

"Maybe, or it could be that I think I've found my groove here, almost. I don't want to jinx it," Abby answers.

"And what does this groove look like?" François asks.

"It's fun, and interesting, and kind of mysterious," Abby answers with a spark in her eye.

"Like you," François says as he folds some cloth napkins.

"What?" Abby asks.

"You just described yourself, so maybe you found you and the groove, non?" François smiles as he gently pats the pile of folded napkins and puts them in a wooden shelf behind the counter.

"That's one of the sweetest things anyone has ever said to me," Abby says, a little taken aback.

"Well, I am the sweetest person, as you know. Except when I'm cranky. Not so sweet." He laughs.

"Still sweet," Abby says. François looks away from the phone, and Abby can hear voices from the kitchen.

"Gotta go? Wholly Crêpe filling up? Line outside?" Abby smiles.

"Oh yes, around the block, as you can see . . ." François pans the camera around the café, and the geriatric regulars are there shuffling to their favorite table.

"Aww, I miss it," Abby says.

"It misses you, too." François smiles. They both say au revoir and hang up.

Abby, still smiling after speaking to François, continues turning the pages of this gorgeous book. With every flip of the page, she sees Paris in a kind of bird's-eye view from the top looking down. She puts her pointer finger on the map inside the cover of the book and traces it out, starting in the 1st arrondissement, then moving to the 2nd and the 3rd, and so on. It is a snail shape, ending with the 20th arrondissement on the snail's outer derriere. This makes her chuckle a bit. Of course, it is an escargot, just like Claire said! As she reads more and more about each of the areas of Paris, she writes down the key descriptive words for each one. She can see how she can formulate these into something that connects but in their own unique ways, which then leads to what Paris is all about— never the same, always chic, and building upon tradition. She stands up and says excitedly and firmly, "Yes! That's it. I got it." She then grabs the little leather book and flips through those gorgeous pages once more. This will work!

Once again in Claudette's smokers' atrium, Abby tries to get ahold of Angélique, but she's not answering the phone. Nonchalantly, she tries to stand next to some people who, given their clothes and mannerisms, look like Claudette's higher-ups. Slyly eavesdropping is not her forte, and eavesdropping in French is most definitely a skill she has not yet honed. She's having fun exhibiting what she thinks are some super sleuth skills, but she resembles a five-year-old playing hide-and-seek behind some short curtains. She leans in on one pair who are talking in hushed tones. Nothing but talk of where to go on holiday. Slowly she meanders over to another pair doing the same. When she hears words like *unfair, tradition*, and *equality*, she stays put. This must be it. These folks must be the au courant people that Jacqueline and Albert are always speaking about.

"Abby?" Abby turns abruptly and ends up elbowing one of her subjects in the side, and they elbow her back without even a pause. All gloves come off in the sacred smoking bowl.

"Bonjour, Jacqueline!"

"What are doing out here? Do you smoke?"

"Uh, non. I don't. I like the fresh air."

"This is hardly fresh," Jacqueline says, puffing out her last inhale before throwing the butt in the approved cigarette waste container. Abby leans in to whisper to Jacqueline and gestures toward the pair standing about a foot from her.

"Au courant," she whispers, smiling devilishly.

"You are ridiculous. Come with me." Jacqueline grabs her arm and pulls her to the other side of the smoky fishbowl.

"What are you doing? You are embarrassing me," Jacqueline says, pulling her further.

"I was trying to get information. I want to help, as I said, and I think I'm on to something, something big that could be great, but I just need some more intel."

"Well, you will not find it here."

"Why are you down here? Don't you usually frequent the higher-up smokers' atrium with the fancy canteen?" Abby asks.

"Oui, I do, but I'm trying to only be around Pierre when there are witnesses. I don't want to give him the opportunity to do anything without others being around to witness it."

"Wow, it's that bad?"

"Yes, it is." They both move out of the smokers' area and into the ladies' restroom.

"I'm so sorry, Jackie," Abby says, not thinking.

"Who is Jackie?" Jacqueline responds sternly.

"Désolée. Jacqueline. I thought we were more friendly now with you telling me about your fear of being fired and everything," Abby says.

"That may be true, but I will never be a Jackie. That name is like a name of a woman that falls over men and laughs too much—you know, those ones in those stupid California beach shows courtesy of your home country."

"Or Jackie Kennedy, a style icon," Abby says, shrugging. Jacqueline takes a beat and shakes her head, her lower lip jutting out slightly while she ponders. Abby checks the first three stalls to make sure no one is in them.

"I have an idea, Jacqueline, that I think could work, but I'll need help and support and people who are willing to take some risks." Abby puts the little leather book on the sink and rubs her hands together in a plotting way. Jacqueline follows the book with her eyes.

"Is this your 'curvy cause' again? I've thought more about it, and although I see your point and from looking at your other account, I can see your passion behind it, which I really respect, I don't have time for it, Abby. No one has time for it, and I must be blunt, no one cares about it but you, and as I told you, you—"

"Are no one. I got that loud and clear. But I beg to differ, mon amie." Abby smiles.

"We are worried about our employment and about being treated fairly and respected for our craft, Abby. This is our life. Working here has been our life for decades now, and Pierre will take it from us. In a flick of an ant."

"Do you mean in the blink of an eye?"

"Does it matter?"

"I guess not."

"He is on a rampage. I can't work like this anymore."

"Then what do you have to lose by doing this?"

"Doing what? You haven't said what it is . . ."

"A good ol' French fashion coup d'état. Let's do this, Jacqueline. Let's bring in some new traditions that promote full representation of women and their bodies at this level of fashion. You are French! Revolution is in your blood! You are talented, you are serious, and you know your stuff, and then I can use my platforms for it all both on Femme Fatale and on Plus-Size Real. We could even get the other influencers in on it. It could be a strong shot in the arm and needed energy in this part of the fashion world. If we did that, it would be well over a few million people seeing this. This could be big."

"Shh, when has a revolution ever happened when talking out loud? It's always done discreetly in secret places with top-secret notes and letters. Being discreet is also in the French blood, and your inability to be discreet glaringly shows our stark cultural differences."

"Okay, I'm sorry. I'll be more discreet. Are you willing to talk about it? Un petit peu?"

"You are so persistent."

"And resistant!" Abby jokes. "I'm a little of both thanks to some major life lessons courtesy of Paris, and of course my mama having cancer for the better part of my tween and adolescent years, but that's for a different day. Let's focus back on this!" Abby says, keeping her eye on the ball, which is taking over the haute couture world, if for only one show.

"Meet me at this café tomorrow night. Don't let anyone see you are there. Please try to dress more mainstream French, as you are a dead giveaway." Jacqueline gives Abby a card with the café's address and details on it.

"Wait! Does Claudette have a fashion police? Who are we hiding from?" Abby asks.

"There are eyes and ears everywhere. Especially when people are forming a group of resistance. The enforcers of the old can smell an impending resistance, so be careful who you trust." Jacqueline turns around, adjusts her shirt into the perfect French tuck, and scurries out of the restroom, smiling a little to herself. Abby, filled with excitement, gives herself a high five in the mirror and then breaks out in some serious dance moves. She's on board. Two down. Three to go. She needs to get to Angélique.

"Bonjour, Abby."

Abby, startled, drops her pen. She hasn't interacted with Sophie face-to-face since she swiped her swag upon her return to the event.

"Bonjour, Sophie, ça va?"

"Where is your next post for Femme Fatale?"

"I'm just finishing it up now and will prep it for Jacqueline to approve."

"Non, I will approve this one this time. Please send me the link by tonight at *dix-huit heures, merci.* And just so you are aware, I've been looking at your other account, the fat lives in fashion one."

"You mean Plus-Size Real?" Abby says as she looks at her straight on, ready to pounce. That's her baby, and there is no way in hell Sophie is going to harm it.

"Yes, that one."

"Why were you looking at it?"

"Maybe I want to see fat fashion. Am I allowed?"

"If you really looked at it, you'd see it's a lot more than fat fashion, which quite frankly is enough to make it great."

"Maybe. I look forward to your post for Femme Fatale."

"Okay. Merci," Abby says, noticing that Sophie's swagger is even more cocky than before. A text comes through on Abby's phone.

> Bonjour, Abby! C'est Dr. Le Vot. I haven't heard from you confirming your first consultation appointment at the end of this week. Please confirm, as I have a very full schedule, but of course not a full stomach. ;) I hope to see you soon! Cordialement, Dr. Le Vot.

Ugh. Abby's got to nail this all down, and now it's going to be a long afternoon getting this ready for Sophie by six. She decides to put off answering Dr. Le Vot for now and starts to type furiously, clicking over her photos in an organized way to show the behind-the-scenes, as they have requested for her to do "surface *caca*," she mutters to herself. After she says that, she stops a second and notices that she still enjoys putting these together. It's what got her here—her ability to put lovely, enticing posts and blogs together. She has a talent for it, so why is she dissing it so much? Perhaps it's not a façade if it makes *her* feel good doing it. Does everything have to be a cause or have depth? Or can some things just be pretty and lovely regardless of body size? She's certainly noticed that the French are masters at pretty and lovely. They basically seem to have trademarked it, and that's nice—it's an honorable way to live. Putting out pretty and lovely are worthy ways to spend time, too.

"Bonjour, not-so-Femme Fatale, how's it going?" Albert comes over and hangs over her cubicle wall.

"It's going. Got to prepare a post for Sophie to approve by dix-huit heures. How about you? What's new?"

"Haven't you heard?"

"About what?"

"There's some kind of political doo-doo going on at the top."

"Details on the doo-doo, please."

"I guess there are rumors that Pierre is trying to sack your lady and her girls for his own. Something about wanting a fresher, younger, trendy crowd."

"Where did you hear that?" Abby looks around to see if anyone is listening.

"In the smokers' area. You were so right. It *all* goes down out there."

"Wait. How did you hear all that? I was just out there earlier, and I got none of that."

"Okay, maybe I overheard it in the men's toilets, or maybe when I was making out with Pierre's exec assistant. I can't be sure." Albert smiles and looks around to make sure no one heard him. Abby can see that Forever Frenchie Muriel, who is two cubicles down, has heard everything by the way she's been positioning her body.

"Albert, are you crazy? That's not going to end well for you."

"But it's so worth it—when in Rome, or I mean Paris." He pushes himself back from the cubicle and then pats his cheeks, which are now red.

"Are you blushing?"

"Indeed I am. Just thinking about it makes me all hot and bothered. The making-out part, not the political part."

"Yeah, I got that, but thanks for clarifying. Anything else the exec assistant said that might be helpful?"

"Helpful for whom?"

"Spill the tea, my friend." Abby is pretty sure he's got more in that fountain of fashion intel.

"I think we should do this at a place that's not here. I'm getting weird half-eyes from a few cubicles back."

Abby slowly turns, pretending to be checking out the TV running nonstop Claudette fashion shows, and sees Muriel trying to look inconspicuous by keeping her eyes right at the level of the top of the cubicle.

"Got it. How about lunch later? We could meet at that corner café down the street—you know, the same place where we had our first lunch?"

"You mean our one and only lunch?"

"Thanks for pointing that out. Yes, that one." Abby smiles.

"Great. See you there." Albert does a dramatic turnaround with a little spin-drop dance move as he leaves Abby's desk. Abby goes back to her post but is very distracted by all she's just heard. First things first. She's got to get this post done and into Sophie by six. Pretty and lovely take precedence. The resistance will have to wait.

TWENTY-FIVE

RESTRICT!

All this intrigue and fashion espionage! It's giving Abby a level of adrenaline that she's not had before, and she loves every second of it. She makes her strange six p.m. Sophie deadline, but not without Jacqueline being pissed because Sophie usurped her by insisting that *she* approve Abby's post. They both feel it's odd that Sophie, out of nowhere, interjected herself into the process, when she's normally one to send nasty emails or texts and leave out the personal one-on-ones. Abby is running on a cocktail of adrenaline, fear, and excitement. The show is around the corner, and if what she's thinking of doing is going to happen, she must move fast on all fronts.

Sitting at the café waiting for Jacqueline to show, she's thinking through what's happening and outlining a mind-map on one of her journal pages. How did she get here? Plotting, scheming, conniving, and more plotting. These people she didn't know before she arrived in Paris have their own lives and their own people, so, basically, they're people she doesn't know at all. Who is she to push this "curvy cause," as Jacqueline called it? She can feel the echoes of a "good ol' scapegoat," to quote her dear daddy. He was always there to help her through, but he won't be there this time. She's on her own with this one if it happens.

Causing a secret coup d'état at a major fashion house while saving the crème de la crème, the première of haute couture and her precious atelier of seamstresses (not forgetting the one token tattooed man) was not what she had planned when she decided to come, and certainly was not a part of her contract. This makes Abby laugh out loud a little because she's learned how much the French love and hate contracts. They treat contracts like they are living beings ready to be created and ready to be torn up but not without a lot of scandal and passionate interactions first.

As Abby keeps mind-mapping and laying out questions on the page, writing word sequences that speak to her indecision and clarifying her purpose with each sentence, she looks out at the street and starts to people-watch meditatively. One by one, she follows them, looking at them from head to toe, taking in their varied looks and colors. She does this for some time and then looks at her watch. It's nearly nine p.m. Jacqueline is an hour late. She doesn't have her number, as they haven't crossed that step in their relationship yet. Just as well. She's guessing that Jacqueline forgot or is still at work. She pays her bill and decides to head home. It's been such a day, and she's desperately in need of some downtime at her apartment to further contemplate and plan. She grabs her phone and calls her mama.

"Bonjour, Abby, how are you, darlin'?" Betty Lou's face is in huge portrait mode.

"Oh my, hey Mama. I'm good."

"What's up, buttercup?"

"I just wanted to call and hear your voice."

"Well, that just made my day. Here's my voice and my face, and here's your daddy." Betty Lou puts the camera to show Steve, and he waves.

"Hey, Daddy. What are you two empty nesters doing today?"

"We are about to head out for some lunch. Any suggestions? Have we ever been to your crêpe place?"

"I don't know. Have you? Not with me, as I recall."

"Maybe we should go there, Stevie, what do you think?" Steve gives a thumb-up without looking up.

"Mama?"

"Abby?"

"If you were in a position to do something that could be really great and really life changing for yourself but mostly for others, would you do it, even if the potential fall-out could be bad and hard and put people's jobs at stake?"

"Good lord, what is going on over there? Are you going on strike? I've been reading about how the French love to strike in those little yellow vests. It just sounds like paid days off when they can go out on the streets and break things without paying for it. Seems a little irresponsible to me," Betty says, attempting a French accent, which makes Abby laugh. If there's one thing she loves about her mama, it's her ability to turn on the silliness and her often wacky sense of humor at the expense of herself. She does it without even trying.

"No strikes for me, but you could say I'm involved with something a little on the down-low with some people over here."

"The down-low? Are you doing drugs? I read that the French do drugs at those clubs. A lot of drugs. Please be careful, Abby. Nancy Reagan always said don't do drugs. Drugs are dangerous."

"Mama, I don't even know who that is, and I am not doing drugs. Seriously, I mean, I'm doing something kind of in secret. Trying to pull something off that not everyone knows about. It's kind of exhilarating."

"Does that mean you are doing something incognito? I just love saying that word. It sounds so spy-like." Betty Lou laughs.

"Kind of, yes. And I'm a little freaked out by it, in a good way, a fun way, but there's some potentially serious implications, as I said. I'm not sure if I should do it. I mean technically I've already started it, but I could back the pickup in reverse and leave it on the side of the road and be done with it."

"I'm glad to see you have retained your ability to use powerful metaphors from home with all that French being spoken." Betty Lou smiles warmly.

"I do miss you both so much."

"We miss you, too, sweet pea. We love your emails, and all the folks down at the lodge love hearing about your latest Parisian adventures during our bingo nights. You're our little celebrity here now, and I wouldn't want it any other way. You are living your life over there and doing your thing, just as you needed to and deserved to do, sweet pea. So, don't you come back until you are sure you are done with it, because it may not come again."

"You don't want me to come back?"

"I didn't say that. I said I want you to do what you want to do. It's your life. Live it. Be happy. Do, do, do. Never look back. We need to always look forward and to always keep our hearts in the right place, which is ahead, progressing, moving forward. There now, that's enough Betty Lou wisdom for today. That wore me out."

"Your mama has been watching way too much Tony Robbins lately. She bought the DVD sets on one of her midnight insomnia QVC sessions. She's all pumped up now," Steve adds in the background.

"That was a lot, Mama, even for you."

"I know it was. I just love Tony. He's like a magician. Gets people from crying and dying back to happy and solid and all positive in like five minutes. It's impressive. Listen, we are hungry, and we need to get going. I'm sure you have many plans you need to do over there in fancy-schmancy Paris. I'm so glad you called, sweet pea. Love you loads. Bye-bye." Betty Lou hangs up before Abby can say goodbye.

"Well, they certainly seem to be doing fine without me," Abby says to herself, noting that they were a little too eager to get off the phone and her mama was a little too positive and engaged. "Something's up," Abby says quietly. However, it was refreshing to see her mama so upbeat and happy. It gives her a little pep in her step, too, which was the desired result she was hoping for, so win-win. *Thanks, Mama.*

⁘·+·✦ ✦ ··⁘

Abby, holding tightly to the little leather book, buzzes Angélique's door and rubs the big golden mermaid knocker for good luck. Once she's buzzed in, she heads up the two big corridors to Angélique's door, which is open just a smidge, with Colette the cat waiting for her. Abby slowly walks in and picks up Colette to pet her, but she squirms and jumps down. Angélique comes in to greet Abby.

"Abby, bonjour. Ça va?" She leans in to do the bisous-bisous and then steps back. "You look different to me. Have you lost weight?" she says, looking her up and down.

"Non, not weight per se but maybe I've lost a little anxiety." Abby smiles.

"Come in, come in. What's that in your hand?" Angélique says as they walk into the main room, where they've had tea before.

"How are you feeling? I was a little worried. I was wondering if you were ill," Abby says genuinely as Angélique heads into the kitchen.

"Oh, don't you worry about me, my dear. I sometimes have spells and I need to rest a little. That's all it was, a little spell, and my daughter came and helped me that day, so all was well." Angélique returns from the kitchen with some Badoit and tea. Abby puts the book on the table. Abby was so engrossed with the book that she didn't hear what Angélique said from the kitchen. "So, you found it?" Angélique asks with a wink.

"I wasn't sure if you dropped it in my bag intentionally or by accident?" Abby asks.

"What do you think?" Angélique smiles.

"Intentionally," Abby responds.

"Well then, shall we talk more about Marie Antionette and her clever ability to slyly change the fashion world?" Angélique asks as she sits back in her chair and slowly drinks her tea. Abby watches her and gets the distinct feeling that although Angélique is getting up in her years, she's still up for an escapade or two, and Abby's all-in as her accomplice.

. .+ .+ + . .

Dressed in a white overcoat with her name embroidered on it, Monique Le Vot—with *Diéticienne* underneath it—steps out of her office with a menacing, rigid flair.

"Abby Allerton?" the woman calls out to the empty room.

"I guess that's me," Abby jokes. The doctor nods and waves her in without responding. Inside the room, there is a camera on a tripod and a desk on the far end with an open laptop and then a white screen against the wall. To Abby it looks like a pared-down photo shop back home without the cheesy props and backdrops.

"So, Abby, I will speak English, oui?" Dr. Le Vot says, looking at Abby for approval.

"Oui! Yes, please. Thank you," Abby says.

"You are nervous?" she says, looking over her glasses.

"Un petit peu. This is not exactly something I'm used to doing. What's the camera for?" Abby points to the camera.

"You will see. So, are you willing to make the change?"

"What change?" Abby asks.

"Your body, your health, increase your level of attractiveness," she says.

"Oh, right. Yes, that change. Angélique tells me you are the Parisian dietician to the stars. Is that true?"

"Oui! Angélique and I have known each other for ages. I've seen her daughter, too, but she is not so receptive. A more rebellious girl than needed for this method. We had to part ways."

"Interesting," Abby says, piecing together a portrait of Angélique's daughter that is getting more and more appealing every day.

"I cannot reveal their names, that would be unprofessional," Dr. Le Vot says.

"Right," Abby says as she looks at all the newspaper clippings on the wall behind the desk.

"I'm a dietician, but I'm not a trained dietician. I have my own method. Nothing in life comes without hard work and discipline, and this method for your body is no exception." She takes out her tape measure and with both hands pulls it back, making a whipping sound. This makes Abby jump back a little.

"Is your method solely based on restricting and measuring?" Abby asks. She's already scared of the answer.

"Oui! Look at how clever you are. Already grasping it. It's simple, n'est-ce pas?"

"Okay, what are we talking? No wine, no bread, no beer?" At that, Dr. Le Vot laughs like a fox ready to pounce on an innocent, unaware bunny. She stands up and waves for Abby to come to the white screen.

"Take off your clothes. You can keep your bra and underwear if you'd like, but I need to see the fat."

"The fat?" Abby asks.

"The fat! Is it not self-explanatory? I find it's better if you expose yourself. I take some pictures and keep them on file, and we see progress or no progress. If progress, we celebrate. If no progress, we have serious conversation. Make sense?"

Abby can see that Dr. Le Vot enjoys her job a little too much.

Abby slowly takes off her clothes. With each movement, she is telling herself that this is for the greater good, not for her. She's telling herself that this experience is one of her body image gremlins on steroids—taking over and preparing for the apocalypse. It's insane and she knows it. This whole culture seems to have a deep sense of anti-fatness, and it's personified in this Dr. Le Vot. Abby is holding steady the parts of her that society has instilled in her, the parts that wonder if this crazy-ass method does in fact work and if this is the reason that most French women she sees in Paris are thin. Are they all coming here, and are all their before-and-after photos still on file in that old laptop on her desk? She doesn't want the pics; she just needs the names. Abby moves over to the white screen in her cute leopard-print bra and underwear. Dr. Le Vot is taking measurements once again, her trendy glasses hanging over her nose.

"You must keep to the restrictions every day. Every hour. You may be hungry, that is true, and you will want to die some days, but you will get the results you want, and you will learn self-control and *restraint*!" She says the final word with emphasis, so it's clear that she's basically copyrighted it for anyone tempted to steal it.

"The French woman's biggest ax in their bag is that they know how to restrict themselves but most importantly when to restrict themselves—this is the key." She uses her pointer finger to relay the message even further.

"The 'ax' in their bag? I don't understand," Abby says.

"Oui! In their bag," she confirms.

"Oh! I think you mean tool in their bag, not ax in their bag."

"It's basically the same thing, non?"

"Not the same thing, but let's move on. So, can we regroup here a second? Are you an actual dietician? Did you earn a degree or take a class?" Abby inquires.

"Non, I have my own method. I took classes but found them to be too weak and not effective for the woman who wants drastic results quickly. It works."

"But can we call starving yourself a method?" Abby cocks her head to the side.

"Non, you do not starve. That would be inhumane. Maybe it will feel like starving, but it is just retraining your brain and stomach to need and want less. I think that will be the most challenging for you based on the body I'm looking at right now."

"No offense, but your whole method feels inhumane to me," Abby quips.

"So honest. Alors! You will live on eight hundred calories a day. Drink only lemon water, but of course you may have your café au lait because it is not life without a café au lait every day, non?" Dr. Le Vot laughs to herself.

"I don't like café au lait. I drink chai lattes. Can I have those?"

"Why not. It will take its place. No problem!"

"You know that eight hundred calories a day is not really living, right? I'd say what you're telling me is the epitome of *not living*," Abby says.

"But you will lose all this!" Dr. Le Vot grabs a backfat roll from Abby's back playfully.

Abby jumps forward. "Whoa. That was not okay," Abby says firmly.

"And you will be so slim and feel so light and so sexy . . ." Dr. Le Vot moves her hips around seductively. She looks like she's doing the hula-hoop.

"And also, you'll be . . ."

Abby jumps in because she's had enough standing there in her skivvies being pinched and prodded. "*Misérable!* I'll be miserable. I'll be hungry and mean and self-critical and unhappy. How can this be worth all that?"

Dr. Le Vot goes to the camera and checks to see all is set up correctly. "That is for you to decide. I can only offer the path. Like Jesus. You must come to the sea to fish," she says.

"I'm not sure that's the correct order of that story, and I'm pretty sure Jesus had his disciples eat more than eight hundred calories a day. With all that bread breaking and walking and discipling . . ."

"We will never know. But I know this works. Consider me a miracle worker." Dr. Le Vot laughs again.

"Like Jesus, yeah, I got that," Abby replies, resigning herself to the fact that there's no disciplining that she could ever do here to make a difference. She needs to get what she came for and take one for the team to get it.

Dr. Le Vot is ready to take pictures. "Now say fromage!"

"Why should I say that? I can't eat it!" Abby forces a smile, but her eyes are dead. She's pretty sure this is her own personal hell on earth and wondering how many women have come before her feeling it, too.

"Are we done? I'd like to get my clothes back on." Abby is now mentally officially done.

"You know you need to love your body more. Not cover it up. Wear things that are tight. That is also part of the method. So that when you see all those rolls bunched up in a tight dress, it will remind you to not to eat and to stay on the method." Dr. Le Vot finishes up the paperwork for Abby to follow—the same paperwork that will be torn up gleefully into tiny little pieces and spread all over the street on the way home.

"Yeah, I don't think that's loving my body—that would be more like loathing my body. Maybe you should call this method 'Loathe your Body to Lose Weight with Eight Hundred Calories or Less,'" Abby says in an informercial tone, using her arms to highlight an image of a billboard.

"Oh, you are a clever one, Abby. Now that will be two hundred euros, please, cash only."

Abby pulls out her new cute wallet she found at a Sunday market with her new, shiny cards. She hands Dr. Le Vot four fifty-euro notes slowly across the desk. Dr. Le Vot takes them, but Abby doesn't release them from her hand. She's having a hard time letting go of two hundred euros just to hear that she's fat (kinda obvious, knew that) and on top of that to have pictures taken of said fat. She stands there and finally releases the money fully to Dr. Le Vot, who quickly shoves the bills in her drawer that she quickly unlocks and locks in a matter of a second.

"Now be clever and *restrict*! Also, I have a kind of group support that I do with some clients. I think you would be good for this. I can add you to one of the group lists if you'd like."

"Yes, please. I will need all the positive reinforcements I can get. Is it a blind copy, or do you put everyone on the email?"

"Why?"

"I'm new to Paris, and I'd love to get to know some people, and if we are all doing this *restrict* together, it might be nice to go for walks or something."

"Aw, that's nice. How about I give you a couple of names that I think will suit you?"

"How about ten or twenty?" Abby smiles big.

"That's a lot of support. But okay. I will check with them and get back to you."

"Could you do it in the next couple of days? Paris is hard, and I could use some friends."

"Ce n'est pas un problème. I'll send you a message introducing you to ten of my clients. Until the next time." Dr. Le Vot gets up, hands her the info papers, and opens the door for her with a wave for her to exit. Abby leaves the office and sees the next client. She's chubby with frightened eyes and is holding her bag tightly close to her. She looks like she's on her way to the guillotine. Abby feels so sorry for her and hates that look in her eye. She wants to barricade herself in front of the door to save her from going in and having her spirit crushed, like she's just experienced. Instead, she smiles warmly at her. The lady shyly dismisses her and goes in for her session with the self-proclaimed successful yet dreadful doctor.

Un Chat Noir

A bby can see Jacqueline sitting in her chair behind her
desk through the office's window walls. She can see her
nervously tapping her thimble on the pane of glass protect-
ing her old antique desk from damage. Abby then sees Pierre
headed that way.

"Jacqueline?" Pierre shrieks as he comes towards Jacqueline's
office with a lady from human resources. Abby sees Jacqueline
tap one last time slowly on her desk, then carefully put the
thimble in her top drawer.

"Oui?"

"Come with us." Pierre doesn't stop at the doorway, and
the woman from human resources follows dutifully behind.
Jacqueline takes her time getting up and scans her office for
things she might take with her. From her desk she grabs her
pen holder containing a letter opener, vintage knitting needles,
and a beautiful antique pen. She holds it tightly to her chest
as she walks behind the other two in a perfectly straight line
through her area of the office. All the seamstresses, interns,
assistants, and administrators stop working to show their
respect, as if they are watching a funeral procession, with their

heads hanging downward in disbelief and bodies inching forward to watch and support without saying a word. Jacqueline's eyes appear to be welling up, but she's keeping it together.

"Jacqueline?" Having gotten wind of what's going on after being out in the smokers' atrium, Abby is running toward the funeral procession, her energy the opposite of stoic. She's all out there, and it breaks the tension.

"What's happening?" Abby asks as she walks alongside the cortege.

"Is it not obvious?" Jacqueline asks with some frustration, as if to say all seemed calm until this grande américaine came along.

"Are they firing you? They can't do that! I won't allow it!" she says, whispering so loudly it's comical.

"Please, let me be, Abby."

"Jacqueline, I'm so sorry. I didn't mean to . . ." Abby steps back and away from the three of them. She turns to look at the line of people, and they all shake their heads in a kind of collective silent shaming. She gets the message.

. ∴+· ✦ + ·∵.

FaceTime is ringing, and Abby looks down at her phone. She's sitting at Café de Flore, trying to journal while nursing her way through the horrible feelings of what's happening at Claudette with a chocolat viennois. She keeps looking at the phone as it rings. It's François. He's called her a couple of times more since their sweet conversation. She's texted him that she's swamped but will call soon. She feels she has no space for him right now, and that feels sad yet kind of freeing. Ironically, a man from the city where she might stay is now a last tie to the place she's always called home. Is he the last thread to home? It seems her parents are clearly enjoying their newfound lease on life without their adult child living with them. Despite all the drama and the difficulties that she's been through, she kind of likes it. It's been, and continues to be, invigorating. She's found that she can maneuver in chaos impressively well and keeps her wits and clarity about her when others may not. Getting to know Claire, and even Albert, has brought a level of fun and curiosity to her life that she had no idea was even inside her. Even though he's French and a part of so many special moments, François is a part of her previous life, one that she's not sure she wants to go back to anymore. Anyway, back to the task at hand . . .

Her phone rings again. It's an unknown number. She picks it up.

"Allô?"

"Abby? It's Albert."

"OMG. Hi, Albert!"

"Where the hell are you?"

"I'm trying to recover from what happened. Where are you?"

"I'm at the office. You need to come back. It's completely crazy here, and I think you should be here. They were asking for you, too."

"Who's 'they'? Is Jacqueline back?"

"Non, but I've heard from my connection, you know that connection I have, the really reliable and really active connection, that one . . ."

"Yes, Albert, I got it. What did you hear?"

"I've heard that Jacqueline is threatening to file a lawsuit for unlawful termination and that Pierre has been brought into HR for that unlawful termination. It's a mess," Albert says, breathing heavily.

"Okay, listen, my mama had cancer for many years, so that's a mess, a life-changing, big ol' hot mess. This is not a mess. This is, well, I don't know what," Abby says, calming herself down with some perspective.

"Can you just get back here, please? I can't take this intensity by myself."

"Aw, I'm touched. You need me there as your friend. That's sweet, Albert."

"Yeah, yeah, whatevs. Just get your not-so-Femme Fatale plus-sized butt back here."

"Okay. On my way." Abby takes one last swig of her drink and waves down the waiter to pay like she's lived in Paris for years. Her confidence in this simple process is palpable, so much so that the waiter complies without even a hitch. Abby notices that she is giving off the vibe that she is just another capable customer in Paris, not a customer smelling of insecurity that he could pounce on accordingly. No fun for him but a huge progress point for her. Does this mean she's officially arrived? She places all her belongings in yet another cool, chic bag that she found at a boutique shop near her apartment and heads off. Back in action, back in the thick of things. She can't help but smile. She really does love it.

· ·+· ✦ + · ·.

Abby walks into Claudette ready to tackle whatever she finds. What she finds is Sophie crying, wiping her eyes daintily with a handkerchief and giving quite a performance for someone who usually comes across as having as much emotion as a rock. She is surrounded by a whole group of seamstresses and her usual entourage of women and of course the one tattooed man consoling her. Abby looks for Albert but can't find him. She pulls out her phone and tries to text him, but it's not going through. She slowly moves closer to Jacqueline's office, hoping she'll find her there as always. It's empty. *Merde.* She walks down the hall to the conference room, where through the glass she sees Pierre ranting and raving with the HR director, the same lawyer who was in her deception meeting, and the CEO of Claudette. Abby's only seen the CEO in pictures, not IRL. She's fascinated that he looks so impish. Like a little elf on steroids, but an elf who's been impeccably dressed by his elfin mother. There are, of course, several beautiful glasses and a bottle of Badoit on the table because even in such scandalous times style and beauty cannot be compromised. Their hands are gesturing fast, and they are expressing themselves so much that the energetic waves of emphasis seem to be swirling around the room, searching for understanding and resolution without anyone to catch them. Abby can't keep up as her French is not up to par, but she does understand a little, surprising herself. She hangs back a bit to try and understand. She pulls out her old class-required, trusty French dictionary that she's had since her high-school French classes from her bag and stands around the corner of the conference room door ready to go. She hears the words *unacceptable, framed, unfair, not admissible,* and *disloyal,* and something about feathers and recordings are all ringing a bell.

"Mmm, maybe my French isn't so bad," she says to herself. She still looks up some words that she overhears, any that she can't understand. They all abruptly stop talking and stand up to leave. Abby hurriedly shoves her dictionary back in her bag and tries to hide behind the space where the door will open so she won't be seen. She has forgotten that the door opens inward, not outward. They all come filing out, and as Pierre stomps out, he flings his flamboyant piece of fabric thing, and it hits Abby in the face. They are all oblivious to her, caught up in their own situation and selves. Abby hurriedly goes around the corner, trying not to be seen, but runs straight into Sophie, now completely fine, all cleaned up and looking as put together as always.

"Bonjour, Sophie, ça va? You looked so upset earlier but look so not upset now . . .That's either strange or hugely manipulative." Abby's eyebrow goes up.

"Bonjour, what are you doing here? You shouldn't be here. The second you showed up, all things went to *sheet*. You are what we call in French *un chat noir*. Trouble follows you everywhere. Just like a black cat," she says with contempt.

"Do you mean to *sheet*? Or do you mean to 'shit'? There's a difference."

"I'm sure you know what I mean."

"Where's Jacqueline?"

"*Je ne sais pas* . . . It's too disappointing to talk about. I don't want to upset myself again. It took forever to pick up the pieces, so now I'm moving on."

"Are we done here?" Sophie asks, frustrated.

"I didn't think we were doing anything to be done with . . . ," Abby retorts.

"Just remember what I said," Sophie says.

"The black cat thing? I love black cats. They always cause a reaction." Abby smiles.

Sophie walks around her and twirls her shawl around her neck, and for the second time, Abby gets hit in the head with it, only this time it's the side of her head. "FFS," she says to herself, sounding like Claire, as she watches Sophie saunter off in her usual style.

Abby decides she's not going to get any info from her and that she needs to find Albert, the man with apparently all the connections but not "those" connections. She walks through the floor, trying to be inconspicuous, but every single person is saying bonjour to her and making it very difficult. She finally reaches the hall where HR is located. She sees a big group going into the office, so she decides to walk by, pretending to look at a pile of blank paper on top of the paper supply boxes. She looks in and sees the smartly dressed elf CEO—and Jacqueline! Thank god! She has a momentary lapse of memory due to her relief and excitement that she is indeed trying to be sly and does a fist pump in the air. Jacqueline sees her and shoos her away frantically. Abby moves past the doorway and makes a prayer sign, and Jacqueline rolls her eyes, but then when Abby is out of sight, Abby can see that it made her smile. Hopefully Jacqueline will get the message that she's revered, even if it is from the perceived troublesome yet well-intentioned américaine.

TWENTY-SEVEN

Merde Encore!

Angélique slowly pours the tea that Abby doesn't like into her cup. Abby watches, and the sound of the tea being poured and the precision with which Angélique does it feels meditative and calming. Abby has come here for one thing and one thing only—to finalize this project of hers. During one of her previous visits, Angélique spent the whole visit showing Abby the originals, truly gorgeous designs from the 1960s, 70s, and a touch of the 80s, but just a touch of the 80s, as Angélique didn't like that era, with its exaggerated shoulder pads and ridiculous pants like parachutes that made people look like they were wearing an elephant's backside, full of garishness and poor design. Those are two things that could never be applied to Angélique. It's what made her start to think it was time for her to retire. Abby, fascinated, laps up every word. She takes a sip of the unwanted tea that she's kind of now gotten used to when, finally, Angélique stands up and says, "Follow me, ma chérie. And bring the book."

They both head down her long hallway, lined with original doors with golden door handles, until they come to the very last door, which is closed. She opens it and says, "Voilà! A lifetime of work, a lifetime ago." Abby steps in and see racks of black bags and shelves of fabric, accessories, and more framed designs. She can't believe that in this one room there is a whole world of design and fashion history. She then notices the big, framed picture of a much younger Angélique holding flowers at a show, surrounded by what looks to be her team of seamstresses, minus a tattooed man this time. All women.

Abby moves closer to it and scrutinizes the faces and the staircase Angélique is standing on. It looks familiar to Abby. The space is very elegant and refined, but it's different from Claudette; it's more subdued.

"See something you like?" Angélique asks.

"This picture is lovely," Abby says warmly.

"Yes, it was a bittersweet day. Happy to move on but sad to leave my life there behind."

"I can relate to that." Abby smiles.

"Can you?"

"I mean, in some way I suppose I'm doing the same, but it's a completely different level."

"I can see your point. Whenever we leave a place in which we've spent so many hours and days and weeks and months and years and decades, it's very difficult to say goodbye. I suppose you leaving home to come here is similar but on a smaller scale, non?"

"Oui, c'est vrai." Abby looks over at the black bags and is literally dying to see what's inside them. Angélique knows this and is up for a little fun. She takes one and unzips it. She pulls an item out and says, "Try it on. The fit should be generous to you."

"Really? You'll trust me with it?"

"I didn't say you could steal it." Angélique laughs.

"I would be honored." Abby takes it delicately, disappears behind the old modesty screen in the corner, and starts to undress. The style is reminiscent of a 60s shift dress but upgraded by the exquisite fabric. It's looks like one of the first day-to-night pieces that are so prevalent now, unique, and special because it was done forty years ago. It has avant-garde patterns in pastels with black outlines. It's dressy with an edge. She pulls it on and is thrilled that it fits her. She comes out and twirls around.

"It looks beautiful on you. It's as if I made it just for you. Look at that. The fit is perfect. You know, those eras' styles were much more forgiving on a woman's body. Look at yourself."

Abby turns around and faces the mirror. She gasps. It is indeed stunning, and seeing herself for the first time in this type of a garment, in Paris, no less, leaves her speechless. She's overwhelmed and starts to cry. Angélique gives her a tissue from the box on the little table by the mirror.

"I keep these here for that exact purpose. I often cry when I see how I've changed."

"I'm crying for another reason."

"And what's that?"

"Because you have been so kind to me when you didn't have to be, and you have shown me what it means to be truly elegant."

"Oh, my dear girl. The pleasure has been all mine. Your maman must be very proud of you."

"I hope so. I hope so." Abby continues to turn around and look at all the angles of the dress. There isn't a bad side, in fact there are only good sides all the way around. This is an ingenious design for a woman with flab. Abby zeroes in on Angélique.

"Angélique, are these the ones?"

"Indeed."

"They are amazing. I'll get changed."

"No need, you can keep it on and enjoy it. If you want, you can go home in it. Just promise to bring it back on the day, will you?"

"Of course I will. I'm going to start crying again."

"The tissues are by the mirror. But first let's take a picture of you." Abby gives Angélique her phone, and she takes the shot. She hands the phone back to Abby for approval. It's beautiful, with the perfect light coming in through the window.

"Enjoy, ma chérie," Angélique says nonchalantly as she leaves the room. Once they are both back in the living room, Abby gets out her *BIG IDEAS* notebook and turns to the page with the heading *Project Parisian Plus-Size Real*.

"So, what I'm thinking is go big or go home, which might be the case for me going home after this, so I want to be sure I go really big on my way out!" Abby looks for a chenille pillow, but it's nowhere to be found.

"Daring, my dear. What's next?" Angélique says.

"Just one more thing, Angélique," Abby says.

"Oui?"

"Why are you helping me?" Abby asks.

"Because of something the great Coco Chanel once said: 'Beauty begins the moment you decide to be yourself.' I saw that moment in you at the library. It was in your eyes. And I want to help design it because I will regret it if I don't, and I have enough regrets in my life."

"Wow. I'm so touched." Abby smiles.

"Let's get started. We've got a lot to do." Angélique smiles, too.

.: ·.+· ╊ ┿ · · ·.

Abby continues to feel like she's the cat's pajamas in this gorgeous dress, walking confidently across Paris, nodding and saying bonjour to all who cross her path, even if they promptly snarl at her and dismiss her before she can even get out the first syllable. Walking and strutting with her AirPods in and taking in all the beautiful architecture makes her feel like she's made it somehow—like she's crossed over a threshold and is finally a part of the beautiful-people scene in Paris. She wonders what she would think about herself if she were sitting at the café across the street doing a session of Parisian people-watching, being a true *flâneuse*, and saw herself strutting by. "Unique, flamboyant, daring, and brave." That's what she would think, and that would be accurate. She might add "sophisticatedly cute," too! She then has an awareness that kind of blows her away. Every woman should feel this, and they should feel that they have many options that make them feel this way. In fact, she gets it. She gets why women "put the dog on," as her mama says, to walk these beautiful streets. It's the perfect combination, this gorgeous city and women who want to feel beautiful walking in it. It's worth the effort, and it brings an instant upgrade to the self like no other place can.

She continues to mull over her conversation with Angélique, and she's excited and scared. Angélique seems so on board, but Abby isn't sure if she'll come through. Doesn't matter! The whole thing is worth the risk, and once again the invigoration it's bringing is making her walk even faster and with more purpose. She's excited to get home and decompress with Claire and show her this amazing dress. She will say, "You are stunners, Abby." Abby's sure of that.

She's almost reached home and stops to get a bottle of Badoit and some berries to munch on, deciding it isn't a day for a pâtisserie but for something a little lighter, and the colors of the fresh fruit on the stands are enticing. Wearing this dress makes life appear in full color, and she wants to enjoy every single minute of it. And then it happens, the familiar oozing of dog poop on her right shoe. She looks down and looks around. No one. Not a dog, not an owner. Just Abby in this beautiful dress with her foot in poop. She stands there, dangling one foot in the air and looking for Angélique to come to the rescue, which she knows won't happen. She looks at the poop and then looks at her dress and makes the connection. The dress is how the world sees Paris, the perfection, the precise way of doing things that are glamourous and pretty. The poop is the reality. The imperfection, the real life that is dirty, gritty, and hard. She's a walking Parisian experience. She decides she can live with that if the dirty, gritty, and hard aren't dog excrement every time and the gorgeous dresses are plentiful. She moves over to the side and takes out the tissues from Angélique's room and lets the cleanup commence. "Disgusting, completely gross, but worth it. So worth it," she says to herself.

. .+. ✦ ✦ . .

Abby and Albert are sitting at their same lunch spot. They are both eating the first slices of baguette that were placed on the table.

"Don't you feel you've just been given a bundle of joy when that basket is put on the table?" Abby asks.

"Mmm, so much joy. But I must cut down," Albert says.

"Why?" Abby asks as she takes another slice.

"I'm getting the Frenchie fanny pack, and I don't mean the ones Claudette sells." He laughs.

"Nothing bad about that. You are in Paris, right? I could give you Dr. Le Vot's number." Abby laughs.

"Indeed." Albert waves to the waiter for another basket. He nods.

They both take a sip of their respective drinks, her a Diet Coke and him a Shirley Temple.

"So, let's get to it. I got my 'group therapy' list of ladies from Dr. Le Vot. We are all good there. I'm formulating my message to them. Any more intel on the J and P situation and what's going on?" Abby asks.

"Yeah, so like P tried to fire J, but she hit him back with an unlawful termination suit because what he had on her was apparently some recording or something that Sophie had acquired that was showing she was insubordinate and was trying to take over his designs for the show or some stupid shit like that." Albert takes another drink. The waiter brings over two soupes à l'oignon for them. They slowly start to pull the cheese from the top around their big spoons, pulling it as high as they can to see who can pull it farther. Abby wins. She laughs and rolls it around her spoon one final time as she dips it in for a spoonful of the broth this time and slurps it up. It is so warm and comforting. Albert watches her.

"You are really into that soupe à l'oignon." He smiles.

"I so am. I think I could marry this soupe à l'oignon," Abby says, laughing.

"You are so weird." Albert smiles.

"But you love me," she says, smiling.

"Mmm, I find you amusing," he says.

"Back to the firing. So, where did your au courant connection say it was now? I mean, it's so close to the wire," Abby says.

"I'm hearing that they worked out an arrangement with J and that she's unfired. Is that a word? Or not fired. And because that recording wasn't consensual, unlike my times with P's assistant, of course, they couldn't use it against her, whatever it was, so it was thrown out. Basically, him trying to screw her made it possible for her to screw him back with all the abuse he was dishing out. Serves him right."

"Go, Jacqueline. That's such a relief. I was so worried about her. Weird about the recording. I wonder what that was and how Sophie got it . . . ," Abby says and then slurps another spoonful of soup into her mouth.

TWENTY-EIGHT

Tout Se Rassemble

It's a fashion flurry backstage. Feathers, quilted jackets with jeans, gaberdine pants, and pleated silk taffeta dresses are all flying around between the head handlers, who are making sure each model is properly fitted and ready for her debut on the runway. Claudette, having been criticized of late for lacking diversity in its fashion shows, has chosen to go with models who are as diverse as possible. Freckles, black skin, brown skin, Asian models, models with mohawk hair, and models with hair all the way down past their asses. It's an eclectic model mix, and the energy is high. Eclectic and diverse is wonderful, but sadly it doesn't cross over into body type. All are stick thin and with the same coat-hanger bodies, as expected. Not one model has a body that's remotely different from the other, despite the valiant effort to show that Claudette is, in fact, versatile and can change with the times. Apparently, that versatility is only applicable to a point, a safe point, and today, there's nothing groundbreaking about it.

As planned, Abby is assisting Jacqueline and her crew at their backstage tables doing last-minute adjustments, which are many, taking photographs, doing any running around or passing over—whatever needs to be done. The music is blaring in the back, and half-naked models are gallivanting around until it's their cue to stand in line and slide into one of the masterpieces. Abby and Jacqueline are actively giving each other eye signals as to what's next, and Jacqueline is constantly looking at her phone. No text.

"Is something wrong, Jacqueline? I mean other than the obviously stressful thing going on around us," Abby asks, concerned.

"Non, I'm just waiting to hear from someone," Jacqueline answers, looking at her phone. Abby notices that Jacqueline's armpits are moist, showing through her crisp white shirt.

"Can I get you anything, Jacqueline?" Abby asks.

"I'm so nervous. Maybe more nervous than I should be. I've done so many of these, like clockwork."

"But this one is a little different." Abby smiles and winks.

"That is true," she answers, putting a wet blanket on Abby's enthusiasm.

Pierre is making his rounds. "Jacqueline?"

"Oui, Pierre. Ça va?"

"Everything looks acceptable. I see you made the required changes, and they are satisfactory," Pierre says, speaking in a super-professional tone.

Watching out the side door, Abby can see based on the number that Angélique's Uber is approaching or rather speeding up to the Grand Palais. It stops just short of hitting a paparazzi photographer. She sees Angélique jump out as fast as a spritely old lady can and yelling at the driver to open the back. He pops it open, and when the black and blue suit bags are passed to Angélique, she almost falls over. Abby starts to go over to her but stops after seeing the driver offering to help her. Angélique shoos him away.

Angélique yells at a paparazzo. "Eh, vous!"

"Oui, madame?"

"Put your offensive weapon down and help me get these to the backstage. It's worth a couple of pictures for you. Capisce? *Allez, allez! Dépêchez-vous!*"

The paparazzo grabs the suit bags and struggles to stay upright under the weight of them, grabbing one of the luggage carts by the door to hang them on. They rush to the side door. Abby rushes over to meet them. Angélique flashes her lifetime Claudette employee card at the bouncers and asks them where the ateliers are located. They direct her. She moves swiftly and carefully so as not to be seen by Pierre and other higher-ups. She reaches the location where she needs to be and stops abruptly.

"A photo, madame?"

"Oui!" Angélique turns to pose with him and takes a selfie with him. At this point, Abby can see that the paparazzo has been duped by a savvy, très élégante old lady. He smiles knowingly and goes on his way.

"Angélique, what was that?" Abby asks as she comes up to her, laughing.

"He asked for a photo. Why should it not be of me? I know a thing or two about these shows. Have you forgotten?"

"Non, I certainly have not. Now, where do I take these? They look like burial cloaks of head designers from the past." Abby laughs.

"They are from the past, that's for sure, but with some elegant and needed updates, as you know. Did you get your part done?"

"Yes, and you'll be happy to hear that I finally went to see Dr. Le Vot, so I guess she is useful for me, just not in the way you originally thought," Abby says.

"We shall see," Angélique says.

Abby and Angélique maneuver backstage through the models, champagne, and flowers until they find the tables. Angélique sees Jacqueline and heads toward her. She stands behind her as she threads a final piece on the model's dress.

"Easy now. Careful. Take your time." Jacqueline, without turning, smiles but remains softly stoic.

"Merci, but I can do it myself without your help. I've been doing this for a long time now. Without you, I might add."

"C'est vrai, but some things never change, ma chérie. And one of those things is Claudette's technique and attention to details. Keep steady. Where do I put these?"

Abby sees Angélique, Jacqueline, and the twenty suit bags. Bingo. All in place. She rushes out to the back door, where twenty curvy, voluptuous models are waiting. All of them were found courtesy of Dr. Le Vot's weight-loss group list and an empowering message for them to join today's event.

"They are here. Just a few more minutes, and we'll get you ready." Abby sees Albert's WTF face, as he was told he was doing something else entirely but is now babysitting a group of loud, curvy women who are a bit unruly. She's guessing his dismay is because he thought his espionage efforts were done with after scouring Dr. Le Vot's files, doing the tedious job of collecting all the ladies' measurements to give to Abby so that she could pass them to Angélique. That was more than he bargained for. Now he's being asked to do this.

"Albert."

"What the Femme Fatale is going on, Abby?"

"I know, I'm sorry. Please trust me. Can you please line them up in the order on this paper, and I will text you when it's time to send one to me? Can you do that?"

"Yes, I'm not an idiot."

"Merci, monsieur. You are a doll."

"So, I've been told," he says. Abby runs back to Angélique. She grabs and starts to push the luggage cart with all the black suit bags. It registers with Abby that Jacqueline and Angélique are conversing as if they know each other. She didn't introduce them, and she's horrified. She rolls back, almost taking out a couple of models, then stops straight in front of them a little abruptly. It's the adrenaline. She's all over the place. Literally and internally.

"Wait, do you two know each other?" They look at each other, confused, and then look at Abby.

"Do you know my maman?" Jacqueline asks.

"Your *maman*?" Abby shakes her head in amazement.

"Oui, c'est ma maman, Abby. Who do you think she is?"

"She's the most amazing seamstress I've ever seen. Just like you. OMG! *You are related.* It all makes sense now. This is amazing. Of course! I can't believe I didn't put it together before now. You have the same eyes. I knew that. How did I not get this earlier?"

"My dear, if you do not get those bags to the proper place, I'm afraid all of us will be kicked out and charges will be drawn against us for trespassing and ruining the fashion world's biggest show on the planet. Run along," Angélique says with an even tone, showing she's a pro at this and has done these shows a hundred times before without a hitch.

"Oui, I'm going." Abby speeds off, pushing the cart.

"Now let's see how this circus plays out, shall we?" Angélique says dryly. She gives Jacqueline another bisous-bisous and heads toward the front row of the runway. The theme of the show this year is Elegantly Empowered Women. The backgrounds and looks all represent women in their various life roles as maman, CEO, artist, wife, teacher, etc., with diverse looks and pieces showing the contrast of daily life with elegance. Sitting in the first row are all the heavy-weight editors from *Vogue*, *Elle*, *Vanity Fair*, major Hollywood celebrities, and the token reality TV star. Abby is preparing the bags she needs in the lineup. Albert has checked in, and all is well outside with the coup d'état crew. All's in place. She sends the first text.

Send in number one, please.

The first voluptuous model scurries in wearing only Honeylove shape wear that Abby was able to get through a sponsorship gig, plus high heels. She hands her the bag and says, "Mettez-le, s'il vous plaît" with a warm smile. The woman takes the dress out and gasps. It's gorgeous and certainly nothing she's ever worn before. She daintily and carefully puts it on. Abby checks in and does the final zip.

"Très jolie, mademoiselle." Abby's eyes well up. "Wait! I know you! You are the woman from Dr. Le Vot's office the day I was there, right? I'm so excited to see you here. Oh my god, this is so meant to be. You are so brave to do this!" she says, excited.

"Oui, c'est moi." The woman smiles. If nothing else comes from this, this moment of seeing this woman look so elegant and beautiful on the same level with the models a few steps away makes it all worth it. Beauty and elegance are not deter-mined by size, and this certainly proves it.

"Alors, what is your name again?" Out of nowhere, Pierre is standing right next to Abby and in front of the curtain with the curvy model straight behind. Abby hurriedly shuts the cur-tains and holds it closed.

"Je suis Abby. Can I help you? Jacqueline is over there if you need her. I'm just finishing up some last-minute things."

"No, no, it is you I want. Our photographer for the show has called and is claiming he's *trop malade* and can't make it today. You will take the photos. You're not as good as him, that's for sure, but you are here and he's not, and I might have scrolled your account with the event, so it'll have to do. Capisce?" Pierre is waiting for a response, but Abby is staring at him as she tries to formulate how she's going to get out of this and simultaneously processing the fact that the head of design at Claudette just told her he "might have scrolled" through her account. This is crazy.

"Hello, lady?" The woman behind the curtain tries to get Abby's attention. Abby keeps the curtain closed and holds it tight. Abby gives off distress signals as big as a ship in the high seas about to go down, way down to Jacqueline. Jacqueline quickly heads over to the rescue.

"Pierre, what do you need?" Jacqueline firmly says. "I need Abby on duty with my items, and the items are behind the curtain, so she can't really leave this space. We are shorthanded, as you know."

"We are down a photographer. She needs to take pictures," he says, again trying to sound professional.

"I'm sure we can find someone else to do that. Where is the other influencer, the gay rainbow one?"

Abby looks at Jacqueline in panic, trying to send her a message telepathically that he's not available because he's involved with their project.

"Um, he's not available because he's doing something else. Something else that you asked him to do, Jacqueline, don't you remember?" Abby says with emphasis so that Jacqueline will get the message.

"Oui, okay. Yes, I remember it now. I did ask him to help with something. You'll just have to look elsewhere. Maybe

Sophie? You both seem to be cut from the same cloth, no pun intended."

Pierre swings his cloth thing around his neck and starts to leave.

"Oh, Pierre?" Jacqueline asks.

"Oui?" he says as he turns around to face her again.

"Don't forget, you have a very important interview with Fashion TV in just a few minutes. I know it's not ideal timing, but all the models are ready, so I can handle the show for you," Jacqueline says, smiling. Pierre puts his hand to his chest and takes a deep breath.

"Oui, I am very aware of this poorly scheduled and planned interview, and I will be there."

"Désolée," Jacqueline says and nods.

Abby lets out a huge sigh of relief and grabs her phone to text Albert.

Send number two, please.

"C'est bon?" Jacqueline looks at Abby.

"Oui, c'est bon. The first one is ready, and it looks truly exquisite. Your maman is amazing."

"Yes, she is. I can see it was a team effort with you two," Jacqueline says.

"When did you know I knew her?" Abby asks.

"The little leather book gave it away." She smiles.

"Right. I missed that detail," Abby says.

"Which is why you could never be an atelier. You must love details," Jacqueline says as she looks over her glasses and winks at her.

"Well, I think it's something you two should consider doing together regularly," Abby says.

"So persistent. I must go back over there now. The show must go on," Jacqueline responds.

The second curvy model comes over and is given her bag while the first one waits. This continues until the first ten are ready to go in record speed, each in stunning outfits with no less wow factor than the ones on the main models prepping for the show.

"*Cinq minutes!*" the show's main producer shouts backstage.

Abby takes some quick photos of her curvy crew. She looks over at Jacqueline across the space with the other models and gives her an affirmative nod that all is well. Jacqueline nods back. The music starts. The models are in line. Jacqueline walks down the line, looking with precision at every piece of clothing hanging on them. She stops at one model at the end of the line.

"Très jolie. This looks beautiful on you," she says in English to the model, a hot six-foot American model newly discovered on the streets of New York.

"It is a team effort, yes? You make it, and I show it to the world," the newbie model replies sweetly.

"Oui, it certainly is. Merci. You are ready." Jacqueline smiles.

"*Une minute*," the producer yells. "Take your places."

The music starts, and images of women from around the world in different life moments start to show on the walls behind the catwalk. Faces and scenes from Ghana, China, Japan, Iceland, and finally Texas . . . ? All offering a feeling of the whole world being in this one space. The energy is contagious. It's electric, and right from the first moment it's clear to everyone that once again Claudette is the best there is. They are masters at making fashion not just something to be worn but something to be experienced.

One by one, the thin, perfect models do what they do best, showing why they are worth the huge contracts they have, sashaying with perfect rhythm to the runway music that the producer has chosen—relevant, upbeat, and with a touch of techno to keep the mood high and enticing. The crowd is swaying and moving to the beat, looking each model up and down and all around, showing this is the one place where the once-over makes sense. It is the perfect setup for what's about to happen next.

The penultimate song starts to play. Albert runs to Abby. Albert takes hold of the curtain, and Abby moves to the stairs that lead to the runway. She gives the DJ the next three songs to play immediately after Claudette's playlist has finished with a hundred-euro note for good measure. He nods. Abby has orchestrated with Jaqueline that Pierre won't come out for his final walk and bow until after the three songs she's just maneuvered. Jacqueline took care of the logistics with the producer, threatening him with a piece of political blackmail that Albert overheard during his little exec assistant rendezvous. All pieces in place. The last song on Claudette's playlist is nearing the end, and the final pieces of Jacqueline's team's work are on the runway now. Albert lines up the curvy coup d'état crew and shuffles them to Abby, who gives the signal to the DJ. The song ends, the runway empties, and there is a pregnant pause; the crowd, which was expecting Pierre to arrive for his applause, is looking around, wondering what's next.

Meghan Trainor's "I Love Me" starts to play at full blast, and curvy model number one struts her stuff down the runway. As she walks the runaway like a small girl coming out on stage for her very first dance recital, smiling broadly, the first image on the huge screen behind her shows a quote by Paulo Coelho that François sent her:

Maybe the journey isn't so much about becoming anything. Maybe it's about unbecoming everything that isn't really you!

She stops and turns. The crowd goes silent, and everyone looks around in disbelief. It's a blank look of "What is this?" It makes curvy model two walk out with much trepidation, so much so she almost trips. She keeps it together but is shaky. At that very moment, serendipity occurs: the new hot model from NY comes out in a black, sleek dress, very vintage, clearly an Angélique masterpiece that Jacqueline maneuvered. The NY hot find looks down at the model and starts to do a fun jig. They give each other a wink and start to walk in perfect synchronized harmony. More phrases appear on the big screen:

All bodies are beautiful.
My body is not your business, but creating
fashion for all bodies definitely is.
There is no perfect body.
All bodies are good enough just the
way they are.

More body-positive phrases fill the screens as the backdrop and the curvy models, along with a few of the beautiful pieces they are wearing, begin to steal the show. The pieces are gorgeous vintage couture from the 60s, 70s, and 80s that have magnificent, roomy, yet tailored structures. All designed and updated by Angélique with Jacqueline's assistance. They worked hours on this, hours they didn't have, and Abby feels a huge debt of gratitude because of it. The models are a walking movement unto themselves. A true revolution walking down the runway, stopping to turn all the way around, so no piece misses its time in the limelight and no woman is left unseen. The crowd finally catches on, with each phrase and each beautiful piece being showcased in fun, vibrant ways. They go wild.

They all stand up, clap, and move with the music. Some of the celebrities are now mouthing the words to "Made You Look" by Meghan Trainor and singing them as a personal anthem, then "About Damn Time" by Lizzo starts to play as the final ten models make their way down the runway.

Pierre has been in the interview feeding his narcissism, talking about himself and his innovative designs, completely oblivious to what is happening on the runway. The roaring affirmations from the crowd are at a level he's not heard before. The interview concludes, and he slowly walks into the backstage space and sees that some of his models are in the back watching what's happening on the back screens of the show. They are all dancing and caught up in the energy of what's happening out on the runway with the curvy twenty.

Abby somehow having eyes all over the place sees Pierre creeping toward the screen and saying, "What is this?" Then she sees him head over toward her near the backstage runway entrance. He is now running over to her.

"Ehhh! What are you doing?" He gets in her face.

"I'm watching change happen. What are you doing?" Abby asks pointedly, hoping to god he doesn't grab her and throw her to the side and ruin this, as he could so easily do. He looks at her and then looks out at the crowd, which is taken over by the amazing scene.

"And who did this?"

"I did, with the help of some very talented women that you totally disregard and dismiss—oh and one token tattooed man, and of course let's not forget Albert. But mostly those women out on that runway are the real heroes. You are watching courage *live* right now. To walk out there in this culture and with this crowd is hard and frightening," Abby says, looking out at them as they all shine. The song is coming to an end, and Abby's almost forgotten how this all ends.

"Stay right there. Don't move, Pierre."

"Where am I going to go, to lunch? It's my show, you idiot." Just then Abby sees Sophie walk up with one of her sinister looks on her face. This can't be good. Abby can't see through the crowd of models but sees someone walking with her. She looks again. By the time she realizes it, it's too late.

"Bonjour, Ms. Allerton. I believe you know this person.," Sophie says with a smirky smile.

"Oui, I certainly do." Abby looks over at Heather.

"I decided to come to Paris. After all, I was invited," Heather says to Abby unconvincingly, trying to be mean.

"Femme Fatale was invited. And that's both of us," Abby says, taking a deep breath. Meanwhile, the music is still going, the models are still walking, Abby can see Pierre is losing his required professionalism fast, and Jacqueline is running up to her to get with the program—her program—as it's going to go to shit any second out there. Pierre runs over and grabs Jacqueline by the arm.

"It was you. I should've known!"

"Non, it's *always* been me, and that's what you should've known, Pierre," Jacqueline says firmly and pulls her arm away. Lizzo's song ends, and as the song ends and the long-legged models head out for the final round around the runway, the DJ plays Meghan Trainor's "Me Too." The curvy models naturally add themselves to the loop so that the group of women walking around the runway one final time represent different sizes, different shapes, different styles, different colors, different looks, but with one thing in common—they are all in Claudette haute couture pieces—vintage redesigns as well as current visionary pieces.

"Abby, we have to deal with this," Jacqueline says.

Abby looks at Heather, sizes up the situation, and says, "Want to join me? As you said, you were invited."

Heather looks at her, then looks at Sophie. "Let's do this. I'm not sure what this lady's vibe is, but I'm so not here for it."

Abby does a fist pump and says, "Follow me, fellow Femme Fatale. Let's bring some closure to this thing."

She and Heather run off with Jacqueline to bring this to a magnificent close. Sophie looks at Pierre, and they both do the "pouf" and follow them.

The song ends, and the screen shows:

Brought to you by Claudette and the founding influencers of Femme Fatale and Plus-Size Real because there is no difference—WE ARE ALL WORTHY OF TAKING UP SPACE, AND WE ALL DESERVE TO SPARKLE NO MATTER WHERE WE LIVE OR WHAT OUR SIZE!

The crowd is still on its feet and yelling universal praise. They don't know it wasn't Pierre that did all this. Abby watches him, in his usual fashion, bow dramatically, as if all of this was him, then turns to Jacqueline. She pulls her shirt down, straightens her hair, and sturdily walks to a more central location on the catwalk with her tape measure and fancy fanny pack still around her waist. They take hands and bow to the ongoing praise. Jacqueline looks at Angélique, who is wiping tears with one of her crisp linen monogrammed handkerchiefs.

"Aw, Maman," she says. The song ends, and the whole place is wanting more. Jacqueline goes and grabs the sleek mic from

Sophie's head. There's a little struggle, but she's victorious and puts it around her own head. The DJ turns the music down.

"*Attention, s'il vous plaît.*" The crowd starts to quiet down. Jacqueline walks back to where her *maman* is sitting.

"Thank you, everyone. There are some things I want to say that I feel I've earned the right to say after so many years. The first one is that this show today has been something out of this world for me and for Claudette. It has embraced everything good about Claudette and all that I and my irreplaceable atelier members work for every day, which is to be original, to magnify beauty where it is not normally seen, and to bring to life designs that are true masterpieces.

"It takes hours, days, weeks, and months to put these together. Pierre, your designs were magnifique, and it was an honor to bring them to light, but you will excuse me if I take some of your spotlight and give it to a woman who dimmed her spotlight so many years ago and today with a little help from *moi* showed it in its full glory. Please give Angélique, former haute couture première seamstress at this design house for over forty-five years, the applause she's been waiting to hear for decades. I'm so proud to be your daughter, and I'm so proud to be a part of your legacy here at Claudette." Jacqueline goes over to the front row and kisses her maman. Abby then brings Pierre, Jacqueline, and Angélique gorgeous bouquets of flowers she arranged for them, then goes back to her more obscure spot. Jacqueline wipes the tears from her cheeks and continues.

"Now, as you know Claudette brought some influencers over to this first-ever influencer event to highlight this show because Fashion Week needed more hype. Right?"

The crowd laughs. "These influencers were bothersome to me; I didn't like them. They were invading my creative spaces with their questions and their proposals of posts, thinking they knew everything, and we knew nothing about how the world of fashion has moved on from what we know to be true. But there is one influencer that I want to mention, because as you see on the big screen, she has officially outed herself to show that she is not what we thought she was and she no longer is, but she is something else entirely. This is someone that I have affectionately, and I'll admit a little rudely, called a no one, but now, seeing her day after day work hard to make this happen, I see she is quite the someone. A someone with vision, with heart, and a strong sense of justice. Abby Allerton, our visiting influencer, merci beaucoup for showing us that following a dream has ripple effects and that those effects are what change the world and may even change a whole industry's ethos. Merci, mon amie. It has been a true pleasure."

Abby's mascara is all over her face now, and wiping with Angélique's handkerchief has only made it worse. She doesn't care. She leans across to hug Angélique.

"You look like a badger, my dear," Angélique says in her ear. Abby laughs. She looks over at Heather. Heather takes her hand, leans over, and whispers to her, "You did it," and smiles.

"I did, didn't I, in the craziest way!" Abby laughs.

The DJ starts the song "Tilted," the one Abby heard at that first fête with Claire, and all the models dance off the runway in a relaxed, fun way. In the back there are selfies, pics, autographs, makeup exchanges, and accessory gifts being passed around. The curvy twenty are playfully taking lessons from the professionals on how to walk the runway while the professionals are enjoying letting it all go and being playful without the stress of having to look perfect. The air of imperfection amid supposed perfection is being lassoed in by everyone, and Abby is doing all she can to enjoy every minute of it, taking picture after picture because, as her mama said, it might not happen again.

"Abby," Angélique says.

"Yes?"

"Stop and take it in."

"I just want to make sure I don't miss anything about this day. I want every piece of my memory with me, and I'm going to post the beejeezus out of it with full disclosure of how it came to be and every step of the way."

"I know, but memories are made from what we feel at the time, so that when we think about it again, we relive it a little bit. That's the beauty of memory, and that can't be captured with an iPhone." Angélique gently pushes Abby's hand to put her iPhone into her dress pocket.

"Look, take in what you've done." She gestures her arm around for her to see the scale of the scene filled with differences, energy, and collective acceptance. Abby takes a deep breath and looks around. She's right. She's been so busy trying to capture it all on her phone that she's missing the enormity of what's happening right before her eyes.

"I couldn't have done it without you. Merci, mon amie." She smiles sweetly and gratefully and kisses Angélique on the cheek.

"Vive la revolution, ma chérie. Marie Antionette would be proud." Angélique slowly walks away and heads toward the door. Abby, watching all that's happening around her, sees Heather and one of the twenty head her way. They both run up to her for her to come join them. Together, they all run back to the crowd and start to dance.

Today is a living dream, a dream Abby didn't even know she had until she arrived in Paris. Now that the dream is here, alive and well, what's next, she wonders.

Four Months Later

J aqueline is carefully positioning and hanging up some eclectic designs on metal rods dangling from the ceiling. Abby is carefully adjusting a sun hat on a real-sized mannequin dressed in one of Angélique's caftan designs. The embroidered phrase *C'est mademoiselle* is on its rim. Jaqueline picks up one of the quaint chenille cross-over bags for a colorful accent to her thin mannequin's outfit. All women are represented here. That's the ethos of this boutique, and it will never change.

Albert is picking out a flamboyant ceramic peacock from a box to put on a shelf on top of the rack. He turns his nose up at it. "What is this? Tacky, that's what it is . . . ," he says quietly.

"I heard that," Abby shouts back, smiling.

There is a huge chandelier hanging in the middle of the shop, and the walls are white stucco with a Provençal feel. Lizzo's song "Special," featuring SZA, is playing through the speakers, and there is a line forming outside the door. Claire is carefully pouring champagne into the glasses at the personal design table with techy chic tablets ready to go, to create personalized designs for any size.

"Are you ready?" Jacqueline asks over her glasses.

"So ready, *et toi?*"

"Oui!" Jacqueline heads over to the door and opens it. *"Bonjour et bienvenue!"* she says, as any self-respecting shop owner in Paris would do. The line of ladies, of all different shapes and sizes, starts to file in with the fun energy of a girls' night out. Due to the press coverage and a few carefully placed interviews, the opening of their boutique was much anticipated and widely followed. Femme Fatale, Plus-Size Real, and Claudette all endorsed it, of course. A trifecta of acceptance is present here.

Later that evening with the sun setting and its vibrant colors framing Paris in its own watercolor scene, Abby, happily exhausted, leaves the shop. Having had no time for lunch due to the many interviews and clients, she's ready to plop herself down somewhere and sit. Thanks to connections via Claudette and their sizable investment, the shop is located on the prestigious rue Saint-Honoré, which gives her an ample selection of places to go for a much-needed reprieve from the crazy yet gorgeous day she's about to leave behind. She heads out toward the Jardin des Tuileries, as she wants to plant herself on those green chairs for a bit. *Zut!* All are taken, so she goes across the park to an enticing-looking corner café with its typical Parisian gingham tablecloths and old wooden silverware stations. She sits down, picking a perfect place to people-watch. She is facing the street, as you do when you are an experienced Parisian, always with her back to the café itself. Tired and finally able to release all the busy and wonderful energy for a bit, she doesn't see the waiter approach. He comes up behind her.

"Bonjour, mademoiselle. Let me guess: a crêpe with crème Chantilly and a Diet Coke?"

Stunned, Abby grabs her scarf. Her eyes start to well up. This better not be a dream. She turns around ever so slowly, and there he is, live and in the flesh. François.

He smiles and says, "Paris is always a good idea, non?"

La Fin

Acknowledgments

The idea for *Plus-Size in Paris* came to me early one morning as I was walking around the Bois de Boulogne in Paris. It was a particularly warm and sunny day, and I was pondering how much I felt like an outsider at that time, having been there a year already. It seemed my larger body was a constant and consistent source of dismissive looks, comments, and discussion. I was tired of it. Then I looked ahead and saw this woman who was around the same size as me, and I wanted to run up to her and ask, "Can we be best friends forever, or at least until I leave Paris?" I kind of chuckled to myself, but it brought a deeper, more vulnerable awareness up in me that I'll never forget. I wanted and needed to feel that I belonged somewhere, not just fit in. I had been trying to fit in. Immediately after that, I had the thought, *I wonder if being plus-size in Paris is hard for her, too.* And I repeated the title again, "*Plus-Size in Paris.*" And then my steps got a little faster. I could feel the creative stars aligning. *Plus-Size in Paris.* That's a title of something. Is it a blog, is it a book, or is it a screenplay, a movie? I couldn't get to what it was meant to be at that time on that walk, but I knew I was on to something. Elizabeth Gilbert's *Big Magic* had just come out around this time, and I knew I had been hit by some Big Magic with that title!

Why am I sharing all this in the acknowledgments section of the book? Because that magic, that feeling of this story or experience being something new, with realness not yet shared, is what all these people who helped me get it to where it is today felt, too, after I would tell them the title of my book.

I wrote this book at different locations in Paris, Dublin, and St. Augustine, Florida, our annual summer vacation spot. I had beta readers in the US, France, Ireland, the UK, and even in Singapore. This book started out as a screenplay that I brought to a weekly screenwriting class over the course of a year, the first year I lived in Dublin after moving there from Paris. During one of those evening classes, after reading my pages for the first time, one of the other writers, Tara, said, "This works, Erin, because it's f-ing real." I will never forget that, Tara. Thank you! That first comment has fueled me ever since.

This is a fiction book, but maybe it's a smidge of autofiction, too. Regardless, it comes from a place of authenticity and sincerity, and that's why I think it resonates and doesn't resonate for some. More on that later.

Back to my acknowledgements. This will be a longer read because I believe in spreading the joy, the light, and the goodness, especially when it comes to creativity. I've learned in the process of formulating this story in whatever form—screenplay, novel, etc.—that spreading the joy and being grateful is the lifeblood and source of it all.

First and foremost, I need to thank my mother, Betty Lou. (She hated the *Lou* part of her name. Sorry, Mom.) She died at the age of fifty-four when I was twenty-three. With everything I've done creatively, I can feel her hand gently on my back nudging me in the right direction, encouraging me and leading me to the right people at the right time. Thank you, Mom, for being the loving, supportive presence from beyond. I owe you so much.

I need to thank my father, Dohn Delano. Dohn was a hard person to love. His generational trauma was strong in our family and did much damage. I know now, also from beyond, that he's mellowed, he's helping, and he was the most well-read redneck I've ever met. I learned so much about so much because of his love of reading and learning. He was always with a book, and now his three granddaughters are, too. That's a good legacy. I feel at peace with him, and a big part of that happened when I started seriously writing.

I want to thank my younger brother, Matthew. Watching the early 90s classic movie *French Kiss*, starring Kevin Kline and Meg Ryan, with you so much that we knew the lines gave me such creative juices for good banter and dialogue, and the memories that came up of our laughs together were heartwarming and helped me write. I miss that.

My first big risk with writing was while living in Paris. I applied for the American Library in Paris novel writing workshop (2016–2017) with Jessica Levine. Jessica was in Paris for one year, and she wanted to find her community of writers as she wrote her second book. I was lucky enough to be chosen to join, and that year, once a month, we all brought our writing submissions to the group. It was so scary, but I will never forget sending that email to her to be considered as a very beginner writer at 4:43 a.m. because I couldn't sleep, thinking about what if I don't send it off? I couldn't shake the deep regret I would have if I didn't. I know my mom nudged me that early morning to finally do it, hearing in my mind, *Don't be wishy-washy, Erin. Just do it!*

That group for me was so many things, but I need to thank them all, because those fellow writers, even with their at times searing criticism, helped me, and it made me keep trying so that my writing really shined and got better. Thank you, Jessica, for being a trusted mentor that believed in this book from the very beginning concept to what it is today. Aoife, my dear friend, I hope you start writing again. Thank you for being a constant voice of support. Thank you for always supporting from afar, and I so enjoyed our Thursday night writing dates when we were both still in Paris at the library and finished up with some soupe a l'oignon around the corner. Thank you to Alexandra, Christine, Eric, Jane, Kay, Lauren, and Nancy. I literally ran to our group meetings, I loved it so much that year! Even though I was sharing a story about Russia with a spy angle in that group, when you told me my writing was horrible (not mentioning names, but you know who you are), it was the seeds of discernment I needed to learn about my work and that readers and their tastes are highly subjective. Thank you!

My second little writing group in Paris was with fellow expat moms. I put myself out there, and you guys did, too. You encouraged me and told me, "You've got something here, keep writing." Thank you, Liz, Jennifer, Mara, and Maia. You were and are part of my target audience, so to have you all unanimously say you loved it meant I needed to carry on. *Merci, mes amies!*

Thank you to Jennifer Hart, my personal trainer in Paris, who helped me walk off those angsty feels when I was trying to find my place in Paris, being well over a size 10. Your reaction to the title the first time I shared it with anyone else was something I'll never forget. Your defiant spirit to make your place in Paris without compromising who you are was inspiring. Thank you!

Moving from Paris to Dublin now and back to the screen-writing group at Flying Turtle Productions. Barry McAvoy, such an a-hole sometimes, and I know I can write that because he'll laugh and appreciate my candor. Barry, you said when I submitted my pages the first time that this story was "fresh and a good new take on Paris, there's something good here." You once again affirmed this time, in a totally different city with a different cultural vibe, that I had something tangible with legs. I will be forever grateful for that First Look night when you headlined the *Plus-Size in Paris* script, and those Irish actors acted out my work, my writing. I felt like I had made it. Truly. I didn't care if it ever went any further. The magic of that night, the audience's reaction, and when they were applauding, you looked over at me, and I saw in your eyes how proud of me you were and how thrilled you were by the reaction it was get-ting, was what it deserved because it was good, risky, and real. Thank you. I'll never forget it.

Aisling, Andy, Aideen, Mary, and Nessa—my screenwrit-ing WhatsApp crew. Couldn't have done it without you all. Aisling, you opened that sarcastic and sensitive heart of yours creatively to me, and I felt so honored to get your very sincere feedback after I handed you that printed-out manuscript at coffee one morning without a folder or bag. I was so nervous for you to read that first draft. You are an agented screenwriter, after all, with all kinds of awards. You sent me the most helpful feedback. You approached it from a place of being invested in it with me and for the story. You helped me see that Abby needed to be empowered, not a victim. I'm so grateful to you. Andy, your humor and true Irish warmth were the fuel in my sometimes-downtrodden tank, always checking in, making sure I was still moving forward. Aideen, you are a spiritual giant. Thank you. Nessa, thank you for reading my draft and for being a willing and helpful heart. You gave me the most well-written, detailed feedback I could've asked for at that time. It was so helpful. I'm here for your YA novel!

I need to thank Helen Downey. My editor of choice in Paris. As I wrote my first draft chapter by chapter, I would send it to her to read and edit. She edited it with love and grace. I will never forget that. She wouldn't let me pay her. Helen did that out of the goodness of her heart, and I'm so honored you shared your time and your effort with me and my different view of your adopted home city. You cheered me on and have stuck with me, making sure to check in and nudge me further. Thank you so much. Your support was life changing for me as a writer.

I need to thank Vanessa Fox O'Loughlin, who writes under the pen name Sam Blake in Ireland and the UK. The International Literary Festival Dublin is what really shot me out of the cannon. Placing in the Date with an Agent competition showed me that this could work in what's called the traditionally published arena. When I met with my assigned agent that day, she told me I was a good writer and that my story was good, and she gave me her contact info to submit to her. I left that conference that day feeling like I had won an Oscar and wanted to dance down Grafton Street in Dublin shouting as such. Again, I was so thrilled, I could've just stopped there. It was a huge affirmation that I had something. I feel I must apologize for the subsequent emails/correspondence to that agent. I was so nervous and so unsure of how to be in this new arena, and now I know some very cringy mistakes were made on my side. Not my best look, but I learned, and I appreciated the learning. Back to Vanessa. With a generous spirit, she responded to all my emails, cheering me on and directing me to other agents in her network who might be interested. She was available every step of the way a whole year and a half after that Date with an Agent competition, right up until I signed with my first literary agent. I believed in me and my story and kept going because she did as well, and I'm forever grateful to her.

I want to thank Lizz Choi, who reached into her Mary Poppins networking bag and connected me with a friend's wife who happened to be a literary agent—Catherine Cho. Catherine was the first agent to read the "polished, ready-to-submit draft" and the first real agent I queried. I'll be forever grateful to her for her wonderful rejection letter, saying in part that there was a lot to admire, but it wasn't in her wheelhouse, and for being willing to pass the manuscript on to her colleague because she saw something promising in it, too. Catherine was a huge part of me finding the query letter inside me that really made my story shine. She was kind and open hearted when she really could have told me to buzz off. Little did I know that three years later I would be moving to Korea, and having had that special experience with her, reading her book *Inferno* (highly recommend), and learning about the Korean culture was going to help me assimilate to Korea in a way I had no idea. Life is so funny sometimes, and the paths we cross—well, we just never know.

I need to thank a whole crew of beta readers that gave me good, solid, thoughtful feedback over the past seven years of writing, rewriting, editing, and writing some more. All their feedback got the novel to where it is today. Nina Hipps, Judith Hammerschmidt, Rosemary Pitts, Deanna Gesuero, Mary Wessels, Michelle Louisor, Dana Thompson, Tamra Dunaway, Shelley Marsh, Brigid Blanco, Elizabeth Milovidov, Claire Matthias, Mara Barth, and Anshu Agrawal. All of you brought such different perspectives to the story that I was then able to find the threads that worked and part with the ones that didn't. I am forever grateful that you all took the time to read it and took the time to tell me such valuable feedback.

And I can't forget Fantine, my French teacher in Seoul, who went through it one final time to make sure the French parts were good and solid. She was a real champ, reading those scenes where French people are depicted less than favorably, keeping balanced within herself, and I considered it a real compliment that she liked and enjoyed this book. It's not easy to read things about one's own culture that are negative or hurtful to others—it takes courage to take it in and mull it over and not shut it down. She did it with an enormous amount of grace, and I'm forever grateful. I want to thank Gianluca Russo for his book *The Power of Plus*. It is an inspiring book on plus-size fashion, and it came out exactly when I needed it to keep going.

I have some dear, never-wavering cheerleaders I need to thank as well. Without the phone calls, the reassuring texts, and constant mirroring that I can do this regardless of the many setbacks in rejection letters when querying and agent feedback sessions, I wouldn't have been able to finish it and get it to this point, the point where I took back control and put it out into the world on my own in my own way. All writers need these people in their lives that believe in them! Thank you, Stefania Gesuero, Isabelle Noura, Hannah Insalco, Sinead Mooney, Nate Jacob, Marta Hobbs, Heidi Wenzler, Lauren Oberham, Julia Rosenberg (Just do it yourself, Erin!), Carly West, Manesha Luthra, Ann Sisson and Jayden, Becky Bangerter, Amanda Beggan, Bonnie Brown (who inspired me to include the influencer Melodie Melodies at #BTSPFW), Tamra Dunaway, Fontayne Fox, Chrissy Edwards, Barbara Segor, Emilie Soto, Beth Appel, Sally Anderson, Taylor Duffy,

Maria Mazlimi, Nanette Johnson, Tanja Crouch, Gabrielle Kelly, Catriona Barry, Laura Mosson, and Maggie North, who kept me off the ledge. Shelley Marsh gets a double mention for being a constant support and texting me off the ledge. Nathalie MacCarthy, my creative soul sister, for our monthly creative support calls, Deanna Vogt, my coach and friend the past twenty years, Donna McEntee, and finally my therapist, Pannill Taylor. Pro tip! Always have a coach and therapist on your side when going through the creative writing process. They will support you to keep your wise self in the forefront when you need it, which in turn will keep your story on track with how it's meant to be.

I want to thank the many literary agents that requested full reads and partial reads, and who gave me thoughtful and helpful feedback along the way with those rejections. The ones who took the time to offer feedback helped me grow as a writer and understand myself more as a storyteller. I learned what's important to keep and protect and what's not. I want to thank my former/first literary agent for feeling the magic of the story and trying the first six months or so to get this ready to submit to editors to be traditionally published. I learned a great deal from you the year we worked together. I also learned that too many people reading for feedback can lead us humans to being overly nitpicky and losing sight of the overall gem before them. Mostly, I learned that I don't want to write from a place of fear, and I don't want to write to everyone's approval or feedback all the time. It sucked the life out of my creative spirit. A huge lesson learned: that I have good, intuitive instincts and I need to trust myself in the process first and foremost. For that, I'm grateful! I want to thank Courtney Maum for the consult we had shortly after I parted ways with my agent. I was feeling low and about to throw in the writer towel. You were great and helped me refocus and recalibrate, affirming that I had something special and it was worth it to keep going. Merci beaucoup! A huge thank you to my production team, Lindsey Alexander and Sal Borriello with The Reading List, and thanks to Sharon Bially with BookSavvy. Liam Fitzgerald with Frequency.ie gets an honorable mention, as he read the whole book to make sure the cover art turned out real and beautiful. Mission accomplished! Thank you all for getting behind this book with your whole hearts. It meant the world!

Finally, and most importantly, I need to thank my own gorgeous globe-trotting family. My husband, Alexander, aka Sasha to me, thank you for being an unwavering support to me with this book. You were there for me with every rejection letter, through the confusing time of needing to separate from my literary agent, who I worked so hard to acquire. You were a great sounding board when I'm sure you just couldn't talk about it anymore, but you found it in you to talk about it anyway. I felt very loved by you with this book. Thank you. To my triple AAA's, Amélie, Ailey, and Aubrey. You three are the reason I persevered. I wanted you to see that you don't give up on your dreams, that you can look to creativity when you are in a tough spot, and that if you stay in touch with your wise self, it'll all work out as it's meant to be. You three are the ultimate muses.

Cover People

Choosing the cover for this book was a global effort! I'm so grateful for the many people in my life all over the world that helped me choose the perfect Abby and the perfect view of Paris for her to step into and take up space.

Thank you for being my "cover people":

Sasha	Julia R.	Barbara	Aoife
Stefania	Fantine	Judy	Siobhan
Gabrielle	Carly	Nathalie	Maggie/Amy
Alyson	Carrie	Aideen	Bonnie
Amanda	Manisha	Nessa	Nina
Jennifer	Shelley	Elizabeth	Maddy
Ann	Ailey	Marissa	Patricia
Pannill	Aubrey	Brigid	Cat
Fontayne	Amélie	Michelle	Mara
Olya	Becky	Lizz	Miriam
Rebecca	Isabelle	Sally	Ruth
Leila	Isabelle P.	Sinead	Tamra
Julie	Taylor	Andy	Laura

About Erin Zhurkin

An American overseas, Erin has lived in five different countries (inclusive of France). Because of these rich and sometimes hard life experiences, she feels called to write stories that resonate across cultures, bringing to light the feeling of *dépaysement* that occurs. She currently lives in Seoul, Korea, with her family and two cats, Coco and Fifi.

Follow her online:
Instagram: @erinzhurkinwrites
Twitter: @ErinZhurkin
Website: erinzhurkin.com

Ingram Content Group UK Ltd.
Milton Keynes UK
UKHW011822040623
422854UK00002B/8